ELISABETH MARRION was born A
Germany. Her father was a corp(
and stationed after the war in th
Germany, where he met her motl

As a child she enjoyed reading
Wilde, Thornton Wilder and never lost her love of reading novels by Ernest Hemingway, or short stories by Guy de Maupassant.

In 1969 she moved to England, where she met her late husband David. Together they established a clothing importing company. Their business gave them the opportunity to travel and work in the Subcontinent and the Far East. A large part of their working life was spent in Bangladesh, where they helped to establish a school in the rural part of the country, training young people in trades such as sign writing, electrical work and repair of computers and televisions.

For inspiration she puts on her running shoes for a long coastal run near the New Forest, where she now lives.

Also by author:

The Night I Danced with Rommel: Hilde's Story
Liverpool Connection: Annie's Story
Cuckoo Clock New York: Ester's Story

the Wight Thing

ELISABETH MARRION

*To Susan
With Best Wishes
Elisabeth.*

SilverWood

Published in 2018 by SilverWood Books

SilverWood Books Ltd
14 Small Street, Bristol, BS1 1DE, United Kingdom
www.silverwoodbooks.co.uk

Copyright © Elisabeth Marrion 2018

The right of Elisabeth Marrion to be identified as the author of this work has been asserted in accordance with the Copyright, Designs and Patents Act 1988 Sections 77 and 78.

All rights reserved. No part of this publication may be reproduced, stored in a retrieval system, or transmitted in any form or by any means, electronic, mechanical, photocopying, recording or otherwise, without prior permission of the copyright holder.

This is a work of fiction. Names, characters, places and incidents either are products of the author's imagination or are used fictitiously. Any resemblance to actual events or locales or persons, living or dead, is entirely coincidental.

This novel was copy-edited by Karenne Griffin, and proofread several times. As an author, I take enormous pride in my books. However, proofreaders are human, so if you notice any errors please let me know by emailing elliK@gmx.co.uk.

ISBN 9781096737582 (KDP paperback)

British Library Cataloguing in Publication Data
A CIP catalogue record for this book is available from the British Library

Page design and typesetting by SilverWood Books
Printed on responsibly sourced paper

For my best friend

PART I THE FRIENDS

Chapter 1

"How do you envisage this to work?" Christine was totally confused by now. Not sure whether it was the effect of her third glass of bubbly or whether she had lost the plot halfway through the evening. Not surprising, really. After all, Steve had literally thrown the idea on the table. After that, everybody got carried away, liking the sound of it. And why not? The longer the evening went on the noisier and livelier the group became. At one stage all talking at once; nothing unusual there.

The strangest 'wake' I have been to, she thought, and had another sip just in case. One never knew when it would be one's last. Look what happened to Patrick. One minute he was here and then *puff*, the next minute he was gone. Isabelle said she'd gone straight upstairs after they had dinner at the new bistro in Wellington Street. She told him she needed to get out of her killer heels and into some comfortable clothes before they both settled for the night with a mug of hot chocolate. Patrick apparently had not felt right all evening during dinner and had not touched his wine.

He said to her he would not stay downstairs and would be up in a second. He wanted to record 'Have I Got News for You'. He hardly ever missed an episode. Next, she heard a thud. Isabelle had called his name and when there was no reply, rushed to find him. There he was, lying next to the grand piano. She grabbed the phone in one hand and with the other kept pushing down on his chest, all the time speaking to the emergency operator. She tried to resuscitate him by giving him mouth-to-mouth while she waited for the ambulance. But there was nothing anybody could have done, the doctor told her at the hospital.

Steve was right on one thing, Christine concluded. People do not spend enough time with their friends. No excuses now since we are all retired. Well, some of us have not worked as long as others.

Look at Nobby, for example. Gave up his profession after he had a cancer scare. Being a surgeon himself, there was no way he wanted to carry on operating on patients. Instead, he'd spent the last few years travelling alone. Giving the impression he was having a great time, when the truth was, they all knew how lonely he felt after Margaret's accident almost eight years ago. He always put his jolly face on, pretending, sending postcards to everybody from everywhere, coming back with his fantastic stories. Who did he think he was kidding?

No wonder he agreed straight away with Steve's idea, branding it a master plan.

"I'll drink to that," he had immediately declared and raised his glass in salute.

Christine now turned her attention to 'Bill and Ben, the flowerpot men'. Their given names were, in fact, William and Benjamin, which was hilarious, both of them being keen gardeners. They had shared their life together for the last thirty-five years. Who said true love never dies? Correct for these two. Still gazing at each other at any given moment. Maybe not always since Ben could drive Bill mad sometimes. They all had witnessed it from time to time. Before their retirement, both worked in the performing arts. Bill was a costume designer whereas Ben was a major producer and had many West End and Broadway musicals to his credit.

"Christine, are you paying attention to anything Steve has suggested?"

Christine was brought back to the buzz at the table. Laura had fired the question at her, shaking her head as she did so.

Now everybody was looking at her. Great!

"Yes. Yes, of course. What do you mean? Steve's idea, yes I am taking it all in."

Steve and Laura used to have their own business specialising in interior design, offering a total service to their customers, and could count famous, or in some cases, infamous names to their client lists. For example, that couple who wanted the inside of their mansion looking exactly like a castle. It already had a turret and stone clad walls. Inside, not one but two iron staircases going to the upstairs rooms. A his and hers, perhaps? Coats of armour on the walls, reproduction medieval trumpets, a long wooden table in the hall, iron chandeliers, candle lighting everywhere else. Four poster beds in sombre looking bedrooms. Not forgetting the customary stone floors downstairs. All that sounded almost normal, considering the rest.

The cellar was to be made into a dungeon with a separate room closed off by a solid wooden door. They claimed that would be their wine cellar. Yeah, right? Who was gullible enough to believe that one? Especially after they requested some large iron rings on the walls. Next to that room was an enormous space. This was to be converted into a bar; the stools were the first to arrive. There seemed no logic to that one. Boxes of pewter beakers were carried down and lined the large shelf behind the counter. Some of them hung from hooks off a wooden construction that, to Christine, looked more like a gallows. But Steve assured her it was not finished. That was on the day when Christine arrived unannounced. Laura's MG Midget had broken down, and she had phoned her from the garage. Laura needed her cheque book. It was typical of her; she never carried any money. Now

Christine had to pick up Steve's house key in a hurry. With him being at the mansion, Christine would have a chance for a quick peep around. When she was eventually escorted off the premises by Steve, she made a point of telling him under no circumstances to invite her to the grand opening of this one, as had become their tradition. She would need counselling for the rest of her life if she went.

The owner of that place was a famous football player. Why was she not surprised? Luckily, Steve and Laura had friends from the theatre world who had helped with that particular project. Nothing was ever too weird for them.

Laura was now kicking her under the table. Christine's input was desperately needed.

"Yes, I mean, how is it actually going to work? There you are, Laura, I asked a question."

Christine took the bottle and refilled her glass, looking over to where Isabelle was sitting next to Rick, who seemed deep in thought.

Isabelle's composure was amazing. Perhaps this is how you are supposed to be if you just lost your husband. Christine would not know since she had not lost hers, unless you count him changing her for a younger model a loss. He did precisely that: swapped her for a photographic model. 'Fiffi l'Amour' as she called her. Fiffi had been one of their imports from France. She'd known there and then that this was a bad idea. *C'est la vie*, good riddance, but not before she made sure her husband paid her over the odds for her part of their modelling business. She also insisted she kept some shares and was ready to move on.

"Pass me the bottle, Chrissie." Rick still called her that, although her 'groupie' days were long behind her. Mind you, he'd lost most of his wealth in his fifth divorce. That one really did take him to the cleaners, they all had seen it coming. That was, everybody, besides Rick.

By now, other guests were looking over towards them, whispering and pointing at their table. They must have recognised Rick. Any minute now the first autograph hunter would appear, she feared. Or worse, somebody was going to ask him to sing. That happened quite often here at this wine bar in Barnes. Maybe that was one of the reasons it had become one of their favourite haunts since the early 70s. She had to admit that although the décor had changed almost as many times as the proprietor, they liked it here. The picture of Georgie Fame was still on the wall.

It had been the day after the engagement party that they had made this place their hangout. Even so, it was a long way from Cambridge where most of them had met as students.

Chapter 2

Christine had first set eyes on Laura when they both signed in for the foundation course in Art at Cambridge University. She had stood in line right in front of her.

"Do you fancy a coffee?" If she recalled correctly, that was what Laura had said to her. Later on, she was not so sure. In any case, she followed her down to the cafeteria. Both seemed to have a lot in common. That is, if not knowing where your studies will eventually take you is what binds you together. They checked their given schedules and were delighted that they were attending the same lectures. That could come in very handy, they agreed. An instant friendship was formed. They even managed to swap their digs at the hall of residence and shared a room for the first year.

Almost immediately, Laura fell in love with young Steve, a handsome example of a Nordic Viking, studying Architecture. His parents lived in Richmond and worked at the Norwegian Consulate.

The back staircase, which led from the female dorm downstairs and out via a solid black iron door, became increasingly busy as the first month of studying passed. Most of the time, Christine had to bunk up with somebody else.

They still laughed about it to this very day, when they recalled the night Steve and Laura got caught by the resident warden.

What the warden wanted in their room that time of day was never established. And who was more shocked, they never found out. The Consulate was immediately informed and Steve's mum and dad arrived. They had an entourage of officials and even a policeman in tow. Christine was glad she hadn't been caught in bed with her boyfriend, Bruce, or was it Frederick? The one with the spiky hair and spiky other bits. Yes, definitely Frederick. Anyway, he was in a mood that night so she found herself without a warm cosy bed. Damn it, time of the month again, hardly her fault, was it? He should be thankful and not sulking, at least they were not as unlucky as one of the new intakes from Hong Kong. She was showing already and had no intention of flying back to her parents' place at the end of the semester. She had made up some story she was travelling to Europe to get ahead of her studies for the next year. Apparently, her parents had swallowed it and kept providing the funds.

With no bed, Christine debated who she could bother or which of the girls were out that evening. She had to crash somewhere. Her room was not an option. That was when she heard the commotion outside. Christine thought a warning was in order and rushed to speak with Laura. It was Steve who introduced her to his parents half-dressed. A diplomatic disaster was avoided when Steve and Laura announced their engagement at exactly that point.

The official party to celebrate this event was something else. Christine travelled down from Cambridge to Richmond with Steve's three friends, Norbert (Nobby), Ben and Bill. She was in the passenger seat next to Nobby who was driving his new red Ford Cortina. She sat completely upright most of the way, afraid that her new sky-blue halter-neck jumpsuit would crease. She had treated herself to it last month. It was Laura who insisted only clothes bought at Carnaby Street would qualify for such an occasion. They'd almost given up and gone back home empty handed when they spotted it. Just what you were looking for, was Laura's opinion. Could have been; it was what Laura had in mind for her. But that outfit, in her size? Too late protesting now. They were here after all, and this was one of Mary Quant's latest creations. Laura, of course, did not allow her any thinking time anyway. Just as Christine fought with the hook fastenings and almost tripped over the humongous bell bottoms, Laura had, to Christine's embarrassment, negotiated a discount with the pimply youth. Was it Laura's hippy outfit, which impressed him? There was no backing out now. However, no more shopping that day, they both decided. They went to the bottom of Carnaby Street, turned left and treated themselves to afternoon tea at Liberty's.

Several times during the journey down from the university, Christine glanced over to Nobby. With his bobbed hairstyle, moustache and white open cheesecloth shirt, he could pass as Sonny Bono's double. Secretly, she fancied him rotten and thought the two of them would make a lovely couple. But best not to let on. She had seen him in deep conversation with fellow female students on many occasions.

They were last to arrive at the house in Richmond. The party was already in full swing. Long wooden tables and benches were set up inside and outside the large marquee. The garden reached all the way to the River Thames. Most of the trees had been decorated with little colourful lanterns. Waiters offering drinks rushed back and forth, caterers were sweating over hot barbecues. Christine had forgotten her invitation and was not immediately allowed inside. Her companions just shrugged their shoulders and left her standing arguing with the butch security guys at the gate. One looked so much like Yul Brynner that Christine would not have minded if he manhandled her. I must be getting desperate, she thought just as Laura came to her rescue.

Laura was positively glowing. The long purple outfit she was wearing was truly amazing. Tight trousers, and a flimsy top, which would have left nothing to anybody's imagination if it hadn't been covered by a silk caftan overlay delicately printed with an array of exotic flowers. The whole ensemble flowed in the light breeze. Christine was mesmerised by the sparkle in Laura's auburn hair, which for this occasion, was not pinned up as usual, but flowed down over her shoulders.

"A Barbara Hulanicki," she whispered.

"What?"

"The dress, I bought it at Biba in Kensington."

After that revelation, Christine was left to her own devices. She dived for the first glass of Babycham before the waiter could disappear, and made a fruitless search for her travelling companions before making a beeline for the buffet. This was too good a chance to miss. She had not eaten a bite all day, worrying that her tight-fitting suit would not have the same effect had she done so. She should have dieted for a couple of weeks beforehand, as Laura had suggested. That was immediately after Christine had forked out most of her monthly allowance from her mum for her outfit.

The band was announced just before midnight: 'Rock Around The Clock'. This was Steve and Laura's favourite hard rock band. Imagine them liking hard rock. They looked more like Scott McKenzie's 'If you're going to San Francisco', standing there at the river's edge, gazing at each other.

To her surprise, the band was not bad at all. There were four members: a drummer, bass guitar, keyboard and Rick played lead guitar and was their singer.

The rest of the evening was a bit of a blur. She shouldn't have sneaked in the hashish she'd saved. Most guests slept where they fell. Unfortunately for Christine, Nobby fell on Shauna, a petite redhead from Dublin. He had been enchanted with her all evening; behaved like a puppy in love. If they now play 'the birdie song' and Nobby does his silly dance, I will throw up, she thought.

Another lonely night for me, and that at one of the most romantic evenings for ages, she was beginning to think when she spotted the photographer who kept following her, snapping pictures of her every move. She quickly checked that she hadn't 'popped out' at the top.

"Are you a model?" he finally asked.

"That's about the lamest chat up line ever," was the best reply Christine could come up with.

"It worked though, didn't it? See, we're talking. I'm Henry, by the way," he said with a grin.

Christine wanted to rip his clothes off that instant, just to show Nobby that she didn't care. She might have done just that, if Nobby had looked even just once in her direction. But instead, she talked with Henry all night.

Chapter 3

Henry had told Christine that his photographic studio was not that far away. She fancied having a look but how could she persuade the others? After all, she relied on their transport. Also, there was the danger of looking too keen. He certainly was no Adonis, but if you squinted and looked at him from the side, there was a little resemblance to James Dean. Well, with a bit of imagination, anyway. Plus, she could not dismiss the fact that he had been the only bloke who had shown some sort of interest in her for at least two weeks.

It was Laura and Steve who came to her rescue. Laura appeared out of nowhere, just as Christine had set out on a fruitless search for Nobby, who was nowhere to be found. Not even with the partygoers down at the river. Early risers, she had thought at first, but looking into their glazed eyes and confused faces, it was clear they hadn't had any sleep. She didn't feel that clever herself.

Laura was fresh as a daisy. How did she do that? Christine was just about to inquire when Steve showed up.

"There you are, my lovely." He reached for Laura and pulled her close.

Christine thought that was her cue to disappear.

"Wait, we were looking for you, do you want to come to Barnes and see that photographer of yours?"

She felt herself blushing. Luck was on her side.

"We'll set off around eleven o'clock. He promised to start developing the photos from last night. Said we should be there at lunchtime."

"Have you seen Nobby?" Christine thought it best to change the subject while she had the chance.

"Last I saw of him, he was saying a passionate goodbye to the Irish beauty he hung around with all night."

"She's gone, then?"

"Yes, her parents had to use all their strength and persuasive powers to drag her away from him. I think she's off to a strict Catholic boarding school in County Donegal."

Christine was now glad that she'd packed her hot pants after all. She almost left them behind, but thought again when she threw her belongings into the small case her granny had given her last Christmas.

She'd had to swallow several times after she ripped the paper off the carefully wrapped present. Her mother should have warned her. She was staring at an artist's impression of a little pigtailed girl, beaming with pride. Kneeling on the floor. An open case in front of her. Her teddy bear leaning against her yellow pleated skirt. She was proudly holding her doll, ready to place it inside her case. Above it in bold letters it said *going to Grandma's*. All that, printed on a red, hard shell overnight case. She was lost for words, which her granny interpreted as being overwhelmed with emotion.

"Oh, Granny, you shouldn't have," she managed to stammer, not daring to look at her brother. There would be endless ribbing from him, for sure.

Granny wiped a tear from her eyes when Christine hugged her and kissed her on the cheek. She blew into her carefully unfolded handkerchief, composed herself and replied, "You deserve it, Chrissie, you going to university and all that." She sniffed again, "One of my grandchildren going to Cambridge. You know, only the best ones get accepted there." That was clearly a dig at Christine's brother who still had not decided what he wanted to do with his life. And he was two years older than her.

❀

She carefully orchestrated it, to be the last one to get to the car. Her outfit, obviously, had the desired effect. Her light blue hot pants, bright pink revealing top. And the *pièce de résistance*, her knee-high, lace-up, shiny patent imitation leather platform boots.

Nobby's lit cigarette fell out of his mouth onto his white Crimplene trousers. The trousers were the latest trend, apparently. He jumped off the seat and out onto the gravel, furiously trying to brush the burning ash away. Angry red skin showed through the hole. He looked perplexed, first at Christine and then back to his pride and joy. Those had set him back at least fifteen pounds. Bill and Ben were hollering with laughter in the back of the car. Serves you right, thought Christine. You could have had all of this and more last night.

Apparently, Steve knew the way, and his car was already at the gate. Nobby had no choice but to put his into gear and follow on. He would inspect the damage to his trousers later. Hopefully his mother would know how to repair them.

They found a couple of parking places in Barnes, at a green with a little pond. How pretty it looked. Christine hoped there would be time to explore the area a little bit later. Whether it was with Henry or Nobby, that didn't matter, considering Nobby hadn't spoken to her during the drive, just given her one of his sullen looks from time to time. They caught up with Laura and Steve and joined them on the pavement, just when Steve said, "Let's go back, there's nobody in. He must have forgotten we were coming."

"Maybe Christine wore him out last night, and he's resting."

Luckily, she was spared further embarrassment when they heard a key turning in the lock from the inside. Henry pushed his head of unkempt hair through the opening of the door.

"Sorry, I was in the dark room. The first photos are

hanging up to dry. Let's go for a quick drink. Hair of the dog so to speak. There's one of those new wine bars about a five-minute walk from here." He looked approvingly at Christine and took her hand to walk ahead. She didn't pull away. As far as she could see, Nobby appeared unaffected by their closeness.

They were delighted to find Rick sitting at a long table in the corner when they entered. He spotted them before they walked through the door and waved them over to join him and the rest of the band. He hugged everyone in turn, including Steve, Bill and Ben. Only Nobby declined. The rest of the musicians had been ready to leave for a while and it seemed to Christine they were glad they could make an exit.

Rick explained that the van had to go back to the rental company and all the gear was still inside. To Laura, he whispered "I usually leave the unloading to them anyway." He would have to turn up at their soundproof cellar tomorrow, mind you. They had a slot booked at the EMI recording studio to start recording the next album and the band desperately needed some practice.

Chapter 4

Henry was something else. He pursued her relentlessly until Christine finally weakened, threw caution to the wind and hoped he had enough money for the constant commute between Cambridge and Barnes.

Instead of studying for her art degree, Christine pursued the art of seduction and secretly scrutinised the Kama Sutra, holding her torch under the blankets. Most activities had to be done by candlelight these days anyway. That prime minister of theirs, Ted Heath, had decided it was wrong to give in to the demands of the striking coal miners. They, on the other hand, had no intention of calling off their action, which had gone on for weeks. Supplies had to run short soon. Although at the beginning it had been proclaimed that there were plenty of coal reserves, nobody had expected that both sides of the dispute would stand their ground for so long. The inevitable announcement followed. Electricity had to be rationed. This was to be done by creating a three-day working week. A rota was in place. On the days when non-essential workplaces received their supply, you worked much longer hours to make up any shortfall. During the 'dark days', offices would open during daylight only. Old equipment was brought from storage and dusted off. In no time, people once again were using manual typewriters, slide rules, and yes, calculations were done using your brain, pen and paper.

An almost wartime atmosphere resurfaced that nobody had foreseen. There was once again comradeship between fellow human beings. Candlelit parties at Cambridge were all the rage. Everybody who owned a battery-operated transistor radio, tape or record player was most welcome. Second in line were those with a good supply of candles and batteries. Drinks were easy to come by; the friends knew of a friendly corner shop. Sharing their supply of hashish helped with price negotiating there. Blaming unfinished work on the darkened conditions became standard practice. Christine confided in Laura that she liked this new arrangement. Henry worked most days in darkness in any case. If he had no new shots to develop, he would stay an extra night, which was no problem now that Laura hardly ever left Steve's' pad. Steve hadn't even complained when she brought the chintz curtains and cushions her mother had made. An additional bonus for Christine was Nobby's displeasure every time Henry turned up. To rub more salt into Nobby's now obvious wound, she sometimes stayed overnight in Barnes.

On one of those stays, Henry took her home to meet his parents who lived in Ealing, West London, just over half an hour away. If Christine worried what his parents might think of her, that was nothing compared to Henry's concern as to what Christine would make of his parents.

The house in Ealing was a Victorian three-storey semi-detached. You walked up a stone outside staircase to the front door. Steve used his key.

"Mum, Dad, are you home?"

There was no reply, which did not surprise him at all. Most likely both were downstairs in the bottom apartment, which had been converted into a studio for his mother. The main entrance for that was on the side of the house, which meant you had to go outside again, turn left at the pavement, down a little slope. No key was ever entrusted to him for this.

"Let's check downstairs," he suggested.

"Can I just have a little look around? This is amazing."

Christine stood inside the large entrance hall. Polished wooden floors led towards a kitchen at the other end. She was drawn to a room on her left, attracted by the ochre wall with the cast iron fireplace surrounded by white painted, elaborate woodwork and an imposing mantelpiece.

Christine exhaled slowly. "Wow."

The whole room was painted using the same warm yellow, setting off the tall windows. These reflected the sunlight towards the top. High above, an ornate white painted plaster ceiling rose matched the rendering and cornices. A sparkling chandelier hung from there. The seating arrangements appeared to have been made from an old bedframe, judging by the size. The bed was covered with a sumptuous blanket and at least a dozen rustic, embroidered cushions. Those and the blanket were a dazzling mixture of warm reds, oranges, browns, yellows and whites, all blended together beautifully. A large carpet covering almost every bit of the dark wooden floor was of a similar design and colour combination. Beanbags were arranged on the floor all over the room.

Painted folding doors, which reached from top to bottom, divided this room from the next, the dining area. To Christine's disappointment this looked quite normal. A door led back into the hall and towards the kitchen, which was quite small for a house this size.

Henry shrugged his shoulders. "Yes, I know. My parents are great fans of Texas Homecare and the orange kitchen cabinets were on special offer. Let's go this way."

There was a back door leading into a surprisingly large garden and a staircase to the downstairs flat.

His mother did not hear them entering. Loud familiar music blasted from a state-of-the-art record player standing on a chest of drawers at the far wall. Christine wanted to walk over and check out the functions of the different buttons and switches, but held herself back.

"Mum, how come the lights are on? It's Thursday."

"There you are, my dears." Henry's mother forced herself

away from her canvas, almost knocking against the bowl of fruits placed next to a dead rabbit, a bird which Christine could not identify, a green and a red cabbage and a couple of onions. Christine glanced from the painting towards the display and could not spot one of the items on the nearly completed artwork.

"Yes, isn't it great?" sighed Henry.

"Come, come, Christine, stand over here next to me and tell me what you see."

From where she now stood the painting came alive. Although it was abstract, she could understand the fascination of it all.

"Christine, I have heard so much about you. Henry never stops telling us how happy you are making him."

Christine felt embarrassed. "Your work is amazing. We went to an art exhibition last week, in Chiswick. Now I realise the paintings were yours. Henry never let on that the artist was his mother."

"Yes, our Henry is a bit conservative. Don't know where he got that from, not from us." His mother laughed.

"What does your husband do?"

"The sculptures over there, those are mine." Henry's father filled the whole door frame, smiling broadly. He walked over and took her in his arms to give her a bear hug. She sneaked a look up and saw his sparkling bright eyes behind the John Lennon glasses. Part of his face was obscured by his long flowing dark hair. When she was released she walked over to the record player and lifted the record cover from the floor.

"We're so glad that Henry finally brought you along. People might have started thinking he's embarrassed by his parents." His chuckle made the white cotton tunic over his loose cotton trousers move up and down. Bare feet and brown sandals. Christine looked at the record cover again. 'Woodstock'. She should have guessed.

Chapter 5

Back at the wine bar, Christine once again was brought back from her reminiscence.

"Christine! Have you given it any thought at all?"

"Given what any thought?"

Laura pursed her lips, exasperated. "You're not even listening."

"Yes, I am. But do you think today is the right day to make a decision which will affect us all?"

"Today is exactly the day we should," added Isabelle quietly.

Christine removed her hand from the champagne flute, which was sure to break if she kept holding on to it so tight. She placed her hand on Isabelle's instead and patted it.

"Would it not be better if we all slept on it for a few days, and if we still think we should do it, we can talk again."

"You do surprise me. I would have thought you'd jump at the chance, being free spirited and all that." Nobby gave her one of his looks, which Christine had learned to ignore a long time ago. She must have stopped caring when he'd introduced Margaret. Christine had felt immediately she was not one of his usual conquests.

"What about the Isle of Wight?" was all she could come up with being put on the spot.

"Isle of Wight? Now that is a thought." Steve had decided it was up to him to push the idea further. The time was right, for his life to take a different direction. He glanced at Laura. "We'll add it to the list and go over it in more detail."

His precise writing had always been slow but Christine started to wonder when she noticed the utter concentration on his face. His tongue poked out a little and moved from side to side, eventually settling on the left. He bent down so far that Christine could not make out whether he was actually moving his pen. She should have paid more attention. She looked at him again and then at Laura, who just shrugged her shoulders. But her expression when she did frightened Christine a little. She sat up straighter to make sure that the others believed she was not yet totally tipsy from all that bubbly she had drunk within a relatively short time.

"Steve, can I have the list?" Thankfully, he pushed it towards her. She had a quick glance and could hardly make out any of the suggestions Steve had written.

"Should we write them out again and next to each list advantages and disadvantages?" she suggested.

"Now you're talking." Rick had stood up a few minutes before and returned with a new bottle of Moët. He leaned over Christine's shoulder and refilled her glass. Christine felt his breath on her cheek, and her face began to glow. Nobby did not fail to notice.

"Romsey. Who suggested that and why?" she wondered out loud and chewed the top of the biro.

"It was our idea," said Ben. "Remember, we told you about it before? It's quaint. Not far from Southampton. Which means easy access to London, everywhere really." Ben's eyes twinkled with excitement. "Besides, it was the home of the Earl of Mountbatten. Broadlands, it's called, and there is an abbey. So, it has a lot of things going for it."

"Plus, lots of good pubs." As far as Bill was concerned, that settled it.

Christine returned to the list. "Next, St Albans in Hertfordshire."

Nobby raised his eyebrows. "We all recall that weekend, surely."

"That would be enough reason to cross it off the list, just in case St Albans remembers us," muttered Laura.

Rick had a coughing fit and the others joined in the laughter, recalling that particular memory.

"Oh, let's not go there." Bill put his arm around Ben's shoulder and looked deep into his eyes.

"It wasn't my fault."

Christine knew if she didn't put a stop to it now, Ben would push his bottom lip forward, put on his best hurt face and sulk for at least an hour.

"It is a lively town." With hindsight Christine shouldn't have said that, now all eyes were on Ben. "It has a cinema, theatre, it's very close to London. Good pubs and restaurants." The last was a mere whisper, but the mention of the pubs raised a few eyebrows.

"Farnham in Surrey," Laura came to her rescue and looked from one to the other. "What do you think?"

"It's really pretty and close to Guildford," said Ben. "The Yvonne Arnaud Theatre is excellent. I directed a couple of shows there. One of them, 'The Importance of Being Earnest', was a great hit." Ben had livened up again, the story about St Albans temporarily shelved.

"Yes, it has almost everything we could hope for. Near London, nice selection of shops, restaurants and, we must not forget the pubs." Christine thought that Steve had spoken very slowly. Did he have as much champagne as herself by now?

"Tell us more about your Isle of Wight, Chrissie." Rick had put his hand on Christine's leg. All eyes were on the two of them, with Nobby trying to work out what the look those two exchanged could possibly mean.

"The island is not very large, we could all go over and have a good look around." Her friends were curiously waiting for her to continue. "How about we spend a weekend there?"

"That's brilliant."

"I always wanted to visit there."

"Have you been before?" It was Nobby who decided to ask Christine. Something about it was bothering him. Laura leaned forward across the table, waiting for Christine's reply; that way she could see deep into Christine's eyes. A familiar expression crossed her face. Only Laura knew the whole story.

"Yes, briefly."

From the expression on Laura's face, Rick realised there was more to it, but he could wait until they had a private moment. He felt it was best to save Christine from what seemed to be a very delicate situation. "I propose a toast to our new coordinator, Christine." He raised his glass and the rest of them followed.

It only dawned on Christine now that once again, she had fallen for it. During the time that she had been deep in thought, the rest had set her up. It had been her friends' intention all along that it would be up to her to do all the donkey work.

Chapter 6

After checking everybody's commitments for the following weeks, they selected the first weekend of July. A hastily arranged meeting for a further discussion was also set. The new coordinator, Christine, made sure she palmed some of the jobs off onto the others before everybody departed.

Ben had already volunteered to be in charge of organising their transport. There was no point, he argued, in taking a couple of cars. He would hire an eight-seater vehicle and Bill would do the driving that weekend. Ben shot a quick glance in Bill's direction when he suggested it. Both had argued many times about Ben renewing his driving licence after it had been suspended for a second time. He would need to go on a government driving scheme and take the test again. Something he would definitely fail, they all agreed.

Nobby's Regency House at Piccotts End, Hemel Hempstead was the biggest and had plenty of rooms to accommodate the friends overnight. Plus, there were plenty of parking spaces. You drove towards the property through a big open iron gate onto a gravel drive, which ended in a circle just before the actual house. If you couldn't park there, the right side of the drive extended towards a row of garages and the mews. The dark green paint on the garage doors had long since faded and was flaking in some places, but this enhanced the ambiance of the courtyard, which was shared between the mews and the garages. Nobby had the house and the mews painted cream about every three years and the friends volunteered each time. They knew Nobby would decline and get the professionals in, but that didn't stop them arriving after the work had been completed. One summer they had decided to dig in the large cellar to find the entry of the, by now, bricked-up trapdoor Nobby had told them about. He was all for it as long as they didn't disturb his carefully stored wine bottles. They must have lifted up eight flagstones and used shovels to remove the dirt, when they reached a layer of cement under two of them, which clearly should have not been there. When Rick drove off in his old silver Jaguar to go in a search of a tool hire company for a couple of pickaxes, Nobby had called a halt and asked them to put everything back. He'd organised a party and guests were already arriving. Rick promised his friends one day they would continue searching. A rumour that there was a secret passageway between the house and the church further down the road was too good a story to let lapse. He quickly painted a red cross on the spot with Isabelle's best nail polish.

Christine sometimes wondered whether this could have all been hers if she'd given in that week all those years ago.

Back those days she'd stayed at the little mews attached to the side of the main house. It was so quaint. You entered through the front door directly into the living room. Two large sash windows gave the room a splendid view over the fields, and you could watch the horses grazing and frisking about. To your left was an enormous fireplace, big enough for even the largest Father Christmas to come down and leave his gifts. To the right was a small kitchen. The window had never closed properly as far as Christine could remember. It had its uses being always slightly open. You could climb in and out if you knew the trick to lift it up. Something which made her smile every time she thought about it. In the living room was a fixed Welsh dresser that reached all the way to the high ceiling. The glossy paint set it off magnificently against the mint green wall. Best of all there was a black iron circular staircase leading to the two bedrooms and bathroom.

However, one night, when Christine was all alone in the mews, waiting for the others to arrive the next day, she decided to go to bed early. She was awoken by footsteps on the staircase, believing for a moment they'd arrived early, or Nobby was trying his luck again. Suddenly the evening turned into a living nightmare. The footsteps stopped right outside her closed bedroom door. All she could hear was heavy breathing. Frozen with fear she held her blanket to her face and believed that her hair stood on end all by itself. She stared at the door and saw the doorknob slowly turning. Not a sound. The doorknob turned back. The movements repeated once more, before the steps could be heard slowly descending. Christine never slept there again, nor did she admit to anybody that she wet the bed that night.

Now that Nobby had resurfaced from his 'walkabouts', he was planning to re-establish his famous garden party. When Margaret was alive these parties were infamous for being large and boisterous. Some of them lasted several days. Christine often wondered how Nobby had been such an excellent surgeon after all the booze he used to consume. But one rainy day changed it all. A drunk driver in broad daylight ploughed into a crowd of shoppers. They were later told that Margaret, in a split second, pushed a young mother with her new-born baby in a pram out of the path of the oncoming vehicle and took the whole impact herself. She became a local hero but this was no consolation for Nobby, his family and friends. Strangers lined the street when the hearse made its way slowly towards the cemetery, the hearse being pulled by four black horses, white feathers on their heads. The funeral director himself walked in front with his top hat and walking stick. People bowed their heads, others threw flowers when Margaret's coffin passed.

Rick, Ben, Bill, Patrick, Steve and Nobby's brother James carried the coffin on their shoulders into the church. Nobby and his son walked behind. The rest of the mourners were already inside, waiting to accompany Margaret on her last journey. Christine was sitting next to Nobby's parents who had flown over from Sierra Leone. Both had worked on the African continent on and off, but had settled there recently working with Médecins Sans Frontières. Although Nobby's father was a cardiologist and had not much experience in general practice, he happily followed his wife everywhere. And it was she, a paediatrician, who wanted to work with expectant mothers in one of the poorest villages.

Nobby's brother James must be the black sheep of the family, Christine had thought when she met him for the first time on that day. Nobby hardly ever spoke about his family, let alone his brother. The funeral was held in a small church Margaret had attended frequently and many of the congregation stood patiently outside, while hastily erected speakers broadcast the service from inside.

The young woman, whose life Margaret had saved, later changed her daughter's name from Mackenzie to Margaret.

Chapter 7

Christine did not know what possessed her when she suggested Rick should look for accommodation on the island for the chosen weekend. But since it was her task to check for properties that would be worth taking a look at, she had to allocate this task to somebody. And why not Rick? Christine smiled at that thought. Yes, why not? She knew he would come up with something nobody else would think of.

Isabelle said they needed some sort of headquarters to gather information and start the ball rolling, if they were really serious about it. She suggested Patrick's old office. This would give her a good reason to go in there without raising suspicion that she was snooping on his former partners, which was silly really. She had known everybody for a very long time.

Christine couldn't wait to get home. She wanted to start the search straight away, and had some idea of what she was looking for and how big the place should be. That aspect the others had not even thought about, she guessed. But mind you, after all that booze, was she really surprised? Maybe their idea would come to nothing anyway when everybody got rid of the hangover they would all have in the morning.

And Isabelle surely had to discuss the matter in great detail with her offspring. Those two were best avoided. Sometimes, she could not believe the twins were really Isabelle and Patrick's. She and Laura often joked that the wrong babies had been laid into their crib at the hospital when they were born. They did not even look like them, being dark haired and slightly olive skinned, whereas Isabelle had lovely blonde hair and so did Patrick in his younger days. A throwback from their ancestors, they used to explain. That both felt an explanation necessary was odd in itself. Christine thought the kids were bordering on hostile lately, the way they spoke to their parents. And what would happen now Isabelle had no Patrick to defend her? At the cremation service they had been just about bearable, but nobody had objected when they decided to leave immediately afterwards. No doubt to go to Patrick's office to establish their position as his heirs. But the friends did not dare ask when Isabelle would summon the courage to show them her husband's last will and testament. Isabelle had confided in her friends that he had changed it only six months prior. She had to face that situation soon anyway, unless those two already knew, which would explain their hasty departure. They'd, in all likelihood, gone off to consult one of those expensive lawyers in town, who would agree to charge all fees to their late father's estate.

Laura and Steve's daughter was a different matter. As far as Christine was concerned, she was away with the fairies. Literally speaking. They must have had an inkling when they named their only daughter Berliot. It was supposed to mean protection and light. Whatever. But Berliot embraced the Old Norwegian customs with enough speed to make you dizzy. Her room as a child was filled with old books about Norway and there were several on the 18th-century Romantic Nationalistic movement. Her prized possessions were books of folk stories. Her favourite of all was fairy tales written by Peter Christen Asbjørnsen and Jørgen Moe. After reading those she told her mother that she was a good witch and would live in Norway when she was bigger. And that is exactly what she did. She dropped out of college and never returned to retake her exams, her original idea of journalism long abandoned. Fairy tales, that was what she wanted to write. Lucky for her she found an equally eccentric husband, Eric. They met at an embassy ball. One look across the dance floor and they knew they were made for each other. Besides Berliot there was nothing to keep Eric in England. He had been abandoned as a child. Dropped outside a monastery on a small island in the middle of the Trondheimsfjord, he was placed in the bottom part of a large suitcase. The top had been removed. He was left there in the middle of the night. It must have been his mother who pulled on the bell to alert the monks inside. They later claimed a young woman was seen running away and jumping on a small boat. Before anybody could reach her, the outboard motor had sprung into action. One man pulled her hastily on board while the second manoeuvred the boat away. Eric's mother had, at least, wrapped him up warmly in a baby blanket, and he was dressed in a hand knitted light blue hat and mittens. His adoptive parents had kept everything for him.

    Nothing could persuade Berliot to exchange their vows in England, and the ceremony was held in the most beautiful little church in Lillehammer, his home town. Christine and her friends flew over from London to Oslo and took the train from there. It only took about two and a half hours to reach their final destination and the scenery on the way was breathtaking. The guests from England had opted for an older, quite large hotel near the historical district, and felt immediately at home while they waited in front of an open fire for their rooms to be cleaned. For the ceremony at the charming red painted wooden church near the River Gausa, a coach had been laid on. Lucky, thought Christine at the time, as the snow and ice would have played havoc with her best stilettos. Why did they have to get married in the winter when the days were short and icy blasts from the north had lasted through the day and the following night? What was wrong with getting married in the summer when the birds were still singing at midnight? When their first child was born not five months after, the reason was clear for all to see and cuddle.

Living in Lillehammer with their ever-expanding family on their newly purchased camping ground saw Berliot blossom from a shy woman into a force to be reckoned with. Even Eric, who was still working in the Research for Energy and Natural Resources Department at the university nearby, often wondered how she fitted so many different things into one single day, and still found time to wander through the woods at full moon in winter and sunrise in the summer.

On her wedding day Berliot had been barefoot, hair decorated with flowers, throwing petals into the air and dancing in a circle. The snow on the ground and freezing cold had no effect on her. She was a good witch, she reminded everybody who cared to ask. Quietly singing to herself, clad in a white flowing gown. With him sitting nearby huddled in blankets, watching.

Laura confided to Christine on one of their evenings together, both having had too much to drink yet again, that Berliot was not wearing a stitch of clothing other than the dress, which was almost see through in any case. Well, that explained a lot. Laura and Steve had six grandchildren, so far.

Chapter 8

Nobby insisted he would drop Christine off on the way home from the wine bar. The taxi could make a little detour to Hanwell. Did he hope he could stop there overnight? No chance, Christine thought when his hand found her knee and slowly moved upwards. She realised the taxi driver was watching them in the mirror. Nobby was out of luck. Christine kissed him briefly on the cheek and waved him goodbye. She watched until the car had disappeared around the corner, put her key into the lock, kicked her shoes off and picked up the post. Her jacket found its way onto one of the hangers on the rack. She made straight for the kitchen and put the kettle on. She checked her watch. Should she have a strong cup of coffee and start the search now, or should she relax in front of the telly? Her neighbour decided for her. The doorbell had stopped working some time ago, and she hadn't heard her knocking. But Mavis next door never gave up easily. She had opened the flap of the letter box.

"Yoo hoo!" her ever cheerful voice echoed through the house. "Are you going to let me in, or do I need to get the spare key from next door?"

Ever since Mavis read the story about a girl called Shanti Devi who had lived in India and who believed she was reincarnated, Mavis had thought if this could happen to a little girl born in Delhi, India, why not her? But Mavis did not have such ability as Shanti Devi claimed to have. Many of Shanti Devi's recollections, which she told her parents from as early as four years of age, proved to be true. One example being, the person she said she was before had died a few days after giving birth to a son in a village called Mathura, a place she later visited. She knew streets and places in a rural area her parents had no connections to. Astonishingly, she also recognised her 'husband' and now grown up 'son'.

Mavis's only bookshelf in her cramped living room contained every book ever written about this girl. "Even Mahatma Gandhi asked a team to investigate this case. So, it has to be true, right?" she insisted every time Christine raised her eyebrows when Mavis turned up with yet another treasure she found at a jumble sale or second-hand bookshop.

The problem with Mavis was, she could not decide who she was supposed to be. It would happen that her inner-self changed several times a week. For a while she called herself Genevieve, because she liked the film. But Christine was totally thrown that she now settled on Olivia: from 'Twelfth Night,' she had explained. When Christine tried to explain that Olivia wasn't real, Mavis shrugged it off.

"Some writers I've read about based their characters on real people, so why not Shakespeare?"

Christine agreed. Whoever Olivia was, she indeed was not a Mavis.

"It's official." Mavis threw a piece of paper onto the little coffee table and plonked herself into the cosy armchair in her most comfortable position, which now had become sitting cross-legged. Christine managed to grab the sheet before it slid off again. Where were her reading glasses, which she seemed to have to rely on more and more?

"It only cost fifteen pounds, you know?"

Christine decided to forget the search for her specs and waited for what Mavis had laid out fifteen pounds. Money she could ill afford.

"Do you have a bottle of Cava left in that large fridge of yours?" Mavis was up again and on her way into the kitchen. She felt comfortable in Christine's house. She was happiest when she was asked to look after it on the few occasions when Christine was off on her travels. How would she ever manage without her? But Mavis did not linger long on that thought. After all, Christine had no intention of moving, living so close to the artists' retirement home in which her former mother-in-law now resided.

"I am now officially called Olivia. There, see for yourself. Cheers."

It was long past midnight when Christine finally managed to close the door behind Mavis, now Olivia. I wonder what the young fellow makes of it, mused Christine. The new lodger; he had only recently moved in. A woman from down the road had approached Christine in the corner shop, just as Christine was negotiating which and how many sweets the shop owner was going to put into the white paper bag. Several large glass jars stood neatly on the counter top having been carefully taken down from a shelf behind her.

"I didn't know Mavis had a son?"

"Mavis doesn't have a son, it is her…yes, five of the pear drops, thank you."

"A nephew then?"

"No to nephew, but yes to ten of the blackjacks." The shop owner received a thankful look from Christine.

"But I saw him move in?" persisted Mrs Nosy.

Christine left the shop with little patience but too many bonbons.

Despite the late hour, Christine laughed out loud. It only now dawned on her. The young man's name was Sebastian. If 'The Bard' put those two characters together, why not here in Hanwell?

Chapter 9

Isabelle did not relish the thought of going home to her empty house, or worse still the possibility that the children would be there to greet her. She should have asked Christine earlier on whether she could stay at her place for the night, but left it too late. She bemoaned her weak bladder. Just when Christine had been getting ready to be off herself and hugged her friend, the Ladies Room beckoned. Isabelle hurried best she could, almost splashing on her expensive footwear. But to no avail. All she saw when rushing out of the wine bar, nearly falling into the arms of a complete stranger, was the back lights of the black taxi. Even worse, Nobby's arm confidently around Christine's shoulders. Oh, somebody might be lucky tonight. She sighed and went back inside where the rest of the group had also gathered their belongings.

Both couples, Steve and Laura plus Bill and Ben, came over to say their goodbyes.

"We're off as well, Isabelle," said Laura.

"I am so glad we managed to make a start and persuaded Christine to take over," whispered Ben into her ear.

"How are you getting back?" Rick inquired. "I might just stop by at the studio. Do you feel up to coming along?"

This was just the distraction she needed. Especially, today. She so bitterly regretted having taken the side of the kids on numerous occasions, just to keep the peace. She had seen the hurt in Patrick's eyes, particularly lately. Going home now, no way. Truth was, she was afraid about the future.

"Let's drink up, and I'll phone the studio to send a car." Rick managed to grab the arm of the new waitress he'd been ogling all evening. She had indicated her interest in return as far as he was aware. But now she was going to dispose of a nearly full bottle of bubbly that had already been paid for. They returned to the corner table, now looking depressingly empty, not helped by the fact that Rick reached for her hand which was clinging to her refilled glass, looked deep into her eye, and gave her one of his looks, raising one eyebrow. She bet he'd been practising this in front of the mirror for many years.

"So, you prefer my company to that of your offspring after all?"

Isabelle needed all her strength to stop herself from sobbing and confessing everything that instant, but luckily, he added, "I often wondered why the two of you did that."

Isabelle almost choked on the sip of champagne she'd just swallowed, coughed and spattered it across the table.

The waitress, who had been watching, rushed over. "Are you all right, madam?" But all the time trying to get Rick's attention. Her boss had told her earlier he was a famous pop star. Not that she had ever heard of him herself, but it could never hurt to be seen in the company of somebody famous, even if he was an old geezer.

"That was quick." Rick noticed a limousine stopping outside, the windows blacked out. Nobody else could be at the studio, he imagined, otherwise Paul would have sent him one of his old bangers, just to annoy him. Or else his agent had already parted with the outrageous sum for his next recording session. He had booked Studio Two for several days, God only knew why.

Isabelle was glad that the attention had now moved away from her, when the waitress flashed her eyelids at Rick, and slapped the latest iPhone into Isabelle's hand.

"Would you mind taking a picture? It's not every day

you meet a famous pop star." With that, she swaggered her hips and pressed them firmly against his body. Isabelle noticed that Rick used his chance to quickly look at her top, which was by now pulled down so far that her generous boobs almost spilled out. She quickly snapped off a few photos, making sure only Rick was fully visible, with only the long-pointed nose of the waitress showing to his left. Isabelle grabbed Rick's arm and pulled him with her, before he could change his mind and decide to stay. She heard the waitress whisper to her colleague, "Who was that bloke again?" before they staggered onto the pavement.

Isabelle was deep in thought throughout the drive through London and only looked out of the window when the car stopped in front of a zebra crossing, which seemed unusually busy for this time of the day. She turned her head slightly to her right. 'Abbey Road', the sign read.

"I didn't know you were back recording here?"

Chapter 10

With the key still in the door Ben was greeted by an over enthusiastic Timmy, who flew into his wide-open arms, licking his face with such vigour that Bill, standing close behind him, became immediately suspicious.

"Those two have been up to something, take my word for it."

"Oh my diddly widdly, come to daddy." Ben simply ignored Bill, who had been unsure about the two dogs. Ben, however, had fully embraced them from the very first day they brought them home. One big rescue dog, that was what they had agreed upon, and Ben had searched online all the centres within a hundred-mile radius. Sometimes, every hour. "You never know how often they might be updated," he'd argued with Bill. As it was, it had taken him nearly a year to persuade Bill to have a dog at all.

Finally, he saw the dog of his dreams, or so he thought. An old English sheepdog named Dudley. Ben already had his newest pride and joy, his latest mobile phone, in his hand. With shaking fingers, he touched the numbers and pressed it to his ear.

"Paddywaggs, what do you want?" a bored voice answered. Before he could reply the phone flew up from his hand and landed with a thud at his feet. Bill had touched him on the shoulder.

"Jesus, you gave me a fright, what did you do that for?" His hands now on his hips and lips pouting, his favourite hurt stance. Ben didn't wait for a reply. Bill could be persuasive, but not this time. No way. He'd fought too hard for this. At one stage Ben had thought Bill might walk out. Bill was unaccustomed to giving in. But this time Ben put it to a test and won the battle.

On his knees, Ben retrieved his mobile. "If it's broken, you pay for a new one. Hello, hello, are you still there? Sorry, I dropped the phone."

Bill stayed where he was, with his back against the white wall in their ground floor living room. Not that much of the wall was visible in any case. Ben couldn't help himself, often standing in front of it marvelling at the photographs of himself holding up prizes for plays he'd directed. Ben with the leading actors, with royalty, certificates and awards. There were a couple with Bill, the latest one taken at last year's award ceremony.

Ben looked up at Bill while speaking. His eyes not leaving him, he could be so unpredictable. It was best not to let him out of his sight right now.

"Paddywaggs. Paddywaggs," he heard again.

"It's Dudley."

"Is he yours? We did our best. About time you came forward, he's costing us a fortune. Do you know how much he eats? Well, indeed you do, if he's yours. You'll have to compensate us, you know, for his stay here. You're lucky you found him now, we've just put him up for adoption and not too soon, if you ask me."

"No, no, you misunderstand, he was not ours before but he is now."

Bill stared at him in disbelief. Ben sounded like the village idiot. It was time to interfere.

"Give me that." He took the phone before Ben had a chance to protest.

"Good afternoon. We have seen Dudley on your website and we're interested in having a look at him. Could we come tomorrow?"

"Today!" mouthed Ben, still sitting on the floor.

"Tomorrow at three o'clock in the afternoon. That will be fine. Yes, we can find it. We'll enter your postcode into our Sat Nav. What? Sorry, the line's breaking up. Pardon?"

"What, what did she say?"

"The reception here is rubbish."

"She said that?"

Bill sighed and stretched his hand out to help Ben up. It was feasible, having to walk a big dog every day might help him with his weight problem. "No, Ben. Our reception here is rubbish. We should switch companies, as I have said on numerous occasions."

"Do you think Dudley will like us?" Gooey eyed, Ben, in his mind, brushed the dog's fur.

"How could he not? You're getting yourself into a right state already."

"Are you sure you have the correct postcode?"

"Yes, Ben."

"You probably typed it in wrong. Let's stop and check. We should have been there ages ago."

"Maybe it's a sign, and we shouldn't have a dog after all."

"I knew it! I knew it! You're doing this on purpose! You don't want me to be happy!" Ben turned his face away and stared out of the window, but not before giving Bill one of his looks.

"There! Stop, I've seen it, over there. It said kennels to the right. Why are you not stopping?"

"Because I have a car right up my bum!"

With pursed lips Ben turned round. "So you have."

Bill drove to the next roundabout, which seemed miles away with a fidgeting, sulking Ben still looking out of the window. Even Bill was relieved when they finally drove onto the bumpy road and stopped in front of a ramshackle building. "This can't be it, surely?"

He had never seen Ben move with such agility from the passenger seat. He was out of the car before Bill could voice his doubts again. Ben waddled past the building and out of sight. He was back before Bill locked the car.

"Yes, yes it is the right place, the entrance is round the corner."

Off he went again. Bill caught up with him at the door which was below a tired looking sign. 'Paddywaggs Dogs Rescue' could be read if you really concentrated.

"We are not having a dog from here."

"You are prepared to leave our Dudley in a place like this?" Ben's hand reached towards the door handle, but suddenly he thought better of it and dug in the pocket of his tight white trousers. A pristine handkerchief retrieved, he shook it out and used it as protection against the grime on the handle.

Ben's face fell. "It doesn't turn. There's nobody here." He was close to tears.

"Yeah, whatcha want?" Rubberboots, as Ben immediately decided to name her, was in danger of dropping her cigarette out of her mouth with the shock of seeing the two strangers.

"D-D-Dudley."

"For goodness' sake, Ben, get a grip. We're here to look at Dudley."

"He's gone."

"What!!!!"

Bill placed a hand on Ben's arm. All he needed now was tears.

"We phoned and told you we were coming at 3pm."

Rubberboots fixed them with a glare. "In case you haven't noticed it's 5pm and we're closed."

"We couldn't find it. So where is the dog?"

"Some other blokes came and got him. To be honest, I thought it was you. They didn't even pay for all the food I gave that mutt for the past week. Frankly, I'm glad I got rid of him when I did."

"I told you we should have come yesterday!" Any minute now Ben would have one of his tantrums.

Bill tried to rescue the situation. "Do you have another dog we could have a look at?"

"No other dogs here."

"But I can hear barking." Ben perked up a little.

"Those, nobody wants those. Have to put them down I'm afraid."

"Noooooo!"

This time Rubberboots did drop her cigarette, which landed inside her filthy wellie.

"Arrrrgh! You idiot, look what you've done!" Boot in her hand, she spat on her grubby hand and wiped over the burn on her calf. "Get off my land. Go on, leave!"

Bill was livid. "We are going to have a look at the dog we can hear whimpering, if not I'll phone the police," he said through gritted teeth and received a grateful look from Ben.

Hand on his hankie to cover his nose, Ben followed her into the back yard. Through another door, and a corridor led them to the end of a windowless passage. There was a cage inside where two small, frightened animals cowered together for warmth and comfort.

"They have no fur," whispered Bill.

"They're Mexican hairless. Proper breed you know. Very expensive, I can tell you. But I can do you a good price if you take them both." Rubberboots undid the bolt and opened the cage. Immediately the dogs cowered further away.

"Get away," snapped Ben. He took off his Hugo Boss linen jacket, wrapped it around the two scared animals and lifted them gently. He felt them trembling in his arms.

"Two hundred pounds if you want them."

"Actually, we are not giving you a penny, but you are going to give us the address of the nearest veterinarian, plus I suggest you retire from your line of work."

Chapter 11

It must be here somewhere. It was the third box Christine had negotiated down the steep ladder leading from the small opening in the ceiling back down to the landing. First, she'd had to search for the pole with the hook at one end. Where was that blasted thing? She was sure she'd seen it recently. That was, of course, when she didn't need it. It happened more and more lately. You come across something, wonder what it is doing there, conclude it is a good place for it after all; easy to locate it if you need it. But, when you do actually want to use it, it is nowhere to be found, although it seemed the perfect location at the time.

And another thing. Don't they say most accidents happen in the home? And why was that? Only too late did she think about the small stool she'd bought for such a purpose. Why did she buy such a short pole anyway? She inspected it when she eventually found it under the bed between two suitcases. She shouldn't have sat up that quickly when she held it up like a trophy. Immediately, her temples started throbbing again and she felt a little light-headed. She'd prefer to forget the amount of alcohol consumed yesterday and then last night. She had remembered the paracetamol trick before she went to bed. Thank God for that, otherwise it would have been curtains for the rest of the day.

Her ankle only hurt a little bit now. She should have remembered that the office chair she'd pulled up to stand on had wheels. That was why she'd bought it, even though it was out of her price range at that time. The loft door had stuck again. She'd had to pull it twice and on the second pull it opened, dropping the flap with speed. She'd lost her balance when the chair rolled back from the impact.

Not in this box either. She should go through them all while she was in the attic and not schlep them all down. She already knew the boxes would remain in her office for several days; if she was honest with herself, several weeks to be more accurate, before she found the energy to put everything back. Or, she would wait until Nobby came by.

She should have replaced the light bulb up there last time, but now she had no spares, and her torchlight only gave several short flickers. She decided to risk it, hangover or not. If she swung her legs through the opening and pulled box after box towards her, there was enough daylight from the room below for her to see. She spotted the old chest bearing her name; the one her dad made for her when she needed one to take to and from boarding school. He had made it in the garage of their cottage in Lymington. She'd insisted on helping, worrying that it wouldn't look like a real pirate chest after all. She even insisted it had to be painted not light blue but grey, with rocks on top where her little mermaid would sit surrounded by shells she had kept from a trip to the seaside the year before. Her mum thought it would be best to place a big net over, so the plastic mermaid wouldn't fall off. Reluctantly, Christine had agreed. She was shocked when her mum and dad unloaded it at her new school in Surrey. All the other chests lined up neatly to the left of the entrance were rectangular, with metal edges, names stencilled on one side. She let go of her mum's hand; no girl at her age entering year 7 would still cling to her mother.

Her brother gave her a push from behind. "Look on the bright side; you've read the brochure over and over again and have been here twice. Unless you still can't read?" he teased her.

"Matthew!" His father's sharp tone stopped him before he could do any more damage.

"I just mean, here, pupils are being treated like individuals. They even call their teachers by their first name. And no uniforms. Not like my stuffy place, Kings." He watched with envy as two boys, about the same age as he, went over and chatted confidently with the prettiest girl he had ever seen. She flicked her long curly hair casually away from her face and over her shoulder. She was looking at him. Matthew immediately prayed the acne cream had done its trick.

"Why am I not going to this school? I could look after Christine."

"Matthew, you and me both, we are looking at the exact reason why you are not here, but at a boys-only school, right?" Christine's father laughed and went ahead followed by her mother.

To Matthew's embarrassment, the girl left the two boys where they stood and floated down some steps. She stopped in front of Christine.

"Hi, I'm Angel, you must be Christine. My, have you got a pretty chest."

"Yours is not bad either," Matthew heard coming out of his mouth, immediately regretting it and feeling the heat rising in his face.

"Dad, wait for me!" He shot past her and caught up with his parents in the main hall.

"There you are." The lady talking to the parents was now looking in his direction.

"Me?" in a flash it came to him, the teacher was speaking to Angel, who had materialised directly behind him.

Angel addressed the woman. "Josephine, I found Christine. I had to promise her that her chest," she shot a quick look at Matthew, who hoped the earth would swallow him right this minute, "is perfectly safe out there. The boys have gone for the cart and will load them in a minute."

The woman smiled as Christine joined the gathering.

"Welcome, young Christine. Say goodbye to Mum and Dad now. Angel will show you around and take you to your room."

"Will I be in the same room as you?"

"No, I'm in year 10 now, you little ones are in a different building." Angel noted Christine's disappointed face and added, "But don't worry, I am assigned to look after you. Taking over the role of your big brother, so to speak."

Matthew thought it best to concentrate on his shoelaces.

Her mother hugged her briefly but gave a lengthy lecture on the do's and don'ts.

Matthew ruffled her hair, pretending it was a daily occurrence that you sent your little sister off all on her own.

This time she did not moan about her brother, but instead revelled in the warm embrace of her dad's strong arms. Only too soon did he let her go, stepping back to overcome a coughing fit. He held her close again and whispered, "Princess, I love you very much, and we'll be back soon. Now you be strong. We'll write as often as we can, and don't forget to meet up with Matthew at Aunty Clare's in the autumn break."

Those were the last words her father ever said to her.

Chapter 12

She could not do it. No, not now. Too many memories in there. Christine pushed the wooden chest back and spotted a worn brown leather strap. One pull and dust specks flew up and danced in the light showing through the tiles on the roof. Her eyes followed them for a while. Somebody has to check that, she thought.

I never even knew I kept this, Christine thought, my trusty rucksack. Yes, if it was anywhere it would be here. She pulled it closer, placed it on her knees before letting it drop through the hatch onto the floor below. More dust floated up. Christine turned around and slowly descended. She was not going to put it back up there. Best to push the ladder into the original position and close the latch. The boxes, already down, could be stacked in the corner. It was a good idea to sort through them anyway. She lifted the rucksack more carefully this time. Avoiding to spread even more dust throughout the house. Her cleaner was not due this week.

A fresh breeze greeted her face when she opened the kitchen door to the small garden. She walked all the way to the back, towards the garden shed. Who would spot her in her old pyjamas? The neighbour on the left? He was too old to care. Several good shakes and she was sure the rucksack was as clean as she could get it. The colour was paler than she remembered. She'd bought it from an old army supply store. They had been all the rage at that time.

I wonder what it feels like now? She put her left arm

through the strap, bent her other arm back. Caught the other loop and shook it into position. A move she had been well practised in. Satisfied, remembering the excitements of those days, she returned to the house through her narrow kitchen and the first door on the right. Her treasured sitting room with the comfy sofa and armchairs. She almost regretted that it was mild outside; lighting the fire now would have made her mood complete.

A coffee might help. She placed her rucksack on the floor. The moment should be savoured. Plus, a fresh cuppa would wake her up completely.

She pulled the little table forward from the side of the settee.

"Blast!" She'd forgotten the coaster. The table had been her dad's favourite piece of furniture and one of the few things her mother had brought back from the Far East. The glass protecting the dragon carvings on the top had long been broken and not been replaced. Christine put her mug of coffee on the carpet, careful not to add yet another stain, and went to get the new coasters she had purchased only two days ago at Daniel's in West Ealing. She loved the old family-run shop. It had been there ever since she could remember. This time she knew exactly where to look. On top of her dining room table. A place hardly ever used to eat a dinner, but ideal to place all your shopping. She'd only wanted two of those coasters but the nice young man in the shop persuaded her otherwise. You cannot break up a set, he'd insisted, even though you could buy them individually. Anyway, the exotic animals matched her mood that day, but she stopped short of buying the additional placemats. The zebra coaster found its place on the coffee table. It was large enough to stop the mug from wobbling. Christine, as usual, sat on the floor, leaning against the settee.

The string holding the top of the rucksack together

seemed brittle, and she took care not to damage it. With both hands she slowly pulled the bag open. The smell of coal tar soap drifted to her nostrils. One of the very few things her mother had taught her; always place a piece of soap with any fabric items you store to keep moths away. Her wardrobes were filled with pieces of soap, most of them the small ones you take away from hotels. Matching hotel shampoos, conditioners and creams lined her bathroom shelf. No need to waste good products, especially if they carried the name of a fancy hotel, such as the Taj Mahal in Bombay. Yes, it did still say Bombay on hers, although the place had been renamed Mumbai for a few years. Christine still called Beijing Peking, but she did like the change from Leningrad back to St Petersburg. It had such a regal sound to it.

On top was her old t-shirt. The grey Rolling Stones one with *the* lips and tongue in red and black. She held it up. This would still fit her. Carefully, she folded it back together and laid it down. Next came a can of 'Hula' drink. Fruit punch soda it read. A smiling Hula girl encouraged you to like it. She also found a flat packet of Curly Wurly and a paper tube of fizzy Spangles. Lost in thought she opened the tube, unwrapped a sweet and placed it in her mouth. She spat it out immediately when the sour fizz exploded on her taste buds.

"Goodness, I used to love this stuff," she sighed. The drink and sweets went to one side with the items she'd decided it was time to part with.

Socks and a baby doll night dress.

"Oh my God," she laughed out loud, almost spitting out the coffee she had just drunk to get rid of the fizzy Spangles taste, not caring whether anybody would hear her and declare her insane. That frilly pink thing. She'd forgotten all about it. And those knickers. These she would have to keep. No way was she going to part with those.

And wearing them with up-to-the-thigh stripy socks and platform yellow boots. What must she have looked like? As she recalled, it hadn't mattered in the sky-high state they all had been in from the hashish they smoked. Images of her running around the field, parting the grass with both her arms. Grass which seemed to have grown as tall as herself in less than a few minutes.

She shook her head in disbelief. Had that really been her in those days? Out came the holder, which you placed around your neck for the items you did not want to lose. A clear plastic front through which she spotted the Ordinance Survey map. The press button flap was still intact, although the button was a little rusty. Careful not to damage it, she opened it slowly, then pulled the map out. She unfolded it to have a closer look. Out fell her treasured black and white Bob Dylan poster and her colourful entry tickets. The massive winged gorilla hovering over New York. Underneath it read, 'Isle of Wight Festival of Music, Saturday 30th August 1969', and on the other one, 31st of August. On the back of each was the list of bands playing that day.

Chapter 13

Isabelle opened first her left eye, then her right. Something was sticking into her back. She reached behind her and pulled one of the cushions away. She sat up and looked around the room. Did she make all that mess? An empty champagne bottle lay on its side on the floor, crisp packets crunched up next to it, a whisky glass still half full.

Bright sunshine penetrated through the patio doors towards the wooden floor. She ought to get up and sit outside for a while. She turned away and looked straight ahead instead. The bedroom door was firmly shut. What time was it anyway? She checked her Rolex but could only make out a faint blur. Her specs should be on the table. She hoped she hadn't lost them yesterday. She relied on them more and more; soon she would need to wear them all the time. She had contemplated investing in some contact lenses or even laser surgery but had put it off again and again. She could fork out for those big glasses, which were all the rage and made you look studious. If she bought them with light sensitivity she could hide behind them like the starlets do with sunglasses. Yes, she would go for those. Just as she retrieved her old pair she heard the key in the front door. A cheerful Rick pushed the door fully open with the metal tip of his cowboy boot, manoeuvring two steaming mugs, one in each hand, a paper bag tightly clutched under his arm.

"You still like your coffee strong, I hope."

"Since when does Starbucks let you take out mugs instead of paper cups?"

"Since your name is Rick, plus I told them I have a guest. After all the custom I bring them, that's the least they can do."

"Any phone calls?"

"If you mean, have your offspring put a frantic search out? Nope!"

He held out one of the beakers, which Isabelle took eagerly. He left the paper bag on the table and walked over to the kitchen part of the room, picking up the empty bottle on the way. He came back with two white plates, opened the bag and placed a large muffin on each.

"Blueberry. Hope that's still your favourite."

"Maybe I should have gone home."

"And then what? To tell you the truth, Isabelle, I think you should stay here for a few days. Let them stew."

"They could do a lot of damage, you know."

"Those two have to wait for the will to go to probate. So, what's the hurry?"

"What if they find out beforehand?"

"I am sure they will. Let's have our breakfast in peace first and while I have a shower, you ring the office and your solicitor. Unless," he looked at her, "you want to come in the shower with me?"

He didn't wait for a reply. He dabbed up the last of the crumbs from his plate and threw her his mobile.

"Yours has no battery life left, you told me last night."

"So, they couldn't reach me anyway."

"Yes, fine. No, I haven't done that, should I come in? Okay, yes, later would be better. About 3pm, alright?"

Rick caught the last of what Isabelle had said. His hair still wet and his jeans felt a little too tight these days. He should have a word with his personal trainer. If his manager really does secure the sponsor, who seemed very keen, they soon would do a UK, or even a European tour. He'd need to be at his fittest at that stage. He checked in the mirror. The Harley Street Hair Transplant Clinic had done a decent job. Luckily, he had gone along with their suggestion in the end. The grey streaks they'd added undeniably made it look natural.

"Who was that?"

"Freddy at the office, said it would be advisable if I stopped by soon. Whatever that is supposed to mean. But I didn't fancy an argument on the phone right now."

Rick frowned. "Now what?"

"Are you busy today?"

"Nothing that can't wait. What have you got in mind?"

"Let's go to my house. With a bit of luck there's nobody there. We'll call a locksmith and have all the locks changed. I also want to call in on the estate agent. He's been pestering us for a while. But you know Patrick, never liked any changes. Now, I am sure, the time has come to do something about it."

"That's my girl."

"And you know what, Rick? I would love to stay here, even if it is on your bumpy old settee."

Chapter 14

Steve was right, and it was time to move on. It had never really felt like home to him. Margaret had insisted they buy it, all those years ago.

Nobby paid for the taxi and unlocked the house, but remained standing in the entrance hall looking around for a while. The staircase was impressive, no doubt about that. The large painting was still there. It had been sold at an auction Laura and Steve held, not long after Margaret's accident, but the new owner never collected it. He should call the auction house about it again. He turned to his right. The only room he seemed to be using these days, and yet his unpacked cases were still standing where he'd dropped them two weeks ago. His old telly stood diagonally in the corner, a settee underneath the window, a small stained coffee table in front. And Margaret's ottoman. Why it was still there he did not know. He would never use it. Plus, it crowded the already tight space. Now is a good time to have a clear out, he realised. But first he needed a drink. It was best to make a new start with a clear head. He went back into the hall and looked up again, half expecting to see the ghost of Lady Hamilton stepping from the painting. Others had said her ghost was there, which was nonsense really. Why would she want to travel to this place, after her death, from Calais all the way to Hemel? There was nothing here for her. Unless, one of her many creditors had lived in the house at the time? That would be a reason to haunt him.

Nobby was sure the bumps in the night coming from the cottage next door proved a point. It was up to him these days to inspect the mews. Nobody lived there now, not since his caretaker had retired last year, and he hadn't bothered to replace him. A company down in the High Street looked after everything for him. Plus, he had the latest up-to-date security system. The red box outside the mews, however, was a fake. The security company said it would do the trick.

Still, when he was woken at night by noises next door, he was drawn towards them, as though pulled by a magnet. He just had to get up irrespective of whatever time of the night it was. Always after midnight. His torch close to hand, next to his alarm clock. His trusted cricket bat hidden just out of view under the bed. In slippers and pyjamas he was at the ready. As soon as he stepped outside his back door, the one leading out of the kitchen with steps down towards the garage and the mews, the security lights would come on. His neighbour, a miserable old git, had complained several times. He'd told him to bugger off and report it to the police if he was that concerned. His neighbour was over a hundred yards away for goodness' sake. The flashlight in his hand was needed to peer through the mews windows. No way would he go inside until the morning. There was this eerie feeling he could never explain. When he did go in the next day it was always the same. An icy blast greeted him. He reasoned with himself that it was the wind through the only partly closed kitchen window. The security company kept promising him to replace the rope on the sash window. To their credit, they had sent a carpenter out on one occasion, who had performed a textbook move. He'd sucked air through his teeth, shaking his head slightly. "Oi, you shouldn't be letting it like that, Mister, to be sure. It's dangerous that is. Oi no, no way." He'd had such a strong Irish accent that Nobby could only estimate that was what he'd said.

❀

Nobby's kettle started to whistle and he took the small cafetière he used from the sink and gave it a quick rinse. The kitchen in the main house was ancient by today's standards. Kept in a 1970s time warp; a look, which was not achieved on purpose, but he'd never bothered to replace it since the day he and Margaret moved in. She had loved it. It was functional, as she'd called it. The great Aga was her pride and joy. He had to admit this was now the only room where he felt really at ease. He pulled one of the chairs out, the metal legs screeching on the tiled floor. He went over to the large fridge with the rounded top. This had been the only new addition when the old one refused to work any longer. But even he could see a modern looking one would never truly fit in. So, he'd invested in one of those retro-looking ones in the palest blue; the colour matching the plastic on the chairs and the Formica table.

He knew Christine liked sitting in his kitchen. That was where they would have a drink on the very few occasions Christine would come over, on her way to somewhere else she would say. But never told him where she was off to.

On her last visit he'd asked why she only stopped by so briefly.

"Nobby, nobody ever knows whether you're actually in the country. I'm here on the off chance. When was the last time you phoned one of us to say you are back?"

She was absolutely right. He had neglected his friends, and couldn't understand what made him so restless. Margaret's sudden death? Yes, it had been a shock. Likewise, his own cancer scare. He hoped now the time had come to settle down again. Oh, he had loved Margaret. No doubt about it. He had to admit that his love for her was not that deep at the beginning. But he had done the right thing when she fell pregnant, and they had married less than a month after she told him. She'd made him the proudest man ever when he'd held Charles in his arms.

The phone in the hall starting ringing and Nobby was glad of the interruption.

"Hi, Nobby, it's Laura. Just wanted to check that you got home all right."

Laura was not normally that concerned. There had to be more to this, he thought.

"Yes, no problem. And you two?"

"We had a couple of errands to run first and just got in. Nobby, what do you think about our idea?"

So that was the reason for her call. "Laura, I think it's brilliant, and I'm glad you suggested it. Although I know the two of you well enough to believe it was not by chance. It's obvious to me that you have thought and talked about it before and just waited for the right moment."

He heard a nervous laugh and Laura shouting to Steve, "Nobby found us out."

Chapter 15

With the map spread out on the floor in front of her, Christine knelt over it for a better look. She retraced her journey with her index finger. Yes, the ferry had carried them from Portsmouth over to Fishbourne. From there they just followed the crowd. English courtesy forgotten, they scrambled onto the next bus to Wootton Bridge. Standing room only, but who cared? She had escaped the protective arms of her aunt. She had lied that she would stay with Lizzie for the weekend. It wasn't a real lie, was it? Lizzie was right here, and they were going to spend the weekend together. True enough. Lizzie's parents believed she was with Christine, which in a matter of speaking, she was. The things we used to get away with in those days. Christine shook her head. Unbelievable really. Are today's youngsters still that free? She doubted it.

They'd walked, like everybody else, for about two miles in the direction of Woodside Bay. The rucksack had pressed into Christine's back; she hadn't dared trying it on at Lizzie's home where they had hidden their bags. What possessed them to take so much food? For surely, you would be able to buy some there on site? Christine could have killed her friend when she confessed on the ferry she'd forgotten to bring the tin opener. It wasn't her fault, she insisted, her mother had queried what she was looking for in the kitchen. Great. Now they'd schlepped all the baked beans for nothing. We can buy one on the Isle, Lizzie suggested. But upon arriving in Fishbourne, there were no shops at the small dock as they'd hoped, and later in Wootton Bridge they had forgotten all about it. Hurrying after the other travellers trying to keep up, they carried the two-man tent between them. They had already decided to chuck it after the event. No point in humping it back.

Christine straightened the site plan, still kneeling on the carpet. The printing was hardly visible after all this time, and it got wet during the rain shower on the second day. She was glad that the poster had survived as good as it did. She shouldn't have folded it this small, but what was done was done. She sat back, took another sip of coffee and checked the plan again. She could just make out from which side they had entered that day and where their campsite was. They had been lucky and found a good spot on Campsite 1, which was near the main stage. Lizzie had been all for just dumping everything where they stood, and getting a good vantage point near all the action. She'd sulked when Christine insisted they'd have to set up first, otherwise they'd lose the spot. She'd seen people arguing over their tent sites already, and she was here to enjoy herself not to fight. However, she agreed just to leave everything inside but not before unpacking the large plastic sheet, which was to serve as their ground sheet. Satisfied that they'd left their belongings as safe as they could, they'd zipped up and headed towards the music.

I wonder whether Lizzie still has the old snaps, mused Christine. She had taken, without asking, her father's best Kodak instamatic. "He won't miss it. Never uses it anyway," she'd confidently announced. It was unfortunate that on that weekend he'd promised to lend it to his neighbour, who had organised a barbecue party in his garden to celebrate his daughter's engagement. Christine had told Lizzie on numerous occasions they wouldn't need a camera. "We'll be too busy to take photos." But Lizzie had insisted she wanted some of The Who and Bob Dylan. Did Christine even know that this would be Bob Dylan's first concert after his accident?

Of course, Lizzie's father telephoned Christine's aunt and asked to speak to his daughter, in the hope she would be able to throw some light on the whereabouts of his camera.

If, after a good search in Lizzie's room, her father had not discovered a newspaper cutting kept in her desk about the festival taking place that week, he most likely would have called the police to report her missing. Lizzie's mother pointed out that both girls were practically adults and off to take up their university places in the autumn. First thing he did was to make a telephone call to reassure Christine's aunt. All hell broke loose when they returned long after the festival had finished.

They had been really close to the stage on both days, mainly because they decided that one of them should keep their place while the other went for toilet breaks. As it was, they didn't eat any of the food they brought along; no point when there were plenty of places to get a large pasty, which kept them going for hours. Other concert goers' drinks were flowing freely, bottles passing from one to another. Up on their feet, jumping with joy, Christine was sure at one time she spotted Lizzie topless. She lost sight of Lizzie for the rest of the night and only caught up again when she became carried along by the flow long after midnight and joined another large group.

She now wondered whether Butlins Holiday Camp was still there. She scrutinised the map in front of her again and decided she would look it up on the website later.

The bloke she'd got involved with on the night at the holiday camp had accompanied both girls back to the site of the festival the following afternoon to gather their things. So, the tins of baked beans would come in handy after all. He wanted to recreate the 'Summer of Love', he convinced them. They and the rest of the group shared the little chalet, conveniently tucked out of sight in a corner, for the week.

He had been in San Francisco in 1967, he proudly told them, after rolling his second joint. If Christine remembered correctly that was when she decided now was a good time to put her frilly baby doll nightie on and prance around outside in the moonlight. Later, she told him she planned to attend the hippie gathering in London at the UFO Club in Tottenham Court Road, but she and Lizzie only managed to go to Speakers' Corner in London in July of that year, to the rally to legalise pot.

Chapter 16

Christine hummed Scott McKenzie's 'San Francisco', gathered her map and poster, scrambled up from the floor and went through the hall into the dining room, which doubled up as her office. She knew there would be time to make a fresh cup of coffee before her old computer had warmed up and decided to spring back into life. She should invest in a new one sooner rather than later, something she had promised herself for too long now. This one she had taken from her office when she left. On it were many useful business files that might come in handy one day. Still, they could all be transferred via a memory stick. She had looked at the computer store in Ealing the other week, almost bought one on the spot. But they only had the display unit and were waiting on a new delivery. She had liked that model. It was of the 'all in one' variety without the separate tower. Plus, with a touch of a button you could use it like a tablet. Yes, she would be going back there to check it out in more detail. She did not phone big companies these days, you got put through to a call centre and never to the store direct. How stupid was that?

In the kitchen, Christine discovered she'd forgotten to stock up on tins of condensed milk, which she preferred in her coffee. Back at her computer, with a cup of black coffee steaming at her side, she typed in 'Butlins Holiday Camp, Woodside Bay, Isle of Wight'. Several sites sprang up. She clicked on the first one. Oh no, it closed in 1980. What a shame. I wonder whether there is anything else I can find? Christine thought. And for a moment she wondered whether it was actually this camp she'd stayed in after all. She clicked on a link, which showed images taken in 2003 and yes, all the buildings were there but almost in ruins. Not one was still intact. She was sure, however, that this had been the place. She tried another site just to be sure. That one redirected her to YouTube links. There were quite a few, that was surprising. First, she clicked on a very short one, which showed how the entrance of the holiday camp looked now, or at least very recently. Next, she selected an old home movie version which came in three parts accompanied by brilliant music. Yes, that was the place. At part two she sang, 'We're All Going on a Summer Holiday' together with the voice of Cliff Richard blasting from her speakers. The third part seemed more professional, like a commercial, so she didn't watch it to the end. She selected one more, again a short one, exactly as she remembered. She felt a little sad watching it and wiped a tear away with her sleeve. Why had she never gone back there? Yes, without fail, she must phone Lizzie. It had been too long since they last spoke. She was sure Lizzie blamed her, and Christine knew she would never really get over it.

Her search engine had come up with another place under Woodside Bay so she clicked on that one. Wow, that was grand, five star no less. Some chalets with a hot tub. Oh my, Rick would love that. She scrolled down the list of accommodation. There were plenty of chalets but only a few with four bedrooms. She decided she'd better check the availability right now for their agreed date. As feared, only one of them was still available. She would have to book it immediately. But was there enough space for all of them? She would have to check with Rick in any case, since she stupidly had put him in charge of booking their accommodation.

Rick's mobile rang twice before it was picked up.

"Rick? Isabelle, what are you doing with Rick's phone?"
"My battery is flat."
"That's not what I meant."
"I know, it's a long story."
"Never mind about that now, you can confess when we meet up, or when you are alone on the phone. I guess Rick is about."
"Yes, yes, sure, do you want to speak with him?"
"Yes please."
"Rick, I'm not checking up on you, or asking what you two have been up to. Not this minute anyway. I have looked on the computer this morning, you know, about our plans. And I've come across this brilliant place we could stay when we go over to the Isle of Wight on our search. It's like a retreat with chalets. All mod cons. Looks fabulous. For you there will even be an outside hot tub. Thing is, there's only one still available with four bedrooms. What do you say?"
"I say go ahead and book it. But why check with me?"
"Rick, you were in charge of finding us a place."
"Was I?"
Christine laughed. "Isabelle has clearly messed with your head. I would love to know the details, but unfortunately, I have no time for idle chit chat. I have rooms to book. Give a hug to Isabelle from me, on second thoughts, best not." She laughed again and ended the call.

I will find out eventually, she thought. Isabelle will spill the beans if I press her a little. The computer had shut itself down. Damn, I hope it doesn't die on me now. Christine pressed the restart button and waited. This old thing reminded her of the days of 'dial-up'. Who now could possibly imagine life without fast broadband? As she waited, she decided it would be a good idea to search for the memory stick – she knew it should be around somewhere. A yellow and white thing, she was sure about that. Ah, found it. Red and black. Fine, that would do. Just quickly book the chalet and download everything. A knock on the door. I don't believe this, now what? She could make out from the shape through the glass panel it was the geezer next door. He annoyed her occasionally when his telly was on so loud she couldn't think straight. But it was not his fault he was going deaf. And having lost his wife a couple of years ago, he kept relying on Christine to help him with small tasks. Normally she didn't mind, but today of all days! And she still had a bit of a dull headache.

"Miss Christine, would you help me with changing my mattress round?"

She let out a loud sigh, but not loud enough for him to hear. She knew the routine, he just craved a bit of company.

"Tell you what, Fred, I'll just finish what I'm doing, after that, I'll be right there."

"WHAT?" He put his hand behind his one good ear.

Christine shouted into it, "Give me ten minutes," and indicated with her hands.

He rewarded her with a toothless smile. "I'll put the kettle on."

Christine slammed the door and went back to the task in hand.

'Book now', it said. Click, here we go. Noooooo! Just my luck, it's gone. She didn't know whether to laugh or cry. There would be no luxurious chalet, and now as well as everything else, she had the task of finding a place for all of them to stay.

Chapter 17

For a second Christine debated phoning Lizzie straight away but put it off once again. Best to sort out where to stay and book it. Done is done.

Just type in what you're looking for and presto, there should be results. She typed 'Holiday home Isle of Wight sleeping eight' and hit the button. Several sites came up. She selected the one which appealed to her most and dozens of accommodations appeared. This is good, just look at the places. She started scrolling down, ignoring the prices and numbers of nights required but concentrated on the number of bedrooms. She wanted a minimum of four. She stopped at the first one, in Seaview. It looked pretty, but she scrolled on. The next one even had a separate annexe. Who would fight to sleep in there? She had an inkling and abandoned that idea but without dismissing it completely. She might have to come back to it.

The one after that was just as good, gorgeous actually. She started to wonder whether all large houses on the Isle of Wight were this magnificent. She noticed pets weren't allowed. Stupid. How could she forget Bill and Ben's little darlings? Back to the properties she had looked at already. No pets allowed in any of those. Time to be more precise with the search.

On the left side you could tick your requirements, so she did that with number of people and pet friendly. Easy, still enough properties showed up. Another one in Seaview and yes, pets were allowed. It was so cute and had an added bonus; you could use the facilities of the hotel, which was part of it. Rick would be glad to have a bar so close by. Isabelle could dip her toes in the sea at the private beach and Bill and Ben could walk their pooches through the acres of grounds as long as they brought enough do-do bags with them. And she knew that Steve and Laura loved swimming in a warm indoor pool. Yes, it would be great. She put it into her favourites. Now for a look at what else was on offer.

A converted barn in St Helens, a farmhouse near Cowes. And wow, she saw it. How beautiful was this one! And in Shanklin of all places. With six bedrooms and all of them with en suite bathrooms. It looked amazing. There was a short driveway leading off a country road with plenty of car parking in front of the house. The house itself looked imposing. Stone cladding up to the first floor, followed by mock Tudor with herringbone brickwork, and several chimneys. Christine scrutinised it all, hoping the fireplaces were still working. To the right there was a patio door leading to the garden. To the back what seemed to be a conservatory. She switched over to look at photos of the inside. Stunning would be the best way to describe them. Wooden floors throughout, massive living area with ornate ceiling, television fixed to the wall, and no cable connection visible. Not like Isabelle's, which hung on the wall, but shouldn't really. The next photo showed a separate smaller beamed sitting room with an enormous open fireplace. The kitchen. Oh my God, a dream come true! But do we need to cook? Separate dining room, it went on and on. Furthermore, there was a balcony with the fabulous views over Luccombe Bay with miles of sea beyond. The price for the week was as staggering as the place itself. Christine didn't give it a second thought that you had to commit for a week, although their plan was just for a long weekend. She clicked 'book now' and paid the five hundred pound deposit. Wow,

I could live there, she thought as she printed the booking. As soon as the confirmation appeared in her e-mail inbox she would forward it to everybody. She felt totally drained, it was time for some toast with peanut butter, and if she felt really peckish, a slice of cheddar cheese on top, washed down with fresh orange juice.

She hoped Lizzie had not changed her telephone number or moved since Christine had last seen her. She knew there was a new bloke around but that was all Lizzie had said at the time. When was that exactly? She couldn't be sure. Somehow, searching for her friend's number would have to wait. What would a few days more matter anyway? She had a more pressing conversation in mind right now. Christine reached for the phone and pressed the speed dial code for Laura.

"It's me," she said when her friend picked up after the third ring.

"Didn't think you would be up this morning."

"Don't joke. Did you find Isabelle odd yesterday?"

"Isabelle is always a bit odd. But specifically yesterday? No, not really. Why do you ask?"

"Would you believe, I rang Rick to tell him about a place on the Isle of Wight for our weekend and..."

"I thought Rick was going to do that?"

"Apparently he has no recollection of that. In any case, Isabelle answered his mobile."

"Did she?"

"Yes."

"Why?"

"No idea, but it looks like she didn't go home to the loving arms of her offspring."

"That is odd."

"I couldn't have put it better. Do you think something is going on?"

"With Rick?"

"No, with the terrible twins."

"What do you mean?"

"I don't know. I just got this feeling." Christine sighed. "Anyway yes, let's go back to our visit to the Isle of Wight. I've found a great place to stay, you'll love it. I've already booked it and paid the deposit. Only thing is I booked it for a whole week."

"Christine!"

"What? We'll just tell the others, right? Could you phone Bill and Ben and tell them to book the car from that Friday for a week?"

"Are you sure about this?"

"Yes, speak to you later."

Christine heard the click of the other phone. Laura had one of those modern reproductions of an old-fashioned phone.

It could be that it was in her imagination, but she'd always thought Isabelle and Patrick had changed after the twins were born. When they'd first announced she was pregnant, she would talk about nothing else. And when they found out it was twins, every time those two kicked inside her, Isabelle would phone around. How many times Christine had to feel her swollen belly, she did not recall. Suddenly everything seemed to change. First, she had put it down to new baby blues. She had talked about it with Laura, but she had been too preoccupied with her own little girl and brushed it aside. But why had Isabelle cut herself off before the birth and had not contacted them for almost a month after? Even though the friends had tried constantly to see her, there was repeatedly one excuse after another, and eventually, when they did all meet up, Isabelle had been pale and withdrawn.

Chapter 18

"You won't believe what Christine did!" Bill turned around expecting Ben still to be engrossed in the newspaper he'd spread out in front of him on the dining room table. The paper was still there but Ben was nowhere to be seen.

"Ben! Ben!" He spotted him at the bottom of their garden. They should trim those trees behind the pond soon, the garden got little enough sunshine as it was. As soon as he opened the patio door, Timmy sped towards him. At least somebody cared about him. He softly scratched behind the dog's ear.

"Ben, what are you doing down there?"

"Look at this, another hole in the fence. If I hadn't spotted it, the dogs could have got out."

Bill doubted that very much, those two were far too comfortable and happy with their home; no chance they would dig a tunnel deep enough to make their escape. But Ben was right on one thing, the fence at the back needed replacing, and he wanted it to be as high as possible. Those new neighbours of theirs were proving a nuisance. They weren't close neighbours exactly; their gardens backed onto each other. There was now a family with six children living there; constantly out there shouting, washing casually thrown onto the washing line. When you stood on the little stool at the back-bedroom window you couldn't fail to notice it. That and the fact that the ball they played with landed over the fence at least once or twice a week.

"I bet those little horrors next door damaged the fence

to crawl through and get in here." Ben was obsessed with his privacy.

"We'll go to Wickes this afternoon and order the new panels. Now let's look on the computer where we will be staying on the Isle of Wight and while we're in the mood, check out the hire car situation."

"Rick found a place already? I would have expected him to still be in bed this time of the day. Did you see the looks that waitress exchanged with him all afternoon? I bet he gave her his address."

"Christine booked it and it was Isabelle who went home with him."

"Whaaaat? Why did you not tell me before? Come on, tell me. What's going on between Isabelle and Rick?" Bill now had Ben's full attention. Ben thrived on gossip. Luckily somebody rang their doorbell before Ben could speculate further. He quickly shut both dogs in the cloakroom near the front door. Maybe he should not have used that pink and lilac wool in the outfits he crocheted only recently for his beloved pooches. People are so ignorant when it comes to this breed of dog. Don't they realise how sensitive they are, having no fur at all? How would it be if we all pranced around outside in the nude come rain or shine. Only too often Ben felt obliged to explain to total strangers why the dogs wore his latest creations in the middle of the summer. But pink and blue crochet jumpers and matching leggings were for the home only.

Ben had always wanted to take up the art of crochet and his dogs gave him the excuse he had been waiting for. He couldn't fool Bill, who had watched him many times, looking at the internet. Ben burst into floods of tears with happiness when as a birthday present he'd received an enrolment into the crochet class at the local community centre. Apparently, it had become all the rage again. That and needlework. It didn't bother him that he was the only male in the class of a dozen or so. Some of the ladies there were so encouraging and two of them, who reminded him a little bit of his mother and aunt, he had regular coffee mornings with. He even persuaded Bill to cook for them one night. How was he to know that both of them were vegans when Bill presented his best beef Wellington? Further embarrassment ensued when Bill, shocked by the expression on their guests' faces, dropped the beef on the floor. Timmy and Tommy had pounced on the unexpected treat in front of them. Bill had hastily booked a table at the ladies' favourite restaurant and the evening turned into a great success, so much so that the four of them often met up.

"The Amazon parcel has arrived. I wouldn't mind viewing some of the DVDs tonight." Ben had already ripped the wrapping from his latest purchase, a selection of Broadway productions, some of them produced by former colleagues.

Bill was engrossed in the computer. "Yes, Christine is right, this is the place to stay."

Ben forgot a moment about the evening's watch list, went to the computer and looked over Bill's shoulder.

"Does she want us to look at it because that is a place we should buy?"

"I don't think so. Look, there are the dates booked."

"A whole week? How can we be away a whole week?"

"There, it clearly states 'Dogs Welcome'."

Ben's mood softened a little when Bill pointed this out to him. "But to be away for so long…what if I get a phone call from the agent about my next possible production while I'm so far away?"

Bill thought it best not to reply. They both had agreed to retire. Plus, Ben hadn't heard anything positive from his agent for over a year now but still jumped every time the phone rang. It was hardly Bill's fault that costume dramas were the in thing on the telly these days and his skills were in demand. And yet he had said no to every offer coming his way, so far. The whole idea about the Isle of Wight seemed perfect timing.

"If Christine has found this fabulous place for us to stay, just think what she might dig up as potential purchases. Yes, let's book our transport straight away."

Chapter 19

Laura had been concerned about Steve for quite a while now. She still didn't know how she should approach the subject. Would he be in denial or even get aggressive, as he did so often these days? She was surprised how he'd kept it together at the wine bar. Nobody seemed to notice. It was only Christine who had shot her several concerned looks. No point in ringing Berliot, she would only half listen, panic, drop everything and try to somehow get back to England. Not the easiest of journeys. Especially since Laura would have to send her the funds for such a journey first; and who, back home, would look after the youngest children? No, best not to worry her. She should speak to Christine instead, or better still, go and see her. Yes, pop in unannounced. That would be best. The only problem was, where would she tell Steve she was going for a whole day? Bagshot to Hanwell was an all-day outing. She put her mug of freshly brewed, steaming hot coffee on the pine table. One of her trusted mugs; bought at Dunkin' Donuts in Anaheim in California in 1989. And here it was, one of the two still intact. If you looked carefully the orange writing was still faintly visible after years of abuse in the dishwasher. She liked her coffee really strong with a small amount of cream. Very continental, she had been told. Steve had gone back to bed. He'd said he was tired, but she'd noticed his hands were shaking more.

Laura heard the bells from the nearby church. She remembered there was a wedding scheduled for this morning.

She had not been there since the vicar threw himself onto the bonfire that cold night in November. What had possessed him to take such desperate action? Little had been said in the village about it, so you would never find out what went on. Sheer desperation, was all she could think of. He had helped so many others and there was nobody he felt he could confide in to help him with his demons. It was very sad.

She now occasionally attended Holy Trinity church in Sunningdale. She'd found it by accident really, the day she'd been looking for the grave of Diana Dors, the actress who had died of cancer in May 1984. She had just seen a documentary, which was called 'Who Got Diana Dors' Millions?' It was fascinating. It focused on the actress having used an ancient code system to hide her possible millions. Miss Dors had previously given her son a scribbled note with part of the code written on it, confiding in him that his father, Alan Lake, had the key to unlock the secret. But Alan, unable to cope with the death of his wife, had committed suicide some five months later, taking the secret with him.

She had asked a woman leaving the church whether she knew where the cemetery was, and they'd ended up walking there together. Her new-found friend, Jill, owned a flower shop and arranged displays in many of the churches in the area. Nowadays, both met as often as they could and together attended many events at South Hill Park, near Bracknell. They had even considered joining a jewellery and silversmith course there, but had never really got around to doing anything about it.

Laura could use her friend as an excuse, just telling Steve they were going on a shopping trip to London. He'd never find out, would he? But still, just dropping in on Christine? That was not such a good idea. She never seemed to be at home these days. She could use the same excuse, phone her and say she would come by on her way into London and confess the true reason when she got there.

Laura thought she heard a noise from upstairs. She turned the small telly off, which was on a bracket on the wall, next to the shelf with all the spices, most of them never used. She left the kitchen and listened in the hallway. Nothing. With a click the telly lit up again. It was her favourite programme, and the only one she didn't like to miss. 'Bargain Hunt'. She and Jill had applied to appear on the show and had been so excited when they'd received a reply from the BBC, telling them they were on the list. As soon as there was a filming scheduled in their area, the BBC would be in touch. That had been over a year ago. They'd heard nothing since.

She checked for a noise from upstairs again. Nothing. Going back into the kitchen she looked around. It would be so good for them if this crazy idea of theirs, all of them moving in together, really did come off. This house was in serious need of updating. It was something they had meant to do for ages, but work had kept them so busy. Renovations had been put off again and again. Nowadays, they didn't dare bring any clients here. What would they think? Steve and Laura came up with the craziest ideas for their houses, but look at their own.

What about the time they'd remodelled the home of that TV presenter, what was his name? It escaped her for a moment but she saw his face clearly in her mind. Yes, his wife had wanted a patio door that would slide down into the ground and disappear from view altogether. It had been done before, but this one presented an extra challenge. The house was built on solid rock up a steep hill. They'd thought to overcome the problem by suggesting to her that they build the swimming pool to the side of the property instead of directly facing the sea. The wife was not having any of it, blaming her best friend for suggesting Laura and Steve as the experts who could handle anything. On and on she went. Laura had never seen Steve that angry and was so proud of him when he rolled up his plans, placed them back into the tube, took his briefcase and said, "We are obviously not the right people for you." Laura and Steve left her standing there, mouth open, and slammed the door behind them. They got the job and the project went smoothly after that.

She heard Steve calling her name. Better go upstairs and see what the problem was.

Chapter 20

Isabelle changed her mind about Rick accompanying her to the house to wait while she had arranged for the locksmith to come over. She needed some time to pack some clothes if she was going to stay at his place for a while. She hailed a taxi instead. It took only about half an hour to get from Kensington to her place in Wandsworth. She didn't believe the twins would be there. Carmella would have put the alarm on before she left the house, after clearing everything away from the wake. The twins had only stayed a little while after the service. She'd had to explain several times that their children found it all too overwhelming. Overwhelming? That was an outright lie. If the move really went ahead, how would she cope without her trusted Carmella? She had nobody now since her son, Antonio, had returned to live in Sicily.

The house looked sad and lonely standing there, partly hidden by the bushes at the front. No, she could no longer live there and the sooner she got away the better. Patrick had invested in some properties on the outskirts of London some years ago. Two flats; one in Cockfosters and one in Epping. That was when the twins were still at school. It must have been foresight. Their children now lived in one each, paying no rent of course; it was their given right, or so they argued when Patrick had approached the subject after a really unpleasant disagreement. It had ended up with them leaving the house in a hurry, slamming the door behind them. Patrick should have arranged to change the locks at that point. They had, however, installed the newest security system.

Where had it all gone wrong? No point in dwelling on it now, Isabelle decided. She was just going to get on with her life. Her Patrick was at peace now, being spared any further nastiness, which she was convinced, was brewing.

The answer phone blinked like crazy, Isabelle noticed when she entered the hall and disarmed the alarm at the box behind the curtain. She had a quick look. Twenty messages. She picked up the post that had been pushed through the letter box in the front door. She flicked through the letters as she walked into the kitchen. Most looked like condolence cards. She dropped them on the kitchen table, but put the letter from her solicitor into her handbag. She retrieved the Yellow Pages from a stack of books standing upright on the dresser, found a locksmith in her area and called for him to come over. Yes, it was an emergency, she explained. That would cost extra, but he promised to come within an hour. She gave him the make and model of the locks now being used and made sure he understood that two new locks were required. Yes, he had some in his van, not to worry. She then phoned Carmella and asked her to come over. There was nothing to worry about, she quickly added, but she was going to stay with friends for a short while and needed to see her beforehand. Isabelle took her black coat off, hung it in the back of the antique wardrobe and went upstairs to pack.

Into her small case she placed three pairs of trousers, debating with herself whether everything she packed should be black or dark, but decided against it. She added two pairs of cropped trousers and removed the dark long ones. Several light sweaters followed her underwear and toiletries. She lifted the case off the bed. Quite heavy, at least fifteen kilos she guessed. Rick might fear that she had decided to move in altogether. But she could also go and stay at Christine's for a while. Who knows?

The locksmith arrived more or less when promised, and she simply ignored his questions about why she required new locks. She was paying over the odds anyway, so no explanation necessary. It was different when Carmella arrived. She gave Carmella Rick's mobile number just in case her own was not charged or she was in an area with no connection. Surprising really, how many areas were still not covered. Soon, she called herself a minicab from the same company they'd always used. There was no point driving her car in London. For a start, there was nowhere to park it at Rick's. The last thing she did was listen to the messages on the answer phone. As anticipated, most were from concerned acquaintances. She deleted them. Only the last message was worrying. Her solicitor had requested her to phone as quickly as possible. She heard the taxi outside, disconnected the answer phone, took a set of new keys with her and locked up firmly.

Isabelle felt so comfortable at Rick's flat, she never wanted to leave. She pondered whether their idea of living on the Isle of Wight was the right thing to do. What about here in Kensington? But she quickly dismissed that thought. Far too expensive and too close to a situation she wanted to get away from. Yes, Isle of Wight sounded good. Outer Hebrides even better. She smiled to herself. She doubted whether her friends would be prepared to move that far away.

"What are you smiling about? Come over here and taste my sauce." Rick wiped his hands on the tea towel he'd casually slung over his shoulder. The striped blue and white apron tied tight behind his back. She knew he loved cooking, but it was something he would never admit to.

Isabelle negotiated her way out of the comfy couch and moved over to the breakfast bar. Rick's flat was beautiful. He had bought it after his last divorce with the money his latest ex had left him with. He'd been lucky. Just when he was about to sign on a poky little terrace in Shepherds Bush, the property market crashed. His estate agent, who had received many commissions from him over the years, immediately went in search of a property nearer to the West End and found this little gem in Kensington; a one-bedroom ground floor flat in need of updating. Laura and Steve had remodelled it skilfully, and created an impression of the place being much larger than it was. From the communal hallway, his front door led straight in to the open-plan living room with a surprisingly large garden beyond. Wooden floors throughout, the fitted kitchen to the left, shiny white cabinets and grey granite work surfaces. To the right, the sitting area; light grey, spacious sofa and armchairs, with a massive television attached to the wall and the latest Bose sound system. Musical instruments in the space next to that. On the far right, the doors to the bedroom and bathroom. Steve had used a dual entry system for the bathroom. One of the doors was en suite and the other provided entry from the sitting room. This only became an issue if you forgot to lock the other door when inside. But that happened only occasionally. Rick only needed one bedroom, he had told everybody and winked at yet another waitress while scribbling his phone number on her lower arm but high enough so it wouldn't wash off when she had to do the dishes, he'd chuckled.

"Promise me not to tell anybody I cook. That would ruin my reputation." He looked into Isabelle's sparkling eyes over the counter. "Your eyes are like little diamonds, you know?"

"Rick, are you practising your latest chat up lines on me? Any young female would wonder whether that was a compliment or an insult."

Rick passed her the open bottle of red wine. "Why don't you pour us another glass, and after that, you can tell me what is really going on with you."

Chapter 21

This was odd, thought Christine. The meeting they had planned at Nobby's had been brought forward. Rick had hastily phoned around but said there was no time to explain. "Let's just meet at the wine bar again in a week's time."

If Christine was disappointed she did not let on. Such is life, somebody must have decided against the plan after all. She wondered who had chickened out. Nobby? Surely not. He was in desperate need of company and would embrace it with open arms. Laura and Steve? No way, since it had been their idea all along. Plus, she has seen the concerned look in Laura's eyes. Bill and Ben possibly. They already lived a contented life, so why uproot? Rick? Yes, that was a thought. Must have been all that champagne, which made him agree to go along. He would never be able to live without his fans and all the associated razzmatazz. Yes, Rick must have talked it over with Isabelle, and she must have agreed to face their friends with him when he backed out.

Now the whole plan would be shelved or scrapped altogether. Was there any point only some of them seeing it through? This was a shame. The idea had grown on Christine. And why not? Also, she had thrown herself into the search for a suitable property with some gusto. She'd been about to contact some of the estate agents when she'd heard from Rick about the new arrangements. Four properties had been on her shortlist, plus a 'wild card'. Yes, property programmes on the telly always presented the prospective buyer at the end with a 'wild card'. The details of that property she was not going to share with the others until they got there.

She put the printed leaflets to one side, thinking about the money she'd just spent on a new laptop and printer. A printer she possibly hadn't needed. But the salesman explained that her old one might not be compatible. Yes, that was the word he used. Was she sure the old one worked wireless? She'd considered for a few seconds. No, she wasn't sure. So, in for a penny in for a pound, as her mother would have said. The young man had winked at her and said he would come around to install it personally. She had declined that kind offer. If all else failed, Sebastian from next door would help. He was a computer geek, a fact the 'new Olivia' would never let on. It didn't fit their image. But with computer work you can earn good money, and even the happiest lovebirds have to eat, right?

She must have got the date wrong after all. She arrived late at the wine bar and none of her friends were in sight. The chap behind the bar noticed her when she entered and made a movement with his head indicating to go right through. She shrugged. Right through to where?

"Back room," he mouthed.

They had a back room? All the years they'd been coming here, and she never knew that before. Nor had there been a need for the friends to meet somewhere presumably more private. She got an uneasy feeling about it but calmed down when she looked around. The wine bar was packed, there had been no room for them. And since Rick was one of their favourite customers, the owner must have felt inclined to give them special treatment. He liked having a famous musician at his place for all to see.

There they were, looking at her when she entered. Around a table with coffee and cakes. Coffee?

"Spill the beans, something isn't right. We're not going, are we?"

"Chrissie, come and sit here. I've kept a chair warm for you." Nobby grinned and pulled the chair into position. She left her shoulder bag with all the information she had brought with her, just in case she'd got it all wrong, against the wall. Took one of the mugs and reached for the coffee.

"Is it still hot?" She decided to wait and let the others fill her in, but looked from one to the other trying to gauge their mood. Sombre was the best description.

Rick cleared his throat ready to speak.

Christine frowned. "Spare us the details, Rick. You've changed your mind, haven't you?"

"Have you really, Rick? Is that what this is all about? I never thought." Ben shrieked and pushed his bottom lip into his best sulking position.

"Let him explain." Bill patted Ben's hand and gave a reassuring glance.

Nobby laid his hand on Christine's. Just to ensure she was in no doubt that he would move into a place with her anytime, just say the word. Or so Christine thought, and pulled her hand away. Both her hands were now safely placed around the mug of lukewarm coffee.

"It's me."

All eyes turned to Isabelle.

"You? Isabelle, don't worry. We understand the shock of losing Patrick and all that," reassured Ben. "It's okay, we can pick the project up next year when you've had time to take a breath. You might be feeling different soon."

"Isabelle has something she would like to share," said Rick.

"I…I don't know where to begin, you will all hate me."

Christine felt Isabelle's discomfort and pain. "Isabelle, we could never hate you. Just start at the beginning."

Isabelle took a deep breath, looked at each person

individually, her hand still holding on to Rick's, and their eyes met.

Realisation shot through Christine's mind. Blimey, who would have guessed? Those two had a thing going all along. And here comes their confession.

"Well…" Isabelle started.

The explanation must have lasted at least forty-five minutes. After Isabelle's brief hesitation she was unstoppable. Story after story poured out of her. The friends sat there open mouthed. Not one of them drank their coffee, let alone dared to reach for a piece of the scrumptious-looking cake. Ben almost interrupted once but even he thought better of it.

You could have heard a pin drop. After a moment's silence Isabelle added, "There you have it, I am really sorry."

All of a sudden, everybody talked at once and Christine went over to give her friend a big hug. "Oh, Isabelle, it is us who should be sorry."

"I think I need a drink," Laura proclaimed.

Chapter 22

It was drizzling, the kind of rain which settled in all day without the slightest glimmer of hope that the sun would ever shine again.

Christine had made up her mind, she must visit Lizzie. Would she be able to get inside the house this time? She hadn't succeeded on her previous attempt. Lizzie had insisted there was the cutest new little bistro not far away and that they go there instead. Her cleaner was busy in the kitchen, she'd added hastily. Christine hadn't met the new fellow who had moved in not so long ago. Why ever not? Lizzie had been adamant that day that the injury to her face was due to hitting herself on a kitchen drawer. She had bent down to pick up her tea towel and forgotten the drawer was still open. Christine had her doubts and now felt extremely guilty for not having done anything about it. On the odd occasions they'd spoken, Lizzie was cheerful. Too cheerful for Christine's liking. But her friend had made it clear she was far too busy to meet up.

Christine's coat was soaked but she remained standing near the school gate, hidden amongst mothers hugging their young children. Occasionally one of them calling their child back. The mother was still clutching the packed lunch, or so it seemed. From where she stood she could observe any comings and goings from Lizzie's house; the house she'd bought from her share of the insurance money when her parents were taken so suddenly. Lizzie had never confided in Christine how it came about that she had not been on the short flight in the light aircraft that day. But Lizzie had not shared anything with Christine for many years.

She had taken the Tube from Ealing Broadway and changed at Bond Street from the Central to the Jubilee Line, alighting at Finchley Road station. From there she walked the short distance to Netherhall Gardens.

The front door to Lizzie's house opened. The chap leaving did not turn round to say goodbye, just slammed the door so hard that some mothers turned round to see where the noise came from. He then hurried to a sleek black sports car. Christine could not make out the make or model from that distance, but it did look expensive. He shot off in the opposite direction and with a screech of tyres disappeared round the corner. Now, Christine thought, before Lizzie might leave the house. She was out of breath when she rang the bell and waited. No answer. Christine tried again, only this time more persistent. Nothing. At that point, she remembered their old ringing code, which used to annoy their parents no end. She tried it, and out of the corner of her eye saw a shadow behind the window to her left.

Christine bent down and opened the flap through which the post fell into a basket attached to the other side of the door.

"Lizzie, I know you are there. You might as well let me in. The neighbours are already watching us because of the commotion that chap of yours made, leaving in such a hurry."

Peeping through the slot, Christine saw Lizzie approaching the front door and stood up again. The door opened slightly.

"Christine, you should have let me know you were coming, I have to go out, sorry." But before Lizzie had the chance to shut the door again, Christine pushed it open and stepped into the hall.

"Jesus, Lizzie. What happened to you this time?"

Tears were forming in the lifeless eyes of her once adventurous friend. Christine put her arms around Lizzie's thin body and held her close. She felt her tremble. "I should have come sooner, I am sorry," she said quietly.

"I never blamed you, not once."

"And I never believed you did," Christine lied.

Inside, the downstairs part of the house was spotless. Was this the same person with whom she had shared, let's say, almost everything? That Lizzie was a scatterbrain and comfortably untidy. Not like this robot she was now following into the kitchen. Remodelled, she surmised; clinical, as had become fashionable lately. Christine went over to the breakfast bar where nobody seemed to have breakfast, and pulled out one of the uncomfortable-looking chrome barstools which must have cost a packet.

"Would you like something to drink?" Lizzie walked over to the wall cabinets and retrieved two of the finest bone china cups and saucers.

"Tell me what you've done to my friend since clearly, you are an imposter?"

One of the cups fell onto the floor, in an explosion which reminded Christine of Stephen Hawking's programme explaining his 'Big Bang' theory. Somehow it had the desired effect on Lizzie. She smiled, sighed and went into the hall. Christine heard a door opening, and rattling and items dropping. Soon Lizzie came back with a dustpan and brush.

"I can never find anything in this house," she exclaimed. And Christine formed her plan. She was not going to leave Lizzie behind again, ever.

They settled on matching settees in the sitting room facing each other, Christine careful not to spill any of the hot chocolate which was in a mug, rather than in cups and saucers. There was an uneasy silence between them until Christine could not stand it any longer.

"Are you going to report him this time?"

Lizzie shook her head and pulled her sleeve further down so that the fresh marks left by very rough hands were no longer visible.

"I think you should. I'll come with you."

"And then what?"

"You can get a restraining order preventing him from coming anywhere near you."

"It will be my word against his. Last month the neighbours called the police in the middle of the night, and when they arrived, they totally ignored me, just took his statement and left."

"What happened next?"

"Nothing."

"Come on? How can that be?"

"Did you not recognise him when he left?"

"I couldn't make out his face. Why, who is he?"

"Does the name Emilio Gassiamos mean anything to you?"

Christine almost choked on the large sip of her delicious drink. "That fancy football trainer?"

"The same."

"Oh my God. That settles it and makes it somehow easier."

"What do you mean?"

"Lizzie, we have him by the short and curlies. We are going to report him right now. Do you have the details from the night when the police came? Do you have a copy of their report?"

"Upstairs somewhere."

Christine followed Lizzie up the polished staircase into the first room on the left. A spacious bedroom. It was immediately apparent the fight had taken place here. The bedding was on the floor next to overturned chairs. The large wall mirror shattered, an object on the floor which must have been thrown against it. And most disturbingly, bloodstains on the bed sheet. Christine had to use all her strength not to cry out but managed to whisper, "Do you have any other injuries?" Lizzie turned her back towards her friend and lifted her sweater.

Chapter 23

They had all agreed, that day at the wine bar, that at least one of them should accompany Isabelle to the solicitor. Rick was the obvious choice. He and Isabelle practically lived together, or at least for the moment. It had taken Isabelle quite a few days to pick up the telephone and make an appointment. And that was only after several text messages from Carmella informing her there had been more messages on the answer phone.

"I should have switched it off, Rick."

"Isabelle, don't be silly. You're not alone in this anymore. Do you think I should wear this shirt?"

Isabelle found it amazing how much money Rick spent on clothing. For his image, he insisted. And as crazy as this outfit was – purple elephants printed on black silk, the cuffs with trees and desert grass, and buttons in zebra stripes – it looked amazing on Rick.

"You'd better carry your jacket, otherwise you won't treat the receptionist to the full effect of your outfit."

Isabelle looked in the hall mirror at her own reflection. Yes, the dark suit would be what any respectable solicitor would expect you to wear under the circumstances. She had, however, changed from a white blouse into lavender to give her outfit a lift. She checked again, her skirt was an itsy bitsy bit too short. She pulled it down hoping to reach her knees when Rick appeared behind her.

Both started laughing. "Oh my God, Rick. I look like your groupie! Let's go before I change my mind."

They had ordered a taxi to take them from Kensington to Holborn. The driver had already rung the bell and Isabelle was half way down the hall when Rick shouted, "Isabelle, your briefcase. Where's your briefcase?"

She retrieved it from under the blouse she had thrown on the floor earlier, closed the apartment door behind her and double locked it with a key hanging from a heart-shaped key ring. In the back of the taxi Rick took Isabelle's hand and nodded his support. Both were silent during the half hour it took to get to Holborn. Traffic in London was as usual very busy at this time of the day.

'Horace Alterman and Associates' it said in big brass letters behind the reception desk. The young girl manning it looked up at them before returning her nail file to the desk drawer. "Can I help you?" she asked with a bored expression.

"Is Nadine not in?"

"She's on annual leave. Who did you say you were?"

The glass door to the left opened and Horace stepped out. He must have seen them arriving. "Isabelle, come in, come in. Sit down. How are you? I have been trying to reach you for days. Did you not get my messages?"

Rick coughed slightly, not wanting to be left outside.

"Horace, this is my friend, Rick."

"Pleased to make your acquaintance. I am a big fan of yours, have been for years. So glad Isabelle brought you along, it is all too much to take in."

He pointed to the vacant chair next to Isabelle and made himself comfortable in his big armchair facing them both.

"Yes, yes, where was I? Isabelle, is it all right if I speak freely?"

Isabelle still had not spoken and just nodded.

"So very unfortunate, so very unfortunate indeed."

Not surprising solicitors bill their clients by the hour; this guy repeats everything three times, was the thought that crossed Rick's mind.

"Where is the paperwork?" He rang the bell attached to the desk and a young legal secretary appeared out of nowhere. "Charlotte, can you get me the file delivered from Browns labelled Iorgovan."

Charlotte went around the desk to the windowsill above which a darkened glass window overlooked Holborn, picked the first file from a large pack, placed it in front of Horace, left the room and quietly closed the door behind her.

"Ah, there it is."

Rick wondered whether the elderly solicitor who had been dealing with all the business matters of Patrick and Isabelle's auction house for many years was the right person to handle such a delicate matter.

He slowly opened the brown folder. "Ahem, Isabelle. Here it says your adopted twins, brother and sister Janette and Edward, have traced their birth parents." He took a deep breath and continued. "However, Mihai and Timia Iorgovan claim that their children were forcefully removed and placed in the orphanage in Timișoara. From there they were smuggled across to what was, at that time, Yugoslavia, which had an open adoption policy."

Horace coughed again. "The loving parents claim they had to leave their remaining eight children to search for their new-born twins, without success."

Rick perked up. "Where are these other eight children?"

"Unfortunately, the parents no longer know but have assured the authorities they have never stopped looking. And now that their beloved Andrei and Ilona have come back to them, they will use some of the money to employ the best person possible in their task."

"What money?"

"Isabelle, as for now, we have managed to put pressure on them not to pursue their original threat to go to the police to report you for kidnapping."

"Could you just repeat that?" Rick felt the heat rising in his face. This was far worse than he'd suspected.

"This is the first I've heard about this," Isabelle whispered.

"Isabelle, did you bring all the papers and original documentation you were given by the Yugoslavian adoption agency?"

Isabelle's hands were shaking. She had the briefcase on her lap; the brown leather one Patrick had given her when she'd returned to work after the twins had settled into their primary school. She couldn't open the little latch and looked apologetically at Rick, who reached over and took it from her. With a click the latch was undone. Rick handed it back and softly placed his hand on her arm before letting the briefcase go.

"This is all I could find." She handed over two copies of British birth certificates, together with a translated copy from the orphanage in Zagreb.

"Mhmmm, what we do know is that the place in Zagreb no longer exists. Plus, the authorities over there categorically deny it ever existed. No way, they said, would our government have allowed foreign adoptions. They are adamant about that, and we have been threatened with a diplomatic incident if we keep insisting. I am afraid to say we cannot pursue any investigations over there." He took a deep breath. "Isabelle, it is quite possible that the children were in fact smuggled out of Romania."

Rick was just about to interrupt when Horace raised his hand to continue. "There is no doubt in anybody's mind that those children were abandoned by their parents and not taken away, as they now claim. Whatever possessed your Janette and Edward to go down this route, I fail to understand. However, they have arranged for DNA tests to be done on the couple in Romania and made their own DNA available to the doctors over there. I may be wrong but it is possible that both your children are over there at the present time. Unless you know otherwise."

Isabelle seemed deflated and shook her head.

"Mr Alterman, what will happen next?" Rick felt it would be best to leave it for today. Isabelle looked very pale.

"Please call me Horace. My advice is to wait and see until we hear further, which I am sure we will in the not so distant future. Meanwhile Isabelle, try not to worry."

Chapter 24

"Why don't you come over for the weekend? The kids would love to see you." Laura had answered the phone after the second ring. Always happy to speak with Christine and even happier to have some relief from the turmoil playing out in her kitchen. Berliot believed in liberal upbringing and it showed. Often Laura complained to Steve that parents let their children run wild these days. That was what had happened the last time she and Steve had planned a quiet dinner in one of their favourite restaurants, the Bel Vedere, an Italian restaurant in the High Street in Bagshot. They had gone there often when it first opened but now Steve declined to go anywhere, unless it was with their trusted group of friends. And even then he sometimes got quite irritable. The shaking of his left hand had increased. But medication could hide it. She knew he sometimes took extra just before they went anywhere. She had a long chat when she saw Christine on her own and told her outright that yes, Steve has Parkinson's. He was trying to play it down, not as successfully as he hoped. She wondered whether Christine would mind telling the others.

"Berliot is over? Were you expecting her?"

"You know our daughter, nothing is ever planned. We get a distress signal that she needs some 'time out' and she arrives. Only this time it's the whole family. A fact she forgot to mention."

"Oh."

"Yes, oh indeed."

"Are you going to tell them about Isabelle's situation?"

"No need for that. In any case it's too close to Eric's own dramatic start in life, and you know what our Berliot can be like. She might try and talk him into exploring his past again."

"What happened last time?"

"Eric was adamant that his birth mother knew what she was doing, and he got the best parents and upbringing any child could wish for. No, it's best left where it is. And if his natural mother ever feels the need to find him, he'll trust the monks to do the right thing."

Christine loved Berliot and Eric. Such kind people. Their children flourished, although somewhat wildly. All home schooled, what else, and with astonishing results. How did Berliot find the time? Christine smiled to herself thinking how simply Berliot thought about things. No need for complications, she'd once said. They'd named their children in alphabetical order, starting with Aage, Bjoote. Caj…Christine gave up after that. And all of them at Laura and Steve's? She hoped there wasn't more to Steve's condition than Laura had led her to believe. Or had the camping ground in Lillehammer run into difficulties again?

The trip they were taking to the Isle of Wight was almost upon them so there was no more time to ponder. Christine needed to ring the agents dealing with their accommodation for the week and go through the list of things they would need to take. They hadn't planned to do any self-catering as such, but now Christine had second thoughts. This would be a great way of finding out whether they could actually live together and Laura had immediately agreed with this suggestion. They would take the cooking in turns. Always two of them. To make it more fun they would draw names out of a hat when they got there, to pair them up for cooking duty. This was perfect because they were eight in number. Still eight at this stage, it was too early to talk to them about her idea concerning Lizzie.

Laura and Christine had discussed a list of basic items they should take with them. At first, they'd thought the items should be distributed to the others with each of them to be responsible for part of the shopping.

"Too complicated," said Laura. "It would simply not happen."

Christine had to admit Laura was right. No, since it was Christine's idea she would go to the Tesco at the new shopping centre. She just wanted to run the list by Laura one more time. They also decided there was no need to tell everybody what was on the list, they would soon see when Christine unpacked her car at Nobby's and reloaded everything into their minibus. Christine hoped there would be enough space and that Nobby would remember to get the breakfast stuff. That had already been agreed on. Christine laughed out loud before she put the receiver down.

Laura was curious. "What's so funny?"

"I pity the person who has to cook with Rick. Can you just picture it? Rick in the kitchen? I hope it isn't me. That reminds me, Isabelle's solicitor told her not to worry."

Chapter 25

"My, you two are pulling today. Timmy! Tommy! Daddy is almost falling over. We'll be there soon enough. No, not through that puddle. You'll get your new outfits dirty."

Bill stayed a few paces behind, rolling his eyes and hoping none of the other walkers overheard Ben.

"I saw that, Bill."

Bill often wondered how Ben did that, he must have eyes in the back of his head.

"Yoo hoo!" Ben had spotted Kenneth about twenty yards in front of them and now hastened his speed. Huffing and puffing, desperate to catch up with him. "Yoo hoo, yoo hoo!"

Kenneth turned around, his own dog obediently sitting down, tail wagging. If he was lucky Timmy and Tommy would be allowed off their leashes, and they could continue their chases round and round the trees.

"No, not today, Buster." Ben bent down and scratched the Boxer behind one ear with his free hand. "You lead my precious little ones into nothing but mischief, and look, they are wearing new outfits. I only just finished them."

Buster tried to look around Ben, checking whether Bill was behind him. He sensed Bill would let the dogs run free. Buster turned his pleading eyes back to Ben.

"Okay, I can never resist you. But if their outfits are ruined I will not give you any of the treats in my pocket." With that he stood up again, patted the pocket of the check jacket and with a sigh unclipped the dogs.

Kenneth greeted them. "I see you're starting a new business venture."

"What do you mean by that?"

"Well, the travel agency."

"Sorry Kenneth, you've lost me there." Bill was curious, especially since Ben had become quiet and was concentrating on searching for the dogs. Concentrating too hard for Bill's liking. That usually meant he'd been up to something which had yet to be confessed.

"You still live on Well Road, don't you? In the big house with parking for two cars in front?"

"Yes, why do you ask?"

Ben decided not to wait for the reply to Bill's question and moved on further across the grass. If he wasn't so worried right now he would enjoy the impressive view across to the trees and bushes beyond. Yes, they were so lucky living this close to Hampstead Heath. It had taken them years of searching to find the ideal house. They'd known which area they wanted to live in but not the exact location. They had moved into a small apartment first, just after they decided to make a go of it and take their relationship further. The apartment at Swiss Cottage was ideal for a bolt hole at the time and from there they could start the search for their permanent home. Mind you, as small as the flat was, it had been big enough to party. Noisy sometimes, and the neighbours underneath them never stopped complaining. That was until the couple below eventually moved out and Lilly and Annette moved in. Bill and Ben knew them from a pub they frequented near Marble Arch. Things were easier after that, but still Bill and Ben continued their quest for their dream home; with wooden floors throughout, where you didn't have to walk around in slippers so as not to disturb downstairs neighbours; the slippers which at Swiss Cottage had been their moving in present from the neighbours below. That was when they were still on speaking terms.

The dream home had to be near Hampstead Heath. That they both had agreed on. Ben took the map of London and drew a circle around the Heath. "There you are, that is our hunting ground." Bill had disregarded north of the Heath straight away. Too far from the action was his reason.

Every free day they'd visited another estate agent, area by area. The search had started to the east first, hence it was furthest away from where they were now. They'd selected three houses to visit, with two different agencies. The one on Parliament Hill they both liked but decided to continue looking. Their luck was in: a conductor, with whom they had worked on many productions in the West End of London, had an uncle who had an estate agency in Hampstead. Instead of Bill and Ben travelling back and forth to the area, the uncle made it his mission to find them their house. They viewed a few and then they saw it. Their home. This was it. On the corner of Well Road. It had been empty for several years, and the agent had somehow managed to track down the owners. They were living in Manhattan and had almost forgotten about a property that a distant relation had left to them. They were quite glad to get rid of it without actually having to travel to England. Yes, the estate agent had done them a favour.

It had been in total disrepair at that time, virtually everything needed to be ripped out and replaced, but that was also the reason why they managed to secure it for less than £180,000.

A bargain even considering at least the same amount needed to be spent to make it theirs. The location was priceless, and close to Hampstead Heath station. So, they went ahead; naturally, it did help to have friends like Laura and Steve, who would take all the worry away. They'd even managed to persuade the local council to replace the pavement at the roadside with angled stone so that the front garden could be converted into two car parking spaces.

To the curiosity of the neighbours on their right and those across the road, their van had arrived with their few belongings from Swiss Cottage, about six months after signing the contract. Ben was immediately conscious that he should not have worn the short dungarees. He'd thought they looked really fetching, but that was in the liberal Swiss Cottage part of London. There nobody would take a second look at you, but here? Would they be accepted in Hampstead? This wasn't something he had worried about before; after all the Act of Parliament, which meant that they could now live free of fear of persecution, had been passed in 1967.

"Do you know in which box I packed the purple overall?" Ben had nervously asked at the time, rushing between the window and several boxes on the shiny floor. He tried to open some of them and wrestled with a large kitchen knife, slicing the tape on one of them, when he heard a knock on the door. Before Ben had a chance to tell Bill not to open it, there he stood accompanied by three people. Ben remained behind the cardboard box hiding his bare legs and shook hands with the elderly woman who moved towards him, having handed a tray of food to what must have been her son, unless she had a toy boy. Her greeting was followed by the seemingly shy younger people still standing in the doorway coughing and venturing, "We thought you might be hungry so just in case we brought these." A girl stepped forward and gave the perplexed Ben a parcel of sandwiches. "We don't know what you like so we made a selection."

Ben rewarded them with a smile. "Thank you, so kind. If you don't mind sitting around the small table on plastic chairs we can polish these off together, and I'll open some bubbly."

"I've seen you on the telly," said the young man, for which he received a stern look from his mother.

❀

"Kenneth, certainly, we still live there. But I still don't get what you mean."

"I saw two blokes arriving in a minibus and parking it there. They locked it up and pushed the key through your letter box. Quickly legged it after that, almost like they were possessed."

"Did it say anything on the outside of the bus?"

"Yes, 'Gay-line Travel'."

Chapter 26

Nobby was feeling cold, although the temperature for outside said twenty-three and that was supposed to be in the shade. He tapped the remote operated weather station. It had not been installed very long, and he wondered whether he'd followed the instructions correctly. More likely not. He'd purchased it online, and like so many things these days the leaflet inside was in any language but English. Tapping on it, like you used to do with the old barometers, did nothing. He should have kept his old one. What had he done with it? Possibly in one of the boxes in the cellar. He searched for the place on the wall where it used to be displayed, but the round dusty mark had disappeared. Maybe he hadn't hung it there at all. Or he'd taken it down before the kitchen had been repainted. A cold shiver started from his head and ran all the way down his back and up again. He pulled his cardigan closer around his body. This cold coffee wouldn't help; besides it was instant since he'd forgotten to replace his beans. He loved freshly ground coffee. He had an impressive display of old coffee grinders lining the top of the fitted kitchen cabinets; out of reach for most people, even Nobby had to stretch himself as high as he could. Either he was getting shorter or the kitchen had grown taller when he wasn't looking. He laughed out loud, and went over to the sink and poured the coffee away.

    He rinsed his mug and turned it upside down for draining. The unit where he kept his mugs was to his left. He moved to the first cupboard door. Wrong again. He did this more often than not, and it worried him. But even he, as a neurosurgeon, could not find a feasible answer. He knew which cupboard he wanted to go to but sure enough opened the door to the one next to it. He was convinced he was wired the wrong way round. Who knows? Or maybe he'd meant to go here all along, although as far as he could remember, plates were kept in this one. He stared at it, had he never noticed it before? Behind all the plates, right at the back, was something that looked so familiar. He took the breakfast plates off the dinner plates and put them on the table by simply twisting his body. The larger plates followed.

He reached for the mug. It felt comfortable and familiar. A white enamel beaker with a blue rim. The handle was a little chipped but the inside undamaged. Christine had said the chips on the handle were caused by the beaker swinging back and forth, being attached to her rucksack by a string. On the other side she'd had a fork and a spoon dangling down. She had collapsed with laughter when she related how she'd stolen her uncle's hand drill, and she and her friend – what was her name? – took it in turn to drill holes into the aluminium cutlery handles. It took them ages, she'd said, they had blisters to show for it. She had showed him her hands and then laughed some more: silly, they had gone by now. That was the night they'd passed the beaker between themselves. Hot chocolate laced with whiskey, sitting in the dark on the floor in his room at the university. Must have been during the three-day working weeks, he pondered. She had fallen asleep in his arms. If he closed his eyes he could feel her and savour her smell. Had he hung onto the beaker for that reason?

Automatically, he went over to the walk-in storage cupboard. He guessed all old houses used to have a massive larder; where else would they have kept all the produce from the fields and garden? He treasured his time as a little boy when his mother used to preserve the fruits from the summer by placing them in large glass jars, sprinkling the fruit with sugar before adding water, or was it the other way round? If it was the pears from the farmer his dad had helped with the last lambing earlier in the season, she would add a cinnamon stick. It undeniably added to the taste. She bought them from the little corner shop or sometimes she sent him. He'd loved that best because the shop always smelled exotic. Mr Patel, the owner, explained the different spices which he kept in little sacks in a glass cabinet. He'd confided that most of his regular customers just told him the dishes they wanted to cook, and he mixed the spices according to his secret formulas. Nobby still had some of the old glass jars, but now he stored small packets of matches in them. Matches he had taken from hotels and restaurants throughout the world. He had no intention of using them. His mother had sat on a stool outside in the back garden; a tea towel on her lap, an old newspaper with thinly peeled skins from the pears which she took from a basket to her right, pear halves cleaned of pips in a bowl on the other side. He often helped unless he heard his friends kicking a ball around at the front of the houses which lined the street tightly packed together, side by side, all the way down to the river. That was too tempting and his mother told him to go and join them. In any case, his mother would not allow any of her children into the narrow kitchen once the boiling process started, not since the neighbour's cousin only just avoided a major disaster when her preserves exploded. The contents were still hot. She had forgotten the metal clips which secured the lid on the jar after you placed the red rubber ring to seal it tight.

He found a box of Cadbury's Bourneville cocoa behind the tins of baked beans. He checked the use by date on it. Only two years out of date, no problem there. He preferred to make his hot chocolate drink the old-fashioned way. Place a small saucepan onto the gas, full fat fresh milk, mix in the cocoa powder and sugar, stirring until it comes to the boil. The only unfortunate thing was the skin on the milk once you poured it into your mug. He hated that. Removed it with a teaspoon and left the spoon in the sink. He took his drink and left the kitchen.

This could be the coldest room, facing north and flanked by the mews on the left and the old stable blocks opposite. His green room faced west and was large and comfortable. The old windows had been cleverly converted into patio doors, which made the room light and airy. Beside that was where his drinks cabinet stood. He did not have to search for the Glenmorangie Original. He unscrewed the top and the aroma filled his nostrils. He poured a generous helping into the metal beaker, smelled it again, and satisfied, he walked to the armchair facing the back garden and the land beyond. He pressed the electric button. The seat reclined, just enough not to spill his drink. He closed his eyes and savoured the moment.

Chapter 27

Lizzie parked the car further away, on the other side, near the school. Christine had told her that was where she'd stood when she saw him leaving and driving off.

Christine had insisted they were going to report the abuse, although Lizzie kept assuring her it was not as bad as it looked. Plus, she had been ignored before, so why bother? It was her word against his, and he could be very persuasive; like the other time the police arrived after the neighbours had phoned. A couple of policemen did arrive some hours later. By then Lizzie had gone to bed and locked herself in. They hadn't even entered the house, or he wouldn't let them in, but Lizzie had heard them and came out of her room. Dressing gown tightly wrapped around her, she listened from the staircase how they all happily chatted and laughed, heard him saying that he and his woman should try to consummate their passion a little bit quieter from now on. You know what some women can be like. Lizzie bet he winked at them. It was something he always did to make himself look more 'macho'. He'd actually had the audacity to say, "I tell you what officers, I am really impressed how our brave police force protect the public and am just sorry you had to waste your valuable time on nothing tonight. Hold on, I can give you a couple of passes for the game next month at Wembley. Just to show my appreciation. I understand you have the occasional police raffle taking place in aid of 'Save the Children'. Good night, officers."

Lizzie had quickly retreated upstairs, double locking the

bedroom door and putting a chair against it, tipping it so it was underneath the door handle. There had been no need; the next thing she heard was the front door slamming and his sports car engine revving. Lizzie had pitied the young girl he would, for certain, pick up that night.

Christine said, "That's it, I have heard enough. We are going." But first she rushed downstairs to rummage in her handbag for her iPhone. She apologised, but was adamant they needed to photograph and record all the marks on Lizzie's body, just in case. Her phone would show the time, date and place where these had been taken. Christine helped Lizzie to get dressed in some comfortable clothing. Lizzie knew that Christine would not take no for an answer and found some loose Karen Millen trousers and a short-sleeved t-shirt in matching grey with a hint of light orange embossing, which Christine, although she tried, could not make out what it said. Plus, a soft light orange hooded cardigan. In normal circumstances, Christine would have taken a step backwards and admired the ensemble, however, this was not the right moment.

Christine had been shocked how fragile Lizzie looked and decided it was best if she drove. With shaking hands Lizzie had handed the keys over and pointed to a red Audi sports car. The latest model. Not easy to get in or out; you almost had to lie down to reach a comfortable position. Upon turning the key, Bob Dylan began to softly sing 'Blowin' in the Wind'. Bob Dylan? Christine shot a quick glance at Lizzie, but she was busy trying to fasten her seatbelt. She fumbled and failed to clip it correctly. Christine undid her own, bent over to secure Lizzie's and fastened hers again.

"Do you have the address of the police station the report was issued from?"

More fumbling, this time in Lizzie's handbag. "Hold on, it's here somewhere. There you are, Finchley Police Station. It's only about ten minutes away. Go down the road and take a right at the end, I'll direct you from there."

Christine stalled the car at the first try and crunched the gears at the second, but eventually eased it out of the tight parking space. By the time she reached the first major road and negotiated joining the very busy traffic, her confidence had returned. Christine spotted the flat building before Lizzie pointed it out and turned into the empty police station car park.

"Looks deserted. You wait here, I'll check what the sign says over there on the door."

Christine tried to open the car door but with a gust of wind it blew back shut. She was in two minds to say something about the car but reconsidered and tried again. This time using both hands she opened the door and managed to slide out without landing in the puddle that was right next to the vehicle; something she hadn't noticed when she'd stopped. Although it was raining she didn't bother to retrieve her coat but ran for the shelter of the building.

"It's closed. Now I have seen everything. A police station closed?" She was damp and out of breath by the time she'd run back to the car and wriggled inside next to Lizzie.

"Let's go home. It was a stupid idea, believing the police might actually be interested."

"No way. Where's the nearest hospital?"

Lizzie took a deep breath. "There's one on Granville Road and there is also a 'walk-in clinic'." Christine followed her friend's directions but missed a turn which was closer than she thought when Lizzie said next left. All the parking places were taken but she spotted somebody just driving off in the street and quickly did a U-turn and backed into a space, to the annoyance of another driver who had hoped the space was his. Christine wanted to give him a well-practised two finger sign but held back on this occasion.

The clinic seemed in chaos. Several patients or their relatives queued in front of what must be the reception desk, but was not visible straight away. Christine feared that Lizzie might bolt at this stage, but having dragged her friend this far was not going to leave without being attended to. She checked around for a comfortable place for her friend to sit. A young man who had a pair of crutches leaning against the wall looked at Lizzie's swollen face and stood up. "Madam," he said with a heavy accent. "Please." And pointed to a seat he was about to vacate.

"No, it's okay."

But Christine quickly pulled her over and Lizzie sank into the armchair. "Thank you, that was very kind of you."

After that Christine waited until it was her turn to check Lizzie in. A kind elderly receptionist listened to Christine's explanation that her friend had been assaulted by her partner.

"I am sorry, but you should really contact the police."

It took Christine all her willpower not to lash out, but she knew that would not get her anywhere. Calmly she said, "We went to the police station but it was closed. This is not the first time my friend has been attacked by this man. And when it was reported the police did nothing. Please just look at her."

The receptionist at first did not react and several people noisily complained that Christine was taking up too much time. This must have been the last straw which had tested the receptionist's patience, Christine realised. She must have had a rough day.

However, the receptionist stood up and opened the latch on the walkthrough counter top, stepped through and closed it again. She looked at Christine and said, "Come on love, you two come with me."

They were guided into a little side room which had a window overlooking a park. The receptionist pointed to seats in front of a desk.

"I'm sorry, but it might take a while until Doctor Callaghan can see you. We are especially busy today. God only knows why. There is the weather, it's lousy, and some of the bums hanging around the park without anything to do have come here just to have a dry place to sit and waste our time, if you ask me. And you don't want to know what I think about local police stations closing all over the country. There soon will not be a safe street to walk on. You mind my words. Would you like a cup of tea or coffee?"

"That is so kind of you. I would love a coffee, but I'll come with you. I spotted a machine outside, and I think my friend could do with a cup of hot chocolate."

Lizzie must have stood near the school for a good twenty minutes. No, his car was definitely nowhere to be seen. She now wished she had not told Christine she would be all right living in her own house. Christine had taken Lizzie home to her place after they'd eventually left the walk-in clinic. They hadn't had to wait as long as they feared for Doctor Callaghan to knock on the door and enter. After introducing herself she apologised that she needed to ask some questions and fill out the forms before she could begin the examination. Only basic details, she explained when Lizzie shot her a frightened look. Lizzie dutifully gave her address, date of birth, name of doctor and no, she had no medical condition. And if Lizzie didn't mind, the doctor wanted another good look at her body. After seeing the state Lizzie was in, she apologised again for having to take some photographic evidence. Lizzie hardly spoke a word and did not protest. After that the kind doctor asked Lizzie to tell her as much as she felt comfortable with. The doctor also wanted a photocopy of the previous police report. She finally asked where Lizzie would be staying, something the friends had not thought about.

"Lizzie will come and stay with me." Christine gave her name and address and her contact details. Doctor Callaghan checked the address. "This is on the west side of London," she said. "But under the circumstances I will make sure you receive a visit from a Scotland Yard detective within the next two days."

Lizzie stayed at Christine's until a restraining order had been issued and handed to Emilio Gassiamos, as well as a request to come in the following day for questioning. He had been reached at the football club's headquarters, where he was negotiating an extension to his contract with the Russian owner of the club.

Chapter 28

Christine had not been comfortable with letting Lizzie go back to her own place. But she was right, she couldn't just crawl away and hide. That would mean Gassiamos had won after all. Lizzie had found some extra strength from somewhere and was ready for him, or so she said. However, she'd had to promise Christine to phone every day and Christine would come over again at the end of the week. Christine hadn't mentioned anything about her forthcoming stay on the Isle of Wight.

She searched for the paperwork with the copies of all the properties she had lined up. That dippy girl Nicky at the estate agent's kept sending her more every day. Granted, some seemed worth consideration, but upon closer inspection were totally unsuitable. Christine had discussed with her, not once, but at least on three occasions, that they wanted to be near the sea. Hopefully with a view and a short distance to all amenities. And what was the point of sending her properties that only had five bedrooms, as nice as the house might be? Six minimum, and that was pushing it. What about visitors?

Christine found the folder underneath the cushion of the old armchair in her bedroom and took it downstairs into the kitchen to make herself some tea. Herbal tea. She'd started to drink it a couple of months ago, when she didn't have any black tea in the house and found a box somebody must have given her at some stage. Something Olivia from next door would bring. That would figure. It said ginger and lemon on the box. To her amazement she actually liked it, and on the strength of this purchased a variety of herbal infusions. She carried the mug into her living room, put it on a coaster on the small table next to the settee and plonked herself down. Feet up ready to get comfy. She reached for her folder. Blast, still in the kitchen. Got up again, retrieved the folder and returned to sit down, hoping there wouldn't be any interruptions. She felt entitled to a few hours of peace and quiet after the stress of the past few days.

The properties in her folder, together with directions how to get there, were sorted by price, which was silly really, since it made more sense to sort them by area. In her folder was also a map of the Isle of Wight which she now spread out on the settee next to her. She took a red pen ready to circle all the places and make a list. They were going to stay in Shanklin, therefore, the first of their visits should be to Bembridge, which was not that far away. Two properties to view. The first one cost over two million pounds and had eight bedrooms. It also had a row of garages and outbuildings, plenty of land, sea views and direct private beach access. Should that be the first her friends should see? What about the other one? Admittedly this only had seven bedrooms, however it also came with a beach hut and a boathouse, amazing views and a private beach. Dippy Nicky had explained that the house could easily be extended to add extra accommodation. As the house was just one and a half million it sounded too good to be true, until Christine realised the beach hut and boathouse had to be negotiated separately.

Ventnor, yes, this one was nice too. Nine bedrooms. A great period house with land and views and less than one million. Aha! Christine picked up the brochure of the old manor house. Eight bedrooms, even had a bar. Rick would like that. And a separate laundry room, manicured garden, plus outbuildings. Christine got a strange feeling every time she looked at it. It felt spooky. The price was just below two million. Upper Bonchurch. Where again was Upper Bonchurch? She took up the map and found it near Ventnor. She circled the area and realised she had forgotten to mark all the other properties. Back to the leaflets she had placed upside down on the floor. Having marked on the map where they could be found she put them back. The one in Upper Bonchurch had fourteen bedrooms, good garden, balconies and decking, views as required and best of all an outdoor heated swimming pool. And all that for less than one million pounds. That would be worth a visit. Another one had eight bedrooms and was at Wootton Bridge. It was right at the waterside, south-facing on a sheltered creek, with its own boat dock. On the leaflet it looked amazing; nearly two million, mind you.

And there was a hotel to consider; with a restaurant. A beautiful Victorian building, set in wonderful grounds with views over Sandown and Shanklin Bay, indoor and outdoor swimming pool and spa. Nicky was supposed to contact the council whether permission would be granted to convert it into a private house. But before she phoned Nicky, Christine wanted to check once more the food items she intended to take and speak with Nobby to ensure he had actually done the shopping for breakfast as promised.

Her items were already on the dining room table: tins of tomatoes, a tube of tomato paste, an onion, herbs, salt, pepper, pasta. Not a lot there she thought, but anything fresh would be bought on the island. What about drinks: soft drink and booze? Had anybody thought about that? Perhaps not. She went back into the kitchen to check her own drink situation. Not a lot left there, polished most of it off when Lizzie was over. However, Nobby had a full cellar, and since they were all going to his place to start the journey, maybe he wouldn't mind them raiding it. No, he wouldn't, she knew him well enough. If he hadn't bought anything for their first morning there she would let him off the hook, visualising the ample drink storage in his large cellar. She would have discussed it with Laura, but she had her own problems at the moment, best not to give her more work. And Isabelle, where could she possibly reach her?

Christine first tried Rick's home number. As she expected, no answer there. She tried Isabelle's mobile phone, and it was picked up after several rings. "Sorry Chrissie, can't speak now, we are at the solicitors again, waiting to be seen any second, call you later." Rick had answered instead of Isabelle. Next, she tried Nobby. No reply. If that dippy Nicky on the island also does not answer today, I give up. But the estate agent was available, eager to confirm all the arrangements which had been made, and said she'd do her best to accommodate the changes to the itinerary Christine now requested. There seemed to be an urgency in the estate agent's voice. Was she trying to avoid the issue of the hotel conversion?

She cleared her throat twice before answering Christine. "I think the council misunderstood and granted a licence, change of use to old people's home."

Chapter 29

Nobby put the empty mug on the floor and picked up his mobile which kept on ringing. He looked at the caller. Christine. He put it back and ignored it. The postcard was on his knees. He looked at it again. A koala bear on a eucalyptus tree. What did the Aussies call it again? Ah yes, gum tree. But why? He could look it up on Google, he guessed. The koala was looking directly at him, or so it seemed. He turned the card round. He looked at the postmark. Posted only ten days ago. That was quick. His only son was not one for many words. 'Hi Dad, guess what? Yes, still here. Are you okay? Are you still coming? Love, Charles and Sophie.'

His grandchildren had long flown the nest. One of them was now, like his father and grandfather, a doctor, working out of a hospital in Perth, but mainly serving the remote communities. He undertook frequent flights to bring back a sick child or an injured gold miner from Kalgoorlie and beyond. One time he had to be flown to a little airfield in Forrest, which boasted a population of two. A distress call had come in. By the time they got their patient to the hospital, the appendix wall had ruptured spreading the infection first to the abdomen and through the entire body, causing sepsis. The little patient had to remain in intensive care for several days.

The other grandson more or less just drifted around. Loved the hippy scene at Byron Bay as far as he remembered. After all, it was only about 320 kilometres away from his parents, who he without a doubt contacted frequently when he needed financial or other assistance. Nobby smiled to himself. Only 320 kilometres in a vast continent like Australia. On the other hand, Noosa and Byron could not be further apart. Upmarket Noosa and hippy Byron. He loved both places, although they had visited Byron only once. That was shortly after their grandson had moved there. He'd been working behind a bar at the former railway station. The railway line there had closed some time ago. Public transport to and from Byron was now by buses and coaches. His grandson's favourite mode of travelling back to Noosa was via Greyhound. Nobby believed the connections were excellent, although he had never tried it himself. Nobby had a soft spot for Byron Bay, it was so hippy and such a throwback to the 1960s, a time he still hankered after. Of all places, his grandson had stayed in a tent at a backpacker's hostel. What was the name again? Nobby closed his eyes, trying to recall it. It was something he always did when trying to remember a place or a person; focussing on a face or landmark, or even a sign, until it became clear in his head. He visualised the entrance, the reception desk, and it came to him in an instant. 'Art Factory'. He almost laughed out loud. What a place. He had never admitted it to Margaret, but he would have preferred to stay there instead of in town. His son had booked them into Hotel Great Northern, which was a classic icon. One of the best features there was the live music scene. But you could also listen to the live music at Rails Friendly Bar at the disused railway station. They should have stayed longer on that visit. He regretted not doing that. He could ask whether his grandson was still there. Goodness that was a thought.

Margaret had this thing about their son's correspondence. She had kept all letters and cards in a cardboard shoe box. Several cardboard shoe boxes actually. Christmas and birthday cards, letters, and drawings from the grandchildren when they were little. Plus, copies of school reports, everything filed in date order. Boxes clearly marked outside with the 'from' and 'to' dates. On special occasions, she would open the boxes and look through them; mostly at Christmas time, when she missed them most. Margaret would sit by the small tree in the television room at the front of the house. It was the smallest room and only used when one or both of them wanted some time out. Margaret had been devastated when Charles told them they were going to emigrate. He had seen a posting in Noosa, Australia and his wife still could not get used to the climate here in England, and had longed to return there for some time. Her parents lived in her family home in Brisbane. The boys were at the stage of their education where uprooting would not present any difficulties, and since they had planned eventually to go and live there, now was the best opportunity. Nobby and Margaret had never reckoned that one day their son would live on the other side of the world. When the announcement came, she took it badly.

Nobby hadn't kept up Margaret's serious collections of correspondence. However, he hadn't disposed of the items he received after her death. They were few and far between. He'd stuffed them in a basket in the kitchen, always intending that, as soon as he found the time, he would put them in the boxes and continue what Margaret had started. But he never did, and in recent years it had lost all its appeal or importance.

Nobby turned his attention away from the postcard towards the back wall. This was where their large Christmas tree used to stand, admired by everybody during the pre-Christmas parties they hosted. He exhaled loudly and started concentrating on breathing in and out, fast at first but then managing to slow down. He put his hand in his trouser pocket and felt the small brown bottle filled with little white pills. He took it out, squinted and tried to count its contents. Plenty still in there. He stood up, looking out over the veranda and the land beyond, all the way down to the little stream. Postcard and bottle in one hand, empty mug in the other, he returned to the kitchen. There stood the wicker basket where he had left it last time. Into it he placed the postcard. He went over to the sink, stared at the bottle again, unscrewed the top and slowly let the contents empty into the sink. He rinsed the mug and the water followed the pills. He left the tap running for a while, watching the pills going round and round in a circle until they disappeared altogether. He felt good. He no longer needed them. He left the kitchen, went into the hall, picked up the phone from the antique davenport desk, and pressed the quick dial for Christine.

Chapter 30

Having Isabelle around had a positive effect on Rick. Sure, it was now more difficult or even downright impossible for him to pull one of the female admirers who were still following him around like little puppy dogs. He was kidding himself on that one. At a glance, they looked more like mature Alsatians. Nevertheless, his fan club seemed as active as ever. It was slightly more difficult to explain his popularity to the young students working in bars, when on the odd occasion he was followed in by a crowd. Still, their faces would light up when he told them his name.

"Yes, I know who you are, my mother has all of your CDs," they would say more often than not.

He would hastily retreat back to the table and join Isabelle with the knowledge that she would have been watching him with amusement. They had by this time developed a routine. If Isabelle stayed at Rick's, which was more often than not, he was in charge of the dinner and afterwards, in fine weather, they would stroll through Kensington Gardens, even stopping for a drink in one of the pubs they passed en route. Like a regular married couple, he once joked and regretted immediately having said that.

After the last visit to the solicitor she had decided to go back to her house for a while. She'd phoned a couple of estate agents from Rick's and made appointments for them to view and value the property. "Too many memories there," she had said to Rick when he suggested now might not be the right time for her to go through even more upheaval.

Isabelle had been adamant, a stubborn and very adorable fact about her which had gone previously unnoticed.

She was so unlike his ex-wives. Not that he was under any illusion that there was a romantic relationship developing between him and Isabelle. All three of his marriages had ended in disaster. Not for the wives, but for him. Whatever made him make the same mistake over and over again? Too much testosterone in his system, was his excuse. He just couldn't help himself. And he prided himself on being 'old school'. You got a girl pregnant, you took the responsibilities. But there was no way he could have married all of them. The current wife at that time would have strongly protested. But he'd been found out every time. Now he not only supported his ex-wives and their offspring, but three more children from one-night stands. Served him right, of course. The only decent thing he had ever done; acknowledge his illegitimate children.

Only on one occasion had a woman he claimed he'd never met insisted he was the father of her child. A money grabber he had called her on live TV interviews. Never laid eyes on her. She hadn't taken to it kindly. A national tabloid paper took up her cause; it made brilliant reading. Headlines no less. As everybody knows, there's no such thing as bad publicity, is there? His fans stood by him, even after the DNA test proved he could no longer be in denial. That had cost him dearly, since it actually went to court despite his solicitor pressing for an out of court settlement. No way, said the woman. She was on a roll. In addition, the papers needed to recover the cost they had invested in her and required new daily revelations about his private life. Very little had remained private after those five days. How could anybody stretch a disputed parentage case out in court for so long? The Old Bailey no less; the courtroom packed with onlookers. Entry was on a 'first come first served' basis. Some had queued for hours. The unlucky ones waited in the street outside. A real circus. Paparazzi pushing for the best positions, having set up the day before. All the best planning had gone to pot as soon as the driver pulled up, got out and opened the rear passenger door to let Rick step onto the pavement. It had been suggested to him that he should enter via the back door through a courtyard, but Rick never shied away from any publicity. Some would say he revelled in it, especially since he would pause and wave at his fans as they shouted words of support. The fans drowned out any possible protest from across the road by a hastily arranged opposition holding homemade cardboard displays. Rick never bothered reading what it said on the placards.

The story had died a few weeks later but not before the same newspaper had wanted to light the fire once more. As it was, by then, Rick had secured frequent access to his son, something the solicitor suggested he should arrange for all his children.

PART II THE SEARCH

Chapter 31

Christine balanced the last of the boxes in her arms, which were already weighed down by her handbag on one and a Tesco shopping bag with fresh fruit on the other. The fruit had been an afterthought. Right this minute she wished she hadn't bothered. She held the bulky purse, from which her car and house keys swung, attached to a small chain, between her teeth. She failed to see why she should have to make an extra trip to the car if she could manage like this, especially since she'd had to park further down the road today. Somebody had left a vehicle right across her drive. A delivery van no less, and the driver nowhere to be seen. She was in two minds about writing down the details and reporting him to his company. No doubt they wouldn't care anyway. That and by the time she complained the driver would have long gone.

She had left her car unlocked, and was anxious now to get back to it. Just her luck, when she'd been about to kick the door shut, the phone had rung. At first, she wanted to ignore it but what if it was Lizzie? She still hadn't confessed to her about the plan; any mention of the Isle of Wight would stir up a lot of painful memories at a time when Lizzie needed to focus. The display on the phone showed a number she didn't recognise. Intrigued, she took the call.

She cursed herself for the third time, frustrated by the delay of the phone call, eventually slamming the front door behind her. At least she could see her car from where she had stood. There had been too many car break-ins in her street lately. Mind you, break-ins only seemed to occur after the pub down the road closed its doors for the night. As far as she knew nothing had been taken from the cars. But still, who would want a broken windscreen or side window?

Earlier she had pushed a scribbled note for Olivia through her letter box. She wanted to tell her in person that she was going now, but for reasons unknown she wasn't there, although she had assured Christine only the night before that she would be. Christine glanced back at her house to ensure everything looked secured and the curtains were drawn, then hurried over to her car. She put everything on the pavement and opened the boot of her yellow Mini. It was amazing how much you could fit in there once you laid the back seats down flat. She stood back and mentally checked all the items. Where was her case? She would have sworn out loud if her elderly neighbour had not come rushing towards her as fast as his walking frame would let him. He must have been standing in his dining room watching her. Only last week she had helped him turn his mattress over, but he would have forgotten that already.

"Miss Christine, are you going away?"

"Fred, can you watch my car for a minute? I have to rush back to the house." She knew he would be proud to be left in charge. He smiled at her, nodding continually. Before he managed to formulate a verbal reply she was gone, dodging around the white van. She noticed too late she had brushed against it with her lacy, light coloured sweater. Blast! What was the matter with van drivers? Had they never heard of brush and water? It seemed they only took action when somebody scribbled something derogatory on their vehicles.

Christine fumbled with her keys in the front door, she had, as it was her habit, double locked it. In at last, and there it stood, her travel case. Big enough to take all her clothes, but small enough if you wanted to carry it on an aircraft as hand luggage. Mind you, it had never been on an aircraft, in fact she hadn't flown anywhere for ages. Christine made a mental note to put an exotic destination on her 'bucket list'. Handle pulled up, she wheeled the case out of the house, locked the door again, and had almost passed the van when she stopped. This was just too tempting. Nobody had written anything in the dirt at the back of the van yet. She stood back, put her finger on her chin and thought. Before she could change her mind, her right index finger wrote 'Dickhead, get a driver's licence and learn to park.' Not up to her usual standard but that would have to do for now.

"Only away a few days." She knew it didn't matter when she replied to Fred's question. The back door to her Mini was still open and he stood guarding it like a bulldog. She shifted the box on top of a plastic container, placed the suitcase in the empty space and shut the door.

"I will look out for your house Miss Christine, and come over when you are back."

Christine was sure he would.

"Mind how you go, Fred. See you soon."

She was ready to set off. If the traffic was light it would take her about one and a half hours to reach Hemel Hempstead. That was if she managed to avoid the school traffic, especially in Harrow on the Hill. She always went that way, past the famous school, in the hope of spotting some of its students. Quite a spectacular sight, a large group wearing their impressive uniform with flat straw boater hats. She pulled out of her parking space, took a right at the end of the road towards Greenford, past the house where she had been told Charlie Chaplin once lived, and was on her way, not knowing how to break the news she'd just received in that last phone call to the rest of the group.

Chapter 32

'The Magic Roundabout' in Hemel Hempstead, as it was often referred to, was permanently busy. Christine was glad you could enter it either way, left, right, straight on; this was the weirdest place, if nothing else. There were smaller roundabouts within this monster you also had to conquer. The whole thing was confusing if it was your first experience. Somebody's brainstorm, no doubt. Most drivers had given up worrying about it, since it was first constructed in 1973. It had been altered once since then, when it was reduced from six exits to five. There had been a survey done some time ago, by an insurance company no less, and it had been declared the second worst roundabout in the country. Which one had won first prize Christine had no idea and did not care to find out. But as all surveys go, there will always be another one by somebody else trying to prove the first one wrong. Sure enough, the magic roundabout, in a later survey, had been voted the very best in Britain by yes, the motorists themselves.

Christine never approached the aforementioned roundabout from the M1 motorway. Instead, she drove through the countryside via Kings Langley. From there she turned right onto the B4141, still expecting to spot the old Kodak building, which had been such a prominent landmark for many years; since 1960, if she remembered right. It was now no longer there, having been replaced by an even taller apartment block, which in her opinion did nothing to enhance the entrance to the town. If she was truthful she would have to admit her indifference to 'New Towns' which had sprung up in various locations after World War II. Hemel Hempstead was no exception.

Understandably, the post-war government had needed to come up with some sort of scheme to house the population displaced by the London blitz. Lucky for Hemel there was still the old town. A hidden gem they said, and Christine could only agree. Its charming streets were often used for television locations. She liked to browse through the quaint stores, including the Antique Centre, and boutique shops, always spending more money than planned. And there was Alberto's, their favourite Italian restaurant. Christine could almost taste their Sardine alla Griglia and Crespoline Vegetariane as she glanced quickly to her right and turned towards Piccotts End.

Laura and Steve's car was parked in front of the house, Rick's at the old stables block, and Christine parked next to it. Isabelle's car was nowhere to been seen. She must have arrived with Rick. Christine left everything in her car for now and entered the house at the back, climbing the stairs to the kitchen. If they were not in there the door would be unlocked in any case.

Nobby entered the kitchen from the hallway the same time as Christine opened the door. "Chrissie, you are here."

They must have been talking about her because Nobby normally would not call her by the shortened version of her name. He had a special name for her, he'd once confessed after the umpteenth glass of bubbly. He had whispered it to her so nobody else could hear. She could still feel his warm breath as he'd kissed her neck at the time.

"Are you all right? You look flushed."

Christine, already recovered, replied, "As I can see the champagne is flowing," nodding at the empty bottle Nobby had placed on the floor before reaching for a new one from the cooling cabinet. Nobby, priding himself a connoisseur, served all his drinks at the perfect temperature.

"Besides Bill and Ben, who should arrive any minute, everybody is assembled."

"We thought we heard voices." Laura together with Isabelle had come to find out who had arrived. Immediately, they came over for a group hug, from which Nobby didn't want to be left out. He took the chance to plant a kiss on Christine's cheek. Armed with a fresh bottle, they returned to the green room and found Rick and Steve in animated conversation, pointing to something at the bottom of the long garden.

"Hi, Chrissie, come here and have a look. Can you see that black animal, there near the stream?"

"Rick, nice to see you too." She gave him a peck as she was trying to make out what he thought he saw. "Are you trying to convince us the elusive puma has reappeared? Don't forget it is nicknamed the 'Surrey puma', and we are in Hertfordshire here."

"I am so glad we are doing this trip, Chrissie." He now hugged her so tight he almost lifted her off the floor. Nobby had handed her one of his best crystal champagne flutes in which a small strawberry danced in time with the bubbles. Christine took a small sip and plonked herself on the sofa next to Isabelle, facing Steve and Laura, Nobby and Rick remained standing. She observed Laura's hand on top of Steve's, trying to contain the shaking of his right arm.

"Listen everybody, we have a problem." Now she had everybody's attention. After a short pause to collect her thoughts Christine explained that just as she was leaving she'd received a phone call from the holiday letting agency on the Isle of Wight, informing her that the property in Shanklin they'd rented for the week all of a sudden had become unavailable. The flimsy excuse was it had apparently been booked by the owners themselves for a family get-together. There was nothing they could do about it; however, they would check whether there was another suitable house available at short notice.

"Shit."

"They can't do that."

"Apparently they can, and before I could get into a long argument with them the woman quickly said the deposit had already been put back into my account and put the phone down."

"Now what?"

"We are still going, aren't we?"

"Why ever not? I brought my laptop with me, we can check all the other holiday accommodation I had previously looked at. I'll get my stuff from the car, and we can start searching."

They all got up to help unloading. Christine had told Laura beforehand what she would bring food-wise for today and Nobby had gone first thing that morning to his well-kept secret, Deb's Organic Micro Bakery. A beautiful display of freshly baked bread and pastries had been laid out on the kitchen table. Delicious smells wafted over to them. Isabelle and Rick had contributed an array of cheeses and cold cuts from a deli in Kensington.

"How about Isabelle and I make the lunch," Laura volunteered.

"Did somebody suggest lunch?" Nobody had heard Bill and Ben parking the minibus in front and entering through the open front door.

"Let's park the bus at the back," suggested Rick. "Easier to load it up afterwards. Meanwhile, I'll fill you in with what's happened."

"Something happened? It's not off, is it?" Ben was panicking, he had been looking forward to taking the dogs on the beaches of the Isle of Wight. Both of the pooches loved water.

"Why don't you let Timmy and Tommy have a quick

run through the field? We'll tell you in a minute."

Ben for once decided not to protest, after all the dogs did indeed need a pee at least. "Where's Christine?"

"In the front room working on her laptop."

Isabelle and Laura had laid out all the food, Nobby had cut some of the bread and Rick had disappeared with Bill to take the minibus round the back. Before Ben let the dogs out he admired the spread. "We are still going out tonight to Alberto's, aren't we?"

"I found something!" the friends heard Christine shouting. They hurried to where she sat. Ben still looked puzzled so Laura quickly told him.

Ben's face fell. "That's just great! And I was worried about the vehicle?"

"Why, what's wrong with the bus?" Nobby was immediately suspicious.

"You don't want to know." Rick had a grin on his face as he and Bill joined the others.

"Look, this one looks fab. It's in Yarmouth. A river cottage and a boathouse, and it's available. The only problem is we can't have it before Monday."

"But Yarmouth is in Norfolk, isn't it?" queried Nobby.

"That's Great Yarmouth," said Christine. "Yarmouth is on the Isle of Wight."

"That's a relief. Let's have a look."

The pall of disappointment hanging over the friends lightened somewhat.

"Wow!"

"We could book the cottage and the boathouse."

"Is it pet friendly?"

"Ben, that was the first thing I typed in."

"Listen, on the River Yar, a few minutes' walk into Yarmouth, breathtaking views from sunrise to sunset. Just look at it, how about that?"

"Book it."

"I'll phone them. That's safer, don't you think?"

They were balancing their fully laden plates on their knees, drinks on little side tables next to them, both dogs curled up on their blankets. Nobby had printed out the details of the Yarmouth property and the sheets of papers were being passed around.

"I tell you what, Christine, this place looks far more exciting than your original choice which was more or less in the middle of nowhere."

Christine felt a little pang at what Rick had just said.

"You shouldn't have left it to me. It was you who had agreed to arrange for the accommodation but conveniently forgot about it."

Rick knew he'd gone too far. "I just mean, look at all the places to eat and drink in town. That's all, Chrissie. Now, the question is what are we going to do with the ferry booking?" He directed his question to Bill, hoping Christine would be distracted.

"What ferry booking?"

Chapter 33

It took about five minutes before the noise in the green room calmed down. It had become clear to all of them nobody had actually been given the task of booking the ferry. Everybody had assumed that either Christine or Bill, or both between them, had sorted it out. Christine knew where their destination was, and Bill and Ben were in charge of the transport. All three of them denied any responsibility, and why should everybody else assume it was up to them anyway?

Rick stepped in to try and make the peace before the situation got out of hand.

"Okay, Chrissie. We pushed a lot towards you, our coordinator." Christine was just about to protest, but Rick raised his hands to stop her. "This was a bit unfair, really, but what choice did we have? You are really good at organising. We know it, you know it." He shrugged his shoulders in surrender. "No kidding, most of us here – yes, that does include you, Nobby – are pretty hopeless these days, plus other events had taken over, so let's take a deep breath. Or better still, let's refill our glasses and rethink."

Christine shot a questioning glance at Isabelle. She had been the only one Christine had confided in about Lizzie. Had Isabelle discussed it with Rick? Isabelle understood Christine's expression and shook her head in denial.

Nobby rose from his chair, went back to the kitchen and returned with a fresh bottle which he handed to Rick to open. Rick stayed where he was, checked the label on the bottle and smiled with approval. He then placed it between his knees, peeled off the gold coloured foil, undid the wire and started to loosen the cork, momentarily distracted by one of the dogs flying off his blanket and racing through the open patio door, all the while barking at something invisible in the garden. Not to be outdone, his brother followed. With a bang like a gunshot the cork flew out and hit the ceiling. Nobby walked over to take a closer look and the friends could no longer contain their laughter. It was clear, the effects of the couple of bottles they had already consumed were beginning to show. There was visibly a dent in Nobby's freshly painted ceiling.

"I think now is a good time for everybody to take a closer look at our proposed mode of transport," said Rick.

They took their glasses with them and walked out through the front door, this time turning left to the side of the house. From there they could see it in all its glory.

Isabelle had left her spectacles inside. "The writing on there, what does it say?"

Laura sniggered. "Gay-line Travel."

"And what's wrong with that?" Ben tried to straighten his leather trousers by pulling at one leg.

"I think we're going to have a great time, even if we stay here until Monday." Rick put his arm around Ben, who was just about to go into one of his sulks. "Anyway, look at the sky." It was beginning to cloud over, so they called the dogs back in and closed the patio door.

"Christine, can you check on your laptop which is the best crossing for us now to get to Yarmouth instead of Fishbourne?"

Bill perked up, what would Ben come up with next?

"Hold on. Ah yes, here it is. Lymington is right opposite Yarmouth and yes, there are car ferries about every thirty minutes."

"I thought so." Ben pulled one of the dogs up to sit on his lap and scratched him behind the ear. He had everybody's attention now.

"Are you thinking it will be easier to book a crossing from there because everywhere else will be busy?" questioned Bill.

Ben took his time for maximum impact. "There is this holiday camp, don't look at me like that. It's a country club, actually." He made a gesture with his hand. "It's a great place. Go on, Bill, tell them."

"You mean we should stay there until Monday?"

"Yes, I do."

Bill cleared his throat. "Ben's right, there is Shorefield, in Milford on Sea. It's a country park with excellent facilities. We stayed there twice, you may remember, with my sister and her family."

They nodded.

"Ben, would you mind having a look?" Christine passed her laptop over and Ben placed Tommy back on the floor. "I'll just put my overnight case in my bedroom. Which one am I using, Nobby?"

"The one opposite mine, I'll show you."

Christine knew exactly where he meant but let him walk ahead of her anyway.

"Well, this is a new development," said Nobby over his shoulder. "And for what it's worth, Rick totally overreacted and I for one am glad you put him right," he rattled on while moving up the staircase.

Christine thought it best not to get involved in any debate. After all, if they moved in together as planned, not every day would go smoothly and the last hour had been a good example. Nobby walked through into her bedroom and placed her case on the bed. The same small case her granny had given her all those years ago and now she would take it everywhere. Christine's room was the nicest of them all, facing the garden, with the river and fields beyond. Sunshine streamed through the large sash window, the earlier cloud having disappeared. Perhaps this was a good omen? she thought.

Nobby still hovered in the doorway.

"I'll just unpack a few items and be right down."

"Are you sure you don't want me to help you unpack your nightie?"

"And you assume I wear one?"

It was Nobby's turn to be thrown off guard. He decided it was best to retreat.

Ben was overexcited by the time Nobby, closely followed by Christine, returned.

"Here, have a look at this! Everybody agrees it's ideal." He stood up and turned the laptop towards Christine. Nobby positioned himself behind her, slightly bending down, so that his face brushed against her hair. She let it pass.

"Let me explain," continued Ben. "These are two wooden lodges, each with three bedrooms, and one of them, wait for it, has a hot tub on the decking."

"Wow!" Nobby exclaimed. "That would be fun."

Christine shot him a look that made him take a step back. "They do look good. And those two are available?"

"Exactly, from tomorrow until Monday. Isn't that great!"

"I'll go along with everybody else, sounds like it could be fun after all." Christine's eyes searched Nobby's face but he was concentrating on a dirty spot on one of the windows.

Chapter 34

They walked down to Alberto's. It normally would have taken about fifteen minutes from the house, but this time the group stopped often, either to go over their new plans or suggest what else they might do. This was a completely new entity now, including Milford on Sea and Lymington. They arrived later than planned and the restaurant was extremely busy. As it was, the place was not overly large and the décor – their famous blue wallpaper printed with pink roses, plus the fact that not all the tables had the same chairs, although the owner did his best to place matching ones at each table – added to the charm and ambiance. Nobby's favourite table was at the window with the wall behind him. From here he could watch the comings and goings within the restaurant and the foot traffic in the High Street.

The owner greeted them at the door and in the continental fashion kissed the women on the cheek, first the left and then the right.

"Ciao, Valentino," was Nobby's greeting.

They stayed longer than planned, enjoying the excellent food and drink. Valentino suggested the wines to accompany every course; a special skill since the choice would have to complement fish and meat, and in Christine's case, the vegetarian option. A generously filled, delicately shaped grappa glass, containing Diciotto Lune' Stravecchia, was served to each of them to finish off the evening, a complimentary gesture from Valentino. Christine was convinced Nobby was singing all the way home, although he denied it vigorously afterwards.

In the morning they loaded up the bus, which took several attempts, packing and removing the items. Nobody wanted to leave the boxes containing wine and bubbly. Everything else they said, besides their suitcases, could be replaced. But as it so happened, it eventually all fitted in, however, only after Ben reluctantly agreed to leave the big dog basket behind, only taking the cushions. And that he would sit right at the back, one dog on his knees and one on the floor. Bill suggested that every hour or so Ben should switch the dogs around, so there would be no jealousy. Ben felt better after that, but he didn't notice Bill rolling his eyes.

None of them liked travelling on motorways these days. The traffic was crazy. It had therefore been agreed they would leave about 10am, hoping the rush hour had passed and the weekend traffic not yet begun. The route to the south of England took them via the M25, M3, and M27 until exit 2 to Lyndhurst. They stopped for a quick coffee at the Welcome Break service station at Fleet. It was time for the dogs to relieve themselves on the grass verge, nearest to the bushes. Outside Lyndhurst there was a hold-up. Ben had worked himself into a frenzy and snapped at Bill at least four times, "I told you not to drive this way. We should have taken the route through the New Forest. Lyndhurst is notorious on this particular stretch."

Bill's patience finally snapped. "If you'd been less pissed that night in St Albans we would not have been stopped by the police, and you would still have your licence. You could have done us the honour of driving today."

Ben immediately turned his hurt face towards the window, lips only slightly quivering, and didn't speak until just after they passed Lymington.

"Left, go left here!" Ben jumped to his feet, almost dropping the dog. "I wanted to go through the village."

"There will be plenty of time for that, we're nearly there now anyway." Bill took a left turn down a narrow lane looking for the entry. Suddenly a sign appeared at the roadside: 'Shorefield Country Club'. At the little roundabout a further sign pointed to reception.

Rick was the first to comment. "You were right, this does look good."

"There's a shop, I wonder whether they have fresh bread in the morning."

"If not, we can go to the village, right?"

Bill was relieved to see how happy his friends were. He parked their vehicle in one of the empty places opposite the shop Laura had pointed out. He got out, walked round the side and pressed the release button for the passenger door. He was amazed that the battered bus seemed to be in such good order. One by one they all climbed out, happy to stretch their legs. Ben, with both dogs on their leashes, looked around to get his bearings. "I think I'll walk the dogs for a bit." He pulled a plastic bag out of his shorts and walked off without another glance at Bill.

"I hope those two make up soon, otherwise I am sharing with you," Nobby whispered to Christine while following Bill who was striding towards the main building. Once inside he glanced back through the glass door, watching Ben walking round the corner. "Hope his male menopause has soon run its course, I don't know how much more I can take."

Rick almost dropped the apple he had taken from Christine's shopping bag and was just about to bite into.

"Can I help you?" A fit looking young female, who had just handed a mother with her small son two red rubber arm bands, now directed her attention towards them.

"Hello, Honey, we have booked two chalets for three nights." Bill said and slid the booking printout towards her.

Christine almost choked, thinking 'Bill, no! We will be thrown out before we have set foot on site.' Relieved, she realised that the name badge on the young woman's chest clearly stated 'Honey'. She visibly relaxed.

"Welcome to Shorefield Country Park." Honey's husky voice sounded well-practised. "The holiday check-ins are in a different place at the moment. See over there?" She pointed through the glass door. "In the mobile unit, second on the left just across from the laundry room. For anything else, please come back, and I will help you. Do you want me to show you round the facilities?"

"Thanks, can we have a look around later?"

"That's fine. Here's a list of this weekend's entertainment. Enjoy your stay."

Ben had waited outside with the dogs. Bill gave them a quick stroke over their heads before they would get too boisterous and start jumping up at him.

The door to the booking office was up a short wooden staircase, and the interior looked too small for all of them to enter. Bill and Christine went in to get the keys.

A much sterner looking, middle-aged man greeted them. "Good afternoon, how can I assist you?"

"We'd like to check in," said Bill. They gave their details, and the man tapped a few keys on the computer. "Ah yes, here we are." He turned to the desk behind him to find the paperwork and the keys. "You have dogs?" He bent over the counter to check.

"My partner has taken them for a walk," Bill volunteered.

"No problem. We have provided plastic bags in the cabins for the dogs." He unfolded a map of the park and spread it on the counter. "Your accommodations are at Amberwood, which is over here." He circled the area he was referring to. "We are here." Another circle. "Where did you park?" Bill pointed on the map to the place near the clubhouse.

"Good. From here, round the roundabout, take the third exit, over a little bridge, left at the bottom. Carry on all the way down. You can park right next to the chalets."

He studied the map more closely and added, "Sorry, but I have to point out to you where the dog bins are. Here, here and here." He marked each with a large X. "Also, there is a strict 'keep your dog on the leash' rule. Have a great time here with us at Shorefield Country Park."

Chapter 35

Ben sighed happily. "The water is really, really warm. Somebody must have heated it up for us." He replaced the cover on the hot tub and went back inside the lodge, closely followed by the dogs, who were now getting over excited, running in circles, barking and jumping on and off the settees.

Bill grabbed both animals by their collars which put a stop to their antics. "Down!"

One sharp command and the dogs obeyed. "Ben, this is not happening. Since when are the dogs allowed to run amok? I tell you what, I wouldn't want to share with us if that is how they behave. And as far as…"

Christine pulled the door open for Nobby to manoeuvre his sturdy frame sideways holding onto the box of champagne which was in danger of slipping from his grip. Ben immediately stepped forward to assist, and Bill let out a sigh of relief.

"We've checked out next door," said Christine. "It's great, but this one is slightly larger, especially the living area. I have it first-hand from Rick that this is where the action is going to be. So Nobby and I are going to settle in with you two. How does that sound?"

"Yes, I always wanted a room with a bunk bed," added Nobby looking into the first bedroom.

"Good, in that case, you don't get any funny ideas should we stagger home in the evening slightly intoxicated," added Christine.

Nobby couldn't believe his luck. "Are you sleeping on top in the same room?"

"You wish. I'm taking this cute little room with two single beds." She put her shopping on the floor and opened a wooden door leading off the sitting room. "Unless you want it, Bill?"

"No, go ahead. We'll have the double."

"If there are two singles in your room, why do I have to sleep on the bottom bunk in the other one?"

"Don't panic, Nobby. There's one more with two single beds, slightly bigger. Just not as cosy as Christine's."

Nobby went back to the bus and unloaded their cases and the boxes containing their food. With Bill's help he carried everything back into their lodge, just before the rest of the group appeared.

Rick checked all the rooms to satisfy himself that besides the layout there was not too much difference. Ben was welcome to the hot tub as long as he could soak in there tonight, under the stars with a glass of bubbly. In his lodge, his room was next to Isabelle's, the additional bonus being that he didn't-have to share with the dogs.

"What's in the boxes?"

"Breakfast cereal, bread, marmalade, honey, things like that."

"Are we not eating at the restaurant?"

This was something nobody had considered until now. They agreed to go and check out the facilities before deciding what they wanted to do. The walk from their accommodations to the entrance took about ten minutes. On the way, they noticed some steps leading to a footpath. A sign read 'To the Beach'. There was also one of the red dog bins. Ben quickly deposited the plastic bag and checked the map he had brought with him. "We just have to follow this path when we walk into Milford tomorrow."

He had obviously decided they would not venture out

tonight. It suited Christine, so she let it pass.

Just outside the main building Ben proclaimed, "It says here on the map that the Milford Room is dog friendly. And it's right next to the Beech Bar, which is over 18's only."

"Tell you what," suggested Rick. "Ben, why don't you settle yourself with your pooches in the dog friendly place, while the rest of us have a good look around. Don't worry, we'll report back and you can mark everything on your map." Rick sounded sharper than he had intended, but he was annoyed that Ben only seemed to follow his own agenda. Had he not noticed how quiet Steve was and how dependent he had become on Laura, who tried her very best to keep up Steve's spirits? He and Isabelle had talked about it earlier when they were alone. They'd decided to keep a close eye on both and thought the time had come for an open and frank discussion.

Ben walked past the reception desk, ignoring the look the girl gave him; the same young lady who had greeted them earlier. He heard Rick say, "Honey, are you ready to give us your guided tour?" before he turned the corner and headed towards the other side of the building.

Honey was only too happy to oblige. Rick had seemed familiar to her so she had checked his name on the list and also Googled him. Wait till her friends heard about it.

They had already spotted the pool area and Christine, Laura and Isabelle stood by the large window checking it out more closely. "There's a sauna, a steam room and Jacuzzi," volunteered Honey. "Upstairs is the Fitness Centre and the Reflections Day Spa. Shall we go upstairs or shall we continue on this floor?" She had positioned herself close to Rick, so close in fact that Isabelle decided it was time to claim him for herself. She linked her arm through his and pulled him along the corridor towards the entertainment area. Christine stopped a moment open mouthed. First looking at Laura, who indicated that she had no idea, and then at Nobby, who either had not noticed or had chosen to ignore this little move of Isabelle's. Rick was clearly revelling in all the attention.

"Michelangelo's does the best pizzas for miles around, and here in the show bar we have live performances. The details are on your list. Tonight, there is bingo. I think it starts at 9pm. It's really popular, you should book a table," Honey went on.

"What is that?" Rick had detached himself from Isabelle. He had spotted an array of flashing lights through a door on his right. Honey grabbed her chance and entered in front of him. This gave her the opportunity to face him again. "It's our amusement arcade. Straight through there are all sorts of slot machines. But it's adults only. We really have to keep an eye on the kids, ever since a mother complained that her teenage son spent all his pocket money in there, hoping to win his fortune. We had to point out, politely of course, that there is a big sign."

Rick was already checking for small change, eager to have a go. But Isabelle had other ideas and pulled him along. 'Tides Bar and Restaurant' said the sign above a nearby doorway.

"As much as I don't like to agree with Ben right now, I think we should stay at the park tonight and eat here. Or if not in there, the adult only bar also serves food," Nobby whispered to Christine, the two of them being the last to enter. Either Honey had heard or she could mind read. "The food is lovely, I eat here often," she said. "Sometimes I even take my mother, you know, on special occasions, like birthdays or Mother's Day." She realised nobody was actually listening and added a bit louder "The Beech Bar has a tapas style menu, if you prefer."

Isabelle decided it was time Honey left them to their own devices. "Thank you for showing us around, Honey." Isabelle took charge. "Why don't you men go and join Ben in the bar, while we do the girlie thing and check out the health club to see whether you lot can treat us to a massage. No, Nobby, we'd rather get massaged by professionals." Christine almost choked laughing. "We'll see you in a moment, you can order our drinks. Double gin and tonic all round, right girls?"

Honey was still hanging around beside Rick. "Can I have your autograph?" She pushed a map of the park towards him. "Right here, next to where you are sleeping."

Chapter 36

It was Steve who won the bingo jackpot. All sixty pounds of it. Laura claimed she should have pocketed the winnings, she had after all marked his card before her own. Steve had been in a really good mood all evening. Still it was best if Laura used the marker on his card, he insisted. His hand, which had been steady during dinner, showed signs of becoming a little bit shaky again. The medicine was wearing off, and he didn't want to take any extra, considering he'd like a couple more drinks. It was the first time Steve had spoken openly about his condition.

They had left the dogs in the lodge, and on their return both were still cuddled up on their bedding. Ben took them out for a quick walk. The friends had decided to call it a night. Breakfast, they said, would be about 9am. Although they'd been told it was not necessary to book a table, Rick thought it prudent to do so anyway. Right at the back of the Tides Bar and Restaurant, the barman had asked Rick whether he was here because of the Milford Art and Music Festival, which apparently had become really popular since it started. If, he said, his memory served him right, it must have been fourteen years ago. Rick was keen to go and hoped there would be a programme he could check, but none could be found behind the bar.

"We could take the dogs with us and walk along the clifftop first," suggested Ben.

"What time are you having your beauty treatments?"

"They're booked for Sunday," Christine replied. "Two

are scheduled for ten o'clock and one for eleven. No heavy breakfast for us beforehand." She mopped up the egg yolk with the last of her toast leaving a sparkly clean plate.

Ben was on top form. "This is so exhilarating, there should be loads of people there. We've been to some of their village fetes before. There used to be a Milford Carnival in August, with floats and music bands coming from all over the county. I looked it up recently on the internet. Turns out that one unfortunately finished some years ago. It didn't say why. Do you think Sally remembers me?"

"Ben, who could possibly forget you? Especially if you wore those dungarees last time you were here." Nobby could not resist.

"Why, what's wrong with them?"

"Just tell us, Ben, who Sally is so we can apologise in advance."

"Sally is an artist." He looked from one to the other, hoping for more questions. They all stared at him but no questions were forthcoming.

"Yes, Sally Hamilton is an established painter, and you have seen some of her artwork. Two of her pictures grace our very own dining room walls. You know, the beach huts and the view towards the Needles. Original watercolours those are." He took another sip of his coffee which by now was cold. It was unlike him not to complain, but he wanted to tell them the whole story and not lose the momentum.

"We got to know her quite well, didn't we Bill?"

"So you did, Ben."

"Do you remember the story she told us?"

"Wait, Ben. Hold on while I order more drinks. This one I want to hear." Christine got up, negotiated past Nobby and went to the bar, placed the order and hurried back. "Ben, you have everybody's undivided attention."

"In that case, here we go. Before Sally had her shop, I believe she ran a small hotel, next door almost. But her circumstances changed and she moved from there to Barton on Sea. You know, walking distance really if you follow the clifftop past the golf club." Ben loved storytelling which they all knew. And frankly most of them, when he was given the chance, were really good. Rick had often commented he should write and publish his short stories as an anthology.

"Sally told us, over a cup of coffee at Polly's Pantry, that she'd had a particularly bad day with a stonking headache. She felt so ill that she had to have a rest on the settee in the flat she had rented. But she could not settle, although she had an ice pack on her forehead, trying to ease the pain. Nothing helped. This image kept popping up in her mind. A small cottage amongst a row of others. And like a bolt it hit her. She must buy it. Convinced it was in Milford on Sea she went into the estate agent opposite the Red Lion pub. 'A cottage has come up for sale, I want to buy it', she insisted. The young man in charge checked all the properties on the list but couldn't find anything closely resembling the building Sally described. Sally wouldn't give up. It was not long before the manager arrived with his camera around his neck and a clipboard with details in his hand. 'That is the one,' Sally told him calmly. 'That is my new home.' It was not even officially on the market yet."

"That's amazing."

"There's more. It was a cottage, not a shop or gallery. Sally simply converted the first floor into selling space, even her kitchen was on display. But she made clever use of it, unless you knew you would never guess. Here comes the best bit. Because she now opened her doors and sold from what to all intents and purposes was her home, this councillor came around to check. To cut a long story short, words were exchanged. Sally insisted her livelihood depended on trading from there. Just wait until you meet Sally, you'll soon find out she is a very determined lady. She has now successfully run her business from there for many years. Furthermore, she called her shop 'Jabulani'."

Nobody had interrupted Ben, but now they threw him questioning looks.

"Jabulani is Zulu and means 'rejoice'."

Chapter 37

They all agreed they didn't want to miss any of the music, or at least that was what Rick had said. With the lodges securely locked up just after 11am the group set off; Bill and Ben each with a dog on a leash. It was best to let them go in front. That way nobody would trip over the dogs and in any case, it was Ben who claimed to know his way around. They had to fall in line one after the other, up the steps and along the small pathway. Ben ahead of them all, which was mainly due to his dog pulling. Bill had his dog totally under control. Laura stayed close to Steve and made sure he used the metal railing for support. They were followed by Isabelle and Rick. Rick stopped halfway to wait for Christine to catch them up. "Ben should have left his very latest, the lime green and purple outfits for the dogs, for a special occasion. Make sure when we get to the village and somebody recognises me, it is not my turn to dispose of the doggy do-do bags."

Ben was ecstatic. "Look at that sight! Isn't it beautiful, and to think we are this close to the Isle of Wight. Yarmouth is just out of view."

Indeed, the uninterrupted view from the clifftop over to the Needles was breathtaking. They marvelled at it before setting off towards the village itself.

"See those flats over there?" Ben pointed to a large four-storey apartment complex to his left. "It has an outdoor heated swimming pool, tennis court and a clubhouse, and who knows what else?"

Nobby was intrigued. "How come you're so well informed?"

"Stompy, the lead in the last musical we produced, has a place there at Camden Hurst. That is what the building is called. Said we could come and stay anytime."

"Stompy?"

"Not his real name, as you can imagine."

Christine had caught up with Ben and both now walked side by side, the dog on his right.

"You are like a local Milford on Sea tour guide, Ben. You seem to know your way around, like an expert."

"I just like it here, that's all."

"Should we consider Milford as a possibility?"

"I already looked, Christine. There are no places for sale that are big enough for all of us."

Christine detected a slight inkling of regret. They walked all the way to the newly erected concrete beach huts. The previous ones had been destroyed by a big storm on St Valentine's Day some years earlier. Ironically the wooden structures a little bit further up had survived. At the Needle's Eye Café they stopped for a coffee. It was sunny and warm and the group was lucky to find two free tables outside which were side by side. Nobby and Rick went inside to order the drinks.

"I don't know why I bothered bringing a cardigan." Laura took hers off, buttoned it up and tied it around her waist. She took a seat opposite Isabelle and Steve.

"This is for you." Rick handed Ben a booklet. 'Milford Art and Music festival programme' it read. Nobby managed to squeeze himself in at the end of the bench next to Christine. Since she hadn't left much space, he had no choice but to sit so close that their bodies touched. Christine tut-tutted and moved slightly. Nobby placed the table number he had been given in the middle of the table and brushed against Christine's upper arm, only just missing her breast.

"Nobby, one more move and you are in a tent somewhere in the wilderness tonight."

Nobby was relieved when he detected the slightest

flicker of a smile in Christine's eyes.

Ben pointed to the half-spread advert in the programme. "Look at this. There's a Dolly Parton tribute tonight. We just have to go. Doesn't she look great?"

"Dolly herself, or the lookalike?"

"Both, here, take a look." Ben slid it across the table towards Laura.

"It starts at 9pm it says, but there's plenty of music throughout the day. Where is it being held anyway?" Laura looked around.

"On the village green," Ben managed to get in before a young man arrived with a laden tray. He put down a generous helping of scones with cream and jams, plates and knives, and disappeared again. Before Ben could dive for a plate, the waiter was back with mugs of coffee, milk and sugar.

"Oh, we do like to be beside the seaside…" Ben tried to sing but was hindered by his mouthful of crumbling scone. No sooner had the table been cleared Ben was ready to go. From the café it was a short walk down Sea Road. Despite his size, Ben managed it in five minutes and was waiting for everybody in front of the chemist.

"Sally's shop is just over there," he shouted, but his words were drowned out by the lively music coming from a lorry parked on the cordoned-off road. The open side of the trailer faced the listeners sitting in the sun on the green. Rick was drawn like a magnet towards the band. Isabelle pulled him back by the sleeve, pointing towards Ben who had rushed ahead down the road, negotiating his way past onlookers and craft stalls which lined the street.

The door was open, and Sally's shop was full of tourists who had come to Milford on Sea for the day. Ben was not easily deterred. He handed Christine the leash with his dog and pushed himself inside. "Yoo hoo, Sally!" was all Christine heard before she realised the dog had just done its business in the gutter. Bill was at the ready and unfolded the plastic bag. "Sorry, Sorry." He cleaned up the mess. "Tell Ben I'll see him later." Bill took both dogs and disappeared in the direction of Sea Road.

Rick used his chance and freed himself from Isabelle's clutches. A young admirer had spotted him and nudged her friend. Both came rushing over and stopped right in front of him, scanning the programme for his name. Rick joined the crowd, closely followed by the two girls who were still searching through their programmes.

"It's too busy for Steve," whispered Laura. "I'll just find Ben and we'll go back too. Steve can have a rest, and we'll come back down later."

Christine nodded. "I'll see what Rick is planning for the rest of the afternoon."

Nobby followed Rick onto the green, leaving Isabelle, Christine and Laura, who were still trying to enter Jabulani. Laura gave up, waved to the others and soon disappeared from view. Ben was in animated conversation with Sally, and had just enough time to introduce his friends before Sally had to attend another customer.

Back on the High Street, they pushed through the crowd to browse around the stalls selling a variety of locally produced crafts. One of them selling knitted babywear seemed especially busy, and Ben almost fell when a toddler got loose from his mother's hold and snatched a little bear from a girl in a pushchair who protested loudly. The toy fell on the ground. Ben bent down to retrieve it, brushed off the dirt and inspected it more closely.

"I wonder whether that Beanie Bear is one from Sarah at The Old Smithy?" He handed it back to the sobbing child and walked towards the shop next to the green, Ben peered into the shop through the side window, trying to spot Sarah inside. His face lit up, he was in luck. He ignored the customers in the equally busy shop and pushed his way towards the till. Christine noticed Sarah's face light up when she recognised him, before Ben picked her up and lifted her off the ground. She lost sight of him after that.

Ben rejoined them outside the butcher's shop just as Nobby was biting into an enormous roll filled with roast pork and crackling. Isabelle wiped apple sauce off Rick's chin with a tissue.

"Where are the dogs and where is Bill?"

"It was too busy here for your pooches, so Bill took them back." Christine quickly changed the subject before Ben could go into one of his fits. "I'm intrigued about you and Beanie Babies."

"You've seen my treasures in the spare room, right?"

"Oh no, not another one of your stories," Rick groaned.

Ben pouted and put on his best hurt face. "Let's just say, that collection would have not been possible without Sarah and The Old Smithy."

Chapter 38

Laura said that Steve felt too weak to go out again in the evening, which raised immediate concern. Christine and Nobby decided to stay at Shorefield to keep them company. They insisted, however, that the rest of them should go down again for the evening, providing they promised to take plenty of photographs. The dogs would now not be alone all night, so even Ben was in agreement. They all left the cabins together and parted at the steps. The four who remained planned to eat at the restaurant on site, and either check out the evening's entertainment at the country club or have a night in just watching TV.

'Dolly Parton' must have worked her magic, since it was almost midnight when the boisterous group returned.

"Sssh! Sssh!" Bill tried to hush the voices, but the excitement of the dogs was too much for Ben. Christine was still awake, having watched Steve struggle to get his movement under control all evening, and decided a cup of camomile tea would calm her nerves just as the two entered.

"You are still up?"

"As you can see, and the dogs had a walk about an hour ago," replied Nobby as he entered the kitchen area, having squeezed his body into the first thing he found on the floor when he got up.

Ben whistled. "I love those, where did you buy them?" Then he stared at Christine, his mouth wide open. Even Bill looked from one to the other several times.

"See you in the morning." Christine left clutching her mug containing the hot brew.

"What were you thinking?" Christine stood in the doorway fully dressed and it was not yet seven in the morning. Nobby lifted his head from underneath the covers, took one look at a cross Christine and pretended he hadn't heard.

"Why are you even up yet?" He turned over and thought it best to ignore her stare.

"I'm going over to check on Steve and Laura." Christine retrieved her underwear from the floor, where Nobby must have dropped it after he realised what he'd put on the night before. She plonked herself on the bed, which had been pushed together to make a double instead of two singles, sitting next to Nobby. Her movement made the mattress bounce up and down, and she smiled recalling the night before. Nobby reached out and took her hand. Christine bent quickly and put her coffee mug on the floor before it could spill and burn Nobby's bare chest. But before Nobby had a chance to pull her gently towards him, two wet dogs stormed through the open door and in unison jumped on his bed, licking his face.

"Serves you right trying to take them over during the time we were out last night." Bill poked his head around the door and raised his eyebrows, his eyes fixed on Christine.

"I was just telling Nobby to get ready."

Steve apparently had a good night's sleep and felt totally refreshed, ready to go, he insisted. He did agree however to have another rest after breakfast while Laura, Christine and Isabelle went for their treatments. Isabelle was going to have a massage and a pedicure. Lovely Donna up at Reflections had agreed to do both, although she wasn't supposed to be working. It was her day off but one of her colleagues had rung in sick. Donna had made plans to take her aunt to Castle Point Shopping Centre for a pre-birthday treat. But that was not until later, she had told Isabelle. As long as she could be on her way to pick up her relative around lunchtime, that would be fine.

The plan was to spend Sunday afternoon in Lymington. Naturally Ben had already planned where the bus could be parked without causing a nuisance. The Waitrose supermarket car park at the top of the High Street shouldn't be too busy on a Sunday, he suggested. The car park had a few free spaces, but the Waitrose had been replaced by a Marks and Spencer, which proved to be popular even on a Sunday. However, they managed to park the minibus at the far end, in a corner next to a white builder's van.

They walked slowly down the street, popping in and out of shops which to their delight were open. Rick wanted to spend extra time in a small antique shop he had noticed not far from a gold painted post box. Curious about the post box and the shop, he had crossed the street without looking and was almost hit by a car. Isabelle was quick to check that he hadn't been injured, ignoring the angry glare of the woman driver. The woman's expression changed to curiosity and delight. She jumped out of the car and started brushing Rick's trousers with her hand to ensure there was no damage. An autograph on the back of her white t-shirt settled any possible dispute. Post box and antique shop forgotten, they joined Nobby and Christine who were standing outside what looked like a boutique hotel; Stanwell House according to the sign above the door. The board next to it displayed the Sunday menu.

"Look at that, Sunday roast. That would be lovely," whispered Christine.

"And the pooches?"

"Leave it to me." Rick was already through the door. He

returned in less than five minutes, grinning broadly. "There is a pavilion at the back that seats about ten customers. And guess what, it was not booked for today, but now it is."

Ben, coming out of Waterstones, the book shop across the road, must have found what he was looking for, judging by the weight of his carry bag. He had told Bill earlier he wanted to purchase a few books about the Isle of Wight. If somebody would carry stock, they surely would. He took Timmy's leash back and after confirmation from Rick, that yes, they could lunch in a separate room, was the first to step through the doorway. He stopped abruptly in front of a table near the exit to the back garden. Four ladies had just lifted their champagne flutes and started a chorus of 'Happy Birthday', much to the embarrassment of the birthday girl who tried in vain to hide her face behind her arm.

Ben stared in amazement. "My goodness, what are you all doing here?"

Delighted to see Ben and Bill, who had stopped at the same time, they rose and kissed them on the cheeks.

"I didn't know you had two dogs?" said the petite brunette.

Christine decided it was best to walk on. She could not, however, resist asking who those lovely ladies were, after they'd found the pavilion and sat down.

"They are my friends," explained Ben. "Rebecca, Gail, Celia and Andrea. They work together at Vision Express in New Milton."

"Are you going to put us out of our misery and explain how you know a group of women who work in Vision Express?"

"We didn't actually meet there, you know. My eyesight is perfectly all right, thank you for asking."

Before he could go off in a tantrum, Bill stepped in. "We met them on a rock 'n' roll night at Shorefield a couple of years back."

❦

After their lunch, which lasted about two hours, everybody wanted to walk further down the road to the harbour. Steve managed the stairs and cobblestones by linking arms with Laura on one side and Christine on the other. Bill, Ben and the dogs had gone ahead and waited at the quay. Laura was enchanted by the whole area and told Christine it reminded her a little bit of Lyme Regis in Dorset, a town she and Steve had visited many summers with Berliot when she was a little girl.

As the friends stood looking over the water Rick pointed towards a large ferry which was just about to leave for the Isle of Wight.

"That will be us tomorrow."

"Let's get back," suggested Nobby. "I want to try the Jacuzzi." He ignored the look Ben shot at him.

When they reached the car park, the van which had stood next to them was no longer there. It was Bill who spotted the scrape on the side of their minibus which must have been caused by the van's front bumper.

"Look at that! What is the matter with some van drivers?"

"Oh my God, how am I going to explain that?" Ben looked horror stricken, his hands covering his mouth, in danger of bursting into tears.

Chapter 39

They were off. Their search for their 'together home' was about to begin. Well, it would have been if the dogs hadn't escaped just as they were ready to leave. Ben had been fussing about the damage to their vehicle all morning. He could not sleep with worry, he complained for the umpteenth time in an hour. There was no point telling him that everybody else heard him snoring loudly, so much so that they couldn't sleep, and the only one who actually had a good night's rest was Ben. He claimed, it wasn't his fault that with all the worry on his mind he'd left the door of the cabin wide open. There was no holding the dogs back once they spotted that rabbit.

Running after them and calling didn't help. It was as though they had gone deaf overnight. Bill knew they would come back eventually but just to keep the peace he went in search of them. The hunt for the rabbit had been too exhausting for the pampered pooches, and he found them both cooling off in the only muddy puddle on the site.

"Oh, my God! Look at their ruined outfits!" Ben was beside himself when Bill returned after a lengthy search, which Ben had apparently been too traumatised to join.

"Now we have to give them a shower. I hope they won't catch a cold. Remember how Timmy sneezed last time he got this wet?"

They all trooped back into the cabin which they had just vacated. Bill disappeared into the bathroom to attend to the dogs.

"Make sure the water is the right temperature," Ben shouted after him before he returned to the bus to get one of the cases. He was back within a few minutes and started unpacking the small case printed with dog bone patterns. "What outfit do you think they should wear, Isabelle?"

"None at all, if you ask me," replied Rick before Isabelle took a deep breath, reached forward and retrieved two of the least offending pieces.

Christine meanwhile had reached for the remote control and was looking for the news channel.

'Emilio Gassiamos beaten up in bar brawl' read the breaking news on the banner at the bottom of the screen.

"Oh, my God. I thought he was still in custody."

"You know this guy?"

"He used to live with Lizzie."

"You're making this up."

"Christine is making what up?" Ben returned to the living area of the cabin with one of the dogs wrapped in a towel supplied by the country club.

Bill was right behind him with the second dog. "Don't worry, Nobby, the dog is clean. We used our own towels first." Nobby let out a sigh of relief.

The television screen now showed a reporter outside a West End drinking establishment interviewing the doorman.

"I didn't recognise him at first, you know, with the baseball cap and all." The doorman now looked directly into the camera, seemingly savouring every minute.

"Hi, Mum, I am on the telly," mocked Ben.

"Shush, I want to hear that," Christine scolded him.

"What's the matter with her?" he quietly mouthed to Nobby, who motioned that he didn't know.

The doorman told the reporter how Emilio Gassiamos had been all over a girl in the bar during the evening, and then they caught him trying to force himself on her in the back alleyway. That was when a customer, who was relieving himself, heard her cry for help. The coverage now showed several police cars with blue flashing lights and Emilio being forced into one of the waiting cars and driven off. The coverage stopped there, and the weathergirl appeared with a smile.

"Now you've made us curious, what is it with Lizzie and this Emilio whatshisname guy?"

"I'll tell you later, I promise, but we'll miss our ferry if we don't leave soon, and believe me, this is a long story. Maybe I should ring Lizzie? No, best not right now."

"Right, that's it! I don't care whether the ferry leaves without us. Tell the story now." It was unusual for Bill to be this forceful but he pulled a chair closer to where Christine sat and put the dog on the floor. Laura and Isabelle stayed where they were. They knew it already, and Christine had also told them a long time ago about her strained relationship with Lizzie over the last decades.

"I think I need a drink first." Christine pleaded with Nobby who reluctantly raised off the couch and hoped nobody else would grab his seat while he went to get a bottle of wine from the back of the vehicle. Rick searched in the kitchen drawer for a bottle-opener and Isabelle fetched the clean wine glasses. Even the dogs were quiet when Christine eventually cleared her throat and started. As soon as the first sentences were out she was unstoppable.

She told them that she had neglected Lizzie for such a long time, something she felt really, really guilty about; and it was only since Patrick's death that she wanted to make amends. She'd decided not to put it off any longer and went to the last address she knew, hoping that Lizzie was still there. She'd stood in the shadow of the school for a while, until she got some suspicious looks from some of the parents picking up their small children. She was just about to give up for the day, when she saw this bloke storming out of the front door where she thought her friend still lived. He got into a flashy sports car and disappeared round the corner with so much commotion that all the parents had turned to watch. Christine related that after several knocks Lizzie opened the door and let her in. Not like last time. Anyway, it was no longer her lively friend in whose kitchen she stood. Lizzie now seemed more like an off-hand stranger. But Lizzie could not keep up the facade for long and broke down. This Emilio apparently was a real nasty piece of work whose party trick was beating up women. Lizzie showed her a police report, but no further action was taken that time.

Christine paused at that stage, and her friends stayed silent. She continued how Lizzie had shown her injuries, that she'd taken her to a hospital and the police had been called. As far as Christine knew, Emilio had been arrested the following day, and had lost his job as a football trainer the following week. Christine had believed he was awaiting trial or something like that.

Rick was the first to respond. "He's famous, no doubt he has a clever lawyer who got him off."

"Where is Lizzie now?"

"She wanted to go back to her own house. I couldn't persuade her otherwise."

Isabelle, who had been very quiet, now came over and spoke softly. "You should call her, Christine. Plus, you should go and see her, what do you think? The Isle of Wight can wait."

"We have enough space, why don't you invite her to come along?" suggested Ben.

"I don't think she'd come to the Isle of Wight, Ben."

Ben let out a loud sigh. "I get the feeling there is more."

Christine sighed and nodded. "Lizzie blames me for the breakup of her marriage."

"Wow!" Nobby was shocked and moved slightly away

from Christine, a pained expression on his face.

Christine's voice was almost a whisper now and the friends had to strain to understand every word.

"We both went to the Isle of Wight music festival, you know, the one with Bob Dylan. Don't forget those were wild times back then, remember the famous 'Summer of Love'? Anyway, we had lost sight of each other for a while over there. She said I left her behind at the stage and went off, which wasn't true. It was she who got carried away in a crowd, topless, and I only spotted her by chance when a group walked to the nearby holiday camp. We stayed with them there for the rest of the trip. After we'd been back home for a while, she discovered she was pregnant. Luckily for her, or so we thought at the time, the abortion act had come into force a couple of years earlier. Only thing was, we didn't go to a normal National Health hospital but scraped the money together, lied to our parents that we were going to check on university places and went to some back-street clinic, who botched the job. She couldn't have children after that."

"That's awful Christine, but how are you to blame for her husband leaving?" Ben wanted to hear it all.

"Her husband was from Rome, from a large Italian Catholic family, and wanted loads and loads of bambinos. When that didn't happen they both had a test. It was not him who was the problem. He blamed her for not being a complete woman and left."

Isabelle pushed herself between Christine and Nobby and took her friend in her arms. Christine was crying uncontrollably. "Hush, hush." She rocked her gently back and forth. "It was not your fault, Christine. Stop blaming yourself."

"But it was, Isabelle, it's all my fault." Christine now let the tears openly run down her cheeks and drop onto one of the dogs who had moved closer and laid at her feet.

Chapter 40

Lizzie picked up the phone after several rings. Christine was just about to press the 'end call' button on her iPhone when she heard Lizzie's voice.

"I heard it on the news," was all Christine said, but Nobby noted her obvious discomfort and went to the back of the cabin to help Bill clean the bathroom. Ben had taken the dogs out for some fresh air, not that they needed any more. Ben had been visibly shaken by Christine's story.

"I am amazed that Christine suggested the Isle of Wight at all," he'd said out of earshot to Rick and Steve.

"We are partly to blame. We pushed her into it and once the idea reached a momentum there was no stopping her."

Laura and Isabelle gave their moral support by staying inside but in the kitchen part. Christine was sitting upright on the settee.

After Christine had listened to her friend for a while, they heard her say, "I am in a place near Lymington." That wasn't a lie. After another pause, "I can leave here today and make my way back, but I don't know what time the train gets into London."

Lizzie must have asked something. "No, I didn't take my car. I'm with Nobby." Not totally untrue. Next, they heard Christine laughing, "No, nothing like that. Look, I'm coming over, and before you ask, yes, I have overnight clothes." There was a longer pause before Christine replied, "Now who's being silly, I am coming back and that is that. I'll ring you when I get to Waterloo Station. Bye." She quickly finished the call before Lizzie could press her further.

"How did it go?" Ben asked Christine when she joined him. Steve and Rick were still outside.

"I have to leave. I am sorry, but Isabelle has the file with all the details of the accommodation in Yarmouth and all the properties we had planned to see."

Nobby and Bill appeared behind her. "Let's just cancel it." Nobby walked past her to the minibus to place a large bin liner containing the wet towels into the storage at the rear. "We can always do it another time."

"No, you go ahead, I'll phone every day, and you can fill me in. And you can WhatsApp me with everything."

"I'll come back with you." Nobby wasn't giving up easily, not now in any case.

"Look, Lizzie knows nothing about our plan. Yes, I really want her to be part of it, and I was hoping to find a suitable moment."

"You could have just told us." Ben was getting quite upset.

"Ben, my newly formed relationship with Lizzie is still rather fragile, and I'm just grateful she has trust in me again. If I would have said anything to her, she might think 'there she goes again, and to the Isle of Wight, of all places'."

"Let's check on the train times from either New Milton or Brockenhurst." Ben had his mobile phone and checked with National Rail. "There's a train leaving in 40 minutes from New Milton. It's not that we want to get rid of you, Chrissie, but I agree, you will have to go and see Lizzie. Try and persuade her to come over with you, when you come back in a couple of days."

They all agreed this was the best plan, and Christine promised to phone as soon as she got to Lizzie's house. Nobby insisted she phone him; none of the others objected. He also insisted she leave her main luggage, after all it was right at the back and they'd need to take everything out to reach it. To Isabelle he later admitted this was a white lie, but if she didn't have enough clothes she'd be back sooner rather than later. Isabelle didn't have the heart to remind him she could go back to her house in Hanwell since it was only about an hour by Tube from Lizzie's.

Even so, Nobby hugged her a little too long, which made Ben again dig Bill in the ribs with his elbow and give him a look which said 'I told you so'.

The train departed and the sombre group returned to their vehicle. Bill was back behind the wheel and this time Ben sat next to him. Silently they drove to Lymington and joined the queue to board the ferry. Their departure time had long passed, but lucky for them the ferry was not very busy and there was room for them. They had to wait, however, since the bus was too large to fit on the top deck and that was the one which was loaded first.

'Wightlink Ferry' it read, painted in large letters. Bill had checked beforehand about the dogs and was assured you could take them upstairs as long as you stayed on the outside deck. When Ben was just going to say what Bill supposed would be something like 'the dogs might catch a cold' he shot him a look which stopped Ben in his tracks. Ben took the smaller of the two dogs in his arms and covered it with the dusky pink sweater he had taken off beforehand and draped casually over his shoulders; a style, he had said, that really suited him.

The crossing from Lymington to Yarmouth was less than fifty minutes but there was enough time for Nobby, Rick and Isabelle to have another cup of coffee. Steve, accompanied by Laura, sat dozing in a corner on a comfy armchair.

"Do we know where exactly the place is when we get off the ferry?"

Isabelle took the folder from her large Gucci bag. "There's a note scribbled here in the front."

"Christine is so organised," marvelled Nobby and looked at the paper on which Christine had noted the directions. "It's quite close to the town. I'll keep this and read out the directions when we've driven off."

"Oh, my God, it's a dream!" exclaimed Ben when the minibus came to a stop outside the cottage. He would have jumped out had Bill not pulled him back by the red braces attached to his tight shorts, which, actually, did not require braces to hold them up.

"Put the dogs on the leashes first, we don't want them to run off again, plus we do not want to alienate the owners."

As it was, the owner had asked them to keep the dogs under control and if possible, could they not use the cottage but the boathouse instead. At first Ben was miffed by this request. The website had said the place was 'pet friendly'. But now upon arrival he marvelled as he stood in front of the boathouse. And for once he was speechless, but not for long. He waited impatiently at the front. "The key, where's the key?"

They looked from one to the other. Where were the keys? That was something they had forgotten to ask Christine.

"I'll ring Christine and ask her." Nobby fumbled for his phone.

"Oh, no you don't," interfered Rick. "Let's see what is says in the notes."

Isabelle retrieved her bag and pulled out the large file again. The clip on the file must have opened and some of the paperwork floated to the ground. Just as Rick was bending down a light gust of wind blew the sheets further away. Rick chased after them, bending down again but not quite reaching them. Off they flew. Isabelle could hardly contain herself and burst out laughing.

"Rick, you're hopeless."

She and Laura went after him, while Steve held onto Nobby and Bill and Ben cuddled a dog each. Breathless,

Rick read out, "When arriving by the Lymington–Yarmouth ferry, drive straight on. Fifty yards on the left park in front of Harris, the estate agent, the key will be held there. After hours ring the bell."

"Spiffing."

"Look, the town is just there – what, 200 yards? Can't be more than that. Let's go for a walk, there's must be a pub or two. We can have a drink, at the same time we suss out the place and see where to go for dinner later."

"Now you're talking." Ben, ready to go, put the dog on the ground and walked off.

"I'll bring the folder with all the information, we should put it back in some sort of order," suggested Isabelle, and tested the handle of the bus to make sure it was locked.

"Christine hasn't phoned yet," she heard Nobby say to Laura. Isabelle raised her eyebrows and looked at the sky, pretending to inspect the cloud formation.

Chapter 41

Rick took charge and collected the set of keys. He asked Ben to walk the dogs a bit further and to his surprise he didn't protest. Bill went along as well, hoping to spot a welcoming pub somewhere nearby.

They soon began to realise how picturesque the whole place was and forgot the search for a drinking hole for a moment, walking the streets instead, delighted at every turn they took. Rick was amazed at the choice of fresh seafood when he pressed his face against the window at the Blue Crab Restaurant in the High Street. He turned around to speak to Nobby, who was a connoisseur, but found he was the only one still standing there. The others had moved on. Uncharacteristically, he broke into a slight jog after them and caught up as they were entering a pub in the Square. They'd noted The Bugle earlier and decided to go there for a drink.

"Wait, wait!" he panted. "I've found a place around the corner for our dinner tonight."

"Nobby, why don't you and Rick book us a table, meanwhile we'll order your drinks. A pint of the best local, right?" Ben had no intention of walking back, relieved by the cool air inside. He'd already spotted a place in the corner which was unoccupied.

Rick and Nobby were in luck. The season was just about to begin, and Monday was their least busy time. There was a table available, big enough to seat them all comfortably. Rick pointed to a sign in the window as they left. 'Pets welcome' it said. "No way!" said the two in unison and laughed out loud.

Nobby found it hard to keep a straight face when he picked up the pint Ben had ordered. "That looks interesting, is it local?"

"Yes. From the oldest brewery on the island, Goddards. Yours is called 'Inspiration', it's their light summer ale," Ben proudly announced.

"And what about yours, local, too?"

"Yes, Fuggle Dee-Dum."

There was no holding back now. Rick and Nobby laughed so much, tears were streaming down their faces. "Oh, Fuggle-Dee-Dum, indeed," Nobby managed to say.

Ben held up his glass against the light coming through the window, examining his drink. Why were they laughing? This looked perfect to him. He gulped it down.

Isabelle had tidied the file Christine had entrusted to her care.

"There are three properties to see in Ventnor; one in Shanklin, one in Wootton Bridge and two in Bembridge," she explained. "I've grouped them together. How about we see the ones in Ventnor tomorrow as planned, followed by the rest on Wednesday. This way we can determine which ones we should go back to with Christine."

"Do you really think she will come over this week?" Nobby asked hopefully.

"Sure, she will. Let's have a look at the first three." Laura reached for the printed sheets Isabelle had spread out on the table. "Isabelle, would you mind phoning the estate agents for the viewings now planned for Wednesday?"

Isabelle reached for her mobile and checked the signal. "There's no reception in here. In any case it's getting late, why don't we go back, unpack and freshen up. I'll phone them in the morning."

The paperwork gathered into the file and their glasses

drained in a hurry, they all agreed it was time to settle into the accommodation. In any case they would go out again in a couple of hours.

"What I really fancy now, is you and me in the hot tub outside, a glass of Nobby's best bubbly and waiting for a spectacular sunset." Ben plonked down on their double bed.

"Look at them, even the dogs are worn out." He propped himself up on his elbow and looked down at the wooden floor, where two tired dogs were having problems keeping their eyes open.

"Yes, but what you'll do instead is take the outfits off the dogs, feed them and spread out their blankets, so that they will be happily asleep when we go out for dinner. And no, before you even go there, they are not coming with us."

"I was not going to suggest anything of the sort, and why are you being so prissy with me anyway?"

"Ben, I'm not in the mood. I'm going to take a cold shower."

When Bill returned, freshened up and changed into clean clothes, he was surprised that Ben had made the effort; he had fed the dogs, cleaned their dishes, set up their bedding and his mood had changed. "I'm starving, to be honest. I'll get ready and see you at the cottage next door. I heard a champagne cork popping."

Bill found the group on the veranda. The sun was beginning to set, the reflection of the orange red light sparkling across the water. It was idyllic. Like the others a few minutes earlier, Bill stood in awe and marvelled.

"My God, what a sight. It's beautiful."

Only now did they spot him. Nobby was whistling a tune which Bill failed to recognise. Could have been 'What shall we do with a drunken sailor'. If so, it was badly out of tune. Without asking, to Bill it was obvious that Christine had phoned.

"What did she say?"

"What did who say?" Ben had also arrived and spotted a free deckchair.

"Christine."

Rick and Nobby exchanged a quick look. No dogs appeared behind Ben.

Nobby filled a couple of glasses, handed one to Bill and one to Ben, and refilled the others before he replied. "Yes, Christine got there, no problem. Lizzie was a little bit shaken but is coping as best as she can. I told her about the plan for the next two days, and she agreed it was a good idea, but still wants to be briefed every evening. She can't wait to hear what we think of the properties and wants loads of pictures."

"Did she say when she's coming over?" Bill wanted to know.

"I thought best not to ask, since we don't know yet how much of our plan she has told Lizzie."

About thirty minutes later they put their glasses in the dishwasher and locked the cottage. Ben strode purposefully towards the boathouse. Nobby and Rick held their breath.

"Where are you going?" Bill wanted to know.

"Have we not forgotten something?" he replied looking back at him. A couple of minutes later he emerged. "There you are. We brought two torches, we might need them later."

The dinner together, at the Blue Crab, was exactly what the friends needed. The food was as splendid as Rick figured it would be. He was the first to enter, undeterred by Ben pulling on his sleeve, jerking him back and pointing to the sign in the window. "Thanks, Rick. That is unless you didn't see this earlier. But don't worry, there was no chance we would have brought the dogs along."

"Ben, you should lighten up. What is it with you lately?" Bill reprimanded him.

They were shown to their table and the reserved sign

was quickly removed. Sitting down Ben was put directly opposite Rick. When Ben was handed his menu, he reached for the glass of water which had been placed at each setting as soon as they had all settled.

He looked at the glass in his hand, then at Rick. Their eyes locked. "Rick, I have been a complete ass today. I am sorry everybody, but that whole Lizzie and Christine business really shook me. I mean, it's really bad what Lizzie had to go through, but Christine kept all this to herself, over so many years, carrying this burden on her own, and we had no idea. What sort of friends are we, if we cannot see the pain one of us is in? And as for you, Isabelle, my heart is broken. I think and dream about the awful situation you are facing. And Patrick, for goodness' sake, he died without being comforted by his friends." Ben could not contain himself any longer, he sniffled and searched his pockets for a handkerchief. Not that he ever carried one with him. So, he tried to use the end of his short sleeve instead. Bill had by now put his arm around him, trying to console him, and took the tissue Laura handed over.

Isabelle reached over and held his hand, "Ben, I wish I had an answer. Maybe in the beginning Patrick and I were so overwhelmed by it all that the time to reveal the truth had passed. When the twins died within me, and we had been given this second chance, I think we lied more to ourselves than to you. It was like a spiral, we slipped further and further down. And to make things worse, you were all so happy for us." Isabelle let her tears run freely. The young female, who had come over to discuss the specials on the menu paused in her tracks, and Nobby quickly handed her the wine list and pointed to a name, making a sign indicating to bring two.

"Now?" she queried without making a sound. And after Nobby's nod, disappeared with speed and returned with two bottles of white wine. For a few seconds she seemed at a loss at what to do, but decided to remove the cork and handed the bottle to Nobby. He studied the label, had a quick taste, gave her a smile of approval and filled his friends' glasses. He raised his own and proclaimed, "This idea of yours, Steve, for all of us to move in together, could not have come at a better time."

"Hear! Hear!" was Rick's reply but his expression still showed great concern at the state Isabelle was clearly in.

Still holding on to Ben, almost in a whisper Isabelle said, "You are the best friends anybody could wish for." She lifted her glass and Ben raised his with a faint 'clink', and the others did the same.

The waitress showed signs of obvious relief when she heard that sound and made her move to come forward with the blackboard. They only half listened to what Nobby thought to be an excellent selection of dishes. He could see he wouldn't get much sense out of the group so he simply ordered for all of them to share, to which nobody objected. It turned out to be an excellent choice; several plates appeared, which were placed in the middle, containing an array of entrees, salads, and chips.

"We have to come back here with Christine," said Nobby as he wiped some dressing off his face with a napkin. And this time, nobody rolled their eyes when Nobby said her name for the umpteenth time that day.

Ben wordlessly handed Rick one of the torches when they entered the short unlit walkway to their accommodation. They all hugged each other before retreating for the night. Isabelle volunteered to set the alarm clock for 7.30am. Breakfast they agreed would be eaten in the little café near the ferry port. In any case they had forgotten about buying milk, bread or butter, so there was very little else they could have besides a mug of a black coffee before setting off.

Chapter 42

Nobody said anything when the dogs came along. Rick even volunteered to take one of the leashes after breakfast when they were ready to get going to the first location. They had studied the leaflets of all three properties at the café. At one stage, the café owner had looked over Nobby's shoulder and spotted the first one they were going to see.

"I think I know this place," he chipped in. "Are you thinking of buying a hotel on the island?"

"No, we..." Steve was interrupted by Laura who replied with a question of her own. "Do you really know it?" She handed him the page containing the most photographs.

He studied it for a while and shook his head. "Sorry, no. Can't say I have come across it after all. Looks haunted to me, have you seen that shadow in the window?" He handed it back. "Any others?"

"No, I think you have helped enough." Nobby shot the owner a look which made him retreat in a hurry.

"Haunted? That's just great, let's skip that one." Laura immediately was unsure about this property, although a few moments ago she had marvelled at the details listed and scrutinised the photo shoot of the outdoor pool for a long time. "I wonder whether it can be heated all year?" she had asked.

The rolling map of the GPS in their bus, apparently, had not been updated for a long time. At one point it sent them the wrong way down a one-way street. The road was narrow and Bill decided to let the local bus coming towards them pass first. There was simply not enough space for both of them. The green bus stopped and the driver pointed to a hedge at the side of the road. Bill looked around but didn't see what he meant. About twenty schoolchildren banged on the window, all pointing in the same direction. Only then, mostly hidden by an overgrown hedge, did he notice something red, a sign just above eye level.

"Shit," he said, and started backing the minibus into a drive, almost knocking against a wheelbarrow filled with fresh grass cuttings. The guy holding onto its handles opened his mouth in surprise, the cigarette he was about to light fell onto the gravel.

"Sorry mate," Bill shouted, did a quick turn and drove back the way they'd come. At a nearby layby he pulled in and stopped. "Phew! That was close."

Laura reached him a bottle of water and Isabelle suggested they find the place the old-fashioned way using a roadmap. They could purchase one at the petrol station which was not far from where they now stood.

"If only we'd thought about it earlier when we filled the tank, there would be no need to go back there." Ben, who had witnessed the incident from the front passenger seat, was shaken; however, he felt partly responsible. After all it was he who had organised their transport. "I am going to tell them about their useless GPS when we get back, in stronger words than these."

"Let's get a map and ask them for directions," suggested Nobby. "Tell you what, if we take today's leaflets with us, they could mark all three locations for us. What do you think?"

"As it so happens I am a first-class map reader." Ben was perking up again.

The young man behind the counter at the little shop which was part of the petrol station was very helpful. He circled on the map all the places they wanted to visit that day. He explained to them which road to take at the bottom of the hill, and after they purchased small bottles of orange juice and several granola bars, even produced a bowl of water for the dogs and showed them a piece of grass at the back where the dogs could go to do their business.

They found the first place without any further problems. A smartly painted sign with the hotel name and an arrow indicating to turn left in three hundred yards was clearly visible in advance. There was plenty of parking in front of the entrance to the building. A small drive led to a car park at one side. Bill drove there; their transport would have stuck out like a sore thumb amongst the shiny vehicles out front. Their estate agent, it seemed, had arrived on time. A bold man, in a dark suit despite the warm weather, was casually leaning against a red Porsche parked right in front of the main entrance. He was checking his watch as he observed them approaching. A very expensive looking watch, Ben noticed.

"It sure does look a bit like a castle," was Isabelle's first reaction.

"We should walk around before we go inside," suggested Rick, taking Isabelle by the arm and guiding her to the side of the property. The estate agent forgotten, the others followed. The estate agent caught up with them when they reached the back of the house.

"Magnificent, isn't it," he puffed, and stretched his hand out to greet Bill who was nearest to him.

"Shane Ryan, pleased to make your acquaintance."

"Call me Bill."

"I will do just that, and you are?" He turned to Ben, who had taken an instant dislike to the Irish man. Perhaps it was the smirk on his face or the flash car, it didn't matter. The only consolation was that the Irish geezer had to look up to Ben when he spoke, and Ben was only 5 foot 8 inches tall. "Is it Shane or Ryan?" Ben simply enquired.

"Oh, my word, oh, no, my dear. Ryan, that is my family name. Oh, my word."

"Where is Nicola? I thought she was meeting us here." Isabelle now introduced herself making sure there was a little distance between Ben and Shane Ryan.

"Ah yes, since it is already later in the day than planned she has gone ahead to the next property. She is waiting for you there. I did not mind hanging around here. Mind you, I was beginning to wonder what happened to you." Looking at his watch again. A Rolex, Ben observed straight away, hoping it was a fake.

"He's doing a lovely job trying to sell us this property," Laura whispered to Steve. They had walked a bit further along and were greeted by a noisy group of elderly guests engrossed in a card game on the veranda at the back. Their banter stopped momentarily.

"Good day to you, are you coming to join us?"

"Not right now," replied Rick, and the guests' attention returned to the game in hand.

From where the friends stood the view was magnificent. Panoramic, uninterrupted towards the sea and the pool area at one side.

"Wow."

"Yes indeed, let's see inside the property. I will introduce you to the owner, after that, I am afraid, I will have to rush off." Another check on his watch.

The reception desk in the entrance hall was attended by a young girl in a light grey uniform. A name tag was attached to her tunic, just above a chest pocket. But before she had the chance to greet them, the owner appeared from the dining room to the right. The receptionist visibly shrank when he touched her shoulder. "It's all right Monica, I'll take it from here."

Introductions were made, the owner's hand limp and clammy. Ben immediately recoiled. The dogs started a low growl and showed their teeth. Bill and Ben picked each one up immediately.

"I hope you don't mind, but the long-term guests are not aware that I have put the property on the market." Doctor Smyth, as he had corrected Shane Ryan when he introduced him as Mister, continued. "I will only be able to show you one bedroom at the moment, but they are more or less all the same, since we have reduced the number of accommodations to include en suite. Yes, indeed, all rooms now come with an en suite bathroom. Some of them even have seats in the shower cubicle," he added proudly.

A group of guests were sitting in large armchairs near the windows in the living room when the visitors entered from the hallway; most of them having nodded off.

"Oh dear, must have been the excellent sherry we served before lunch."

From there a door led into the dining room, which was in the process of being set up. Nobby mentally counted the number of place settings. Far too many for the number of rooms available, even if all had double occupancy.

"Are you fully booked?" he asked, still looking at the tables.

The good doctor followed his glance. "Not completely, however we always set the tables to full capacity of the kitchen. Sometimes visitors turn up and we have not been notified beforehand."

An elderly man watched them intently from a barstool, holding his glass. He got up and walked over. "Are you the family to reclaim her body?"

"No, George, go back and enjoy your drink, there is no body to collect."

Isabelle moved closer to Rick and he took her hand and gave it a quick squeeze. They continued through a large kitchen which seemed spotlessly clean and empty of any staff. Isabelle turned back to take another look. No sign or smell of food ever having been prepared in here.

Nobby declined Rick's suggestion to ride on the chairlift to the floor above. Sure enough, the bedroom they were shown was pleasant, with light pine furniture, too many items for this to be just a hotel room. There was beside two single beds, a wardrobe, a large armchair facing the open window, overlooking the garden towards the sea. Also, a table with two chairs, a bookshelf, a chest of drawers, but no television. There must have previously been one on the wall, since the wiring still showed.

"Ah yes, our residents prefer to watch television together downstairs in the living room. We have a film one evening each month," Smyth volunteered.

"I bet you do." It was unlike Steve to voice his opinion outright. Rick gave him a nod of approval.

"Thank you for showing us around, we'll be in touch with the agent." Rick quickly shook his hand before following the others to the car. Bill and Ben had not even bothered to say goodbye.

They gave the property a last look as they sped down the lane.

"What on earth?"

"It's haunted," proclaimed Laura.

Chapter 43

The second property was only a ten-minute drive away and a young woman, whom they assumed to be Nicola, was exiting her car having seen them arriving. Bill parked next to her battered Honda, but not too close. Looking at the bumps and grazes on the car he wondered about Nicola's parking skills. Her elegant, demure appearance didn't fit with the vehicle she arrived in.

Nicola's engaging smile immediately won them over. Her warm, firm handshake and softly spoken voice even appealed to the ever-critical Ben. She had noticed Bill's inspection of her ten-year-old banger and laughed. "Yes, my son's. He has a job interview today on the mainland, so I let him borrow mine. Mind you, looking at his car, I am starting to worry in what state mine will be returned tomorrow."

The Victorian detached villa looked charming, from the outside at least. A well-maintained drive led towards the entrance, again plenty of parking out front. Manicured gardens on each side of the drive which seemed to extend a long way to the back of the house.

"Shall we have a look inside first?" Nicola suggested. The dogs were once more carried, although dog hairs on any carpets or rugs would have not been an issue with their breed of dog.

From the front door, they walked immediately into a large carpeted reception room. From there a white painted wooden staircase led upstairs. Walking straight on, the drawing room was at the back of the property. It felt so welcoming that Laura and Steve could not resist sitting in the two comfortable high-backed armchairs at the bay window, enjoying the view over the lush back garden, over the roofs of houses, towards the sea beyond. Bill inspected the ornate high ceilings before taking a closer look at the marble open fireplace which was large enough to step inside, bent down and looked up the chimney.

Nicola must have arrived a while before them, since she had ensured that the French doors to the south-facing terrace had been opened and the dust sheets were removed from the furniture. Standing outside under the white painted ironwork veranda, which ran across the whole of the back of the house with balconies above, Isabelle pointed to the plants next to the palm trees. "Are those banana plants?"

"Yes, but sadly they don't bear fruit," Nicola confirmed.

"Where are the present owners?" Nobby inquired.

"The couple are from Australia, and are planning to return to live there. Presently they are looking at properties over there. Noosa, I believe."

"Noosa? My son lives there," Nobby exclaimed.

Before Nicola could reply, Bill, who had been quiet throughout the viewing so far, closed in on Nicola. "We have met your Shaun or Ryan or whoever at the other property."

"Oh, dear, I am so sorry." They all laughed when they detected a twinkle in her eyes.

"Let's show you the dining room and the kitchen and have a look upstairs, shall we?"

"Do you want to stay here, since there would be two sets of stairs to climb?" Isabelle had walked over to Laura and Steve.

"I have to take plenty of snapshots for Christine."

All bedrooms on the first floor had an en suite bathroom,

were tastefully decorated, and the south-facing ones had doors onto the balconies. One of the bathrooms had a free-standing bath in the middle and a shower cubicle to one side. "That's mine," Isabelle said to Rick.

On the top floor a bathroom was shared, but the rooms were light and airy despite having angled ceilings.

"What do you think?" Nicola must have promised to report back to the owners.

Isabelle looked around and decided to make herself the spokesperson. "I believe we all really like it." Nicola's face lit up, but changed when Isabelle added. "The only problem I can see is not having a bedroom with bathroom downstairs for Steve and Laura."

They were given directions to a popular pub in Bonchurch, which happened to be dog friendly, and was known for its variety of great food. She would meet them in one and a half hours at the last house for the day, which was only a few minutes away from there.

The drive that led towards the pub looked narrow, so Bill drove a little bit further on and found a layby in the shadow of some trees. Other cars had already parked there. This would also give the dogs an opportunity to have a short walk.

"I would never have believed the Isle of Wight had so much charm if I hadn't witnessed it myself," Rick told them, once they all had a drink in front of them sitting outside in the courtyard.

"You must have been part of the Music Festival Christine told us about?"

"Only too true, but as she reminded us, it was the Summer of Love. That, plus the LSD was handed round like dolly mixture sweets at the time. I have to admit I don't remember ever being on the island. I mean look around you, these wonderful ancient buildings, grey traditional local stone no less. And have you seen the inside of the pub, with all its original beams and massive fireplace? I had a good look at the old photographs displayed on the walls."

"It says here on the menu that the pub dates back to 1840."

"Let's just order a selection of sandwiches. We are going out tonight, right?"

As soon as the food order was placed, Steve asked what everybody thought about the second place they had viewed.

"We all agreed the first one is a definite no-no. It was weird and that has nothing to do with Laura's ghost."

Ben shook his head in disbelief. "Did the old fellow really ask whether we were there to collect a body?"

"He sure did, it still gives me goose-bumps just thinking about the place." Laura placed her hand on Steve's and he squeezed it gently.

Isabelle said out loud what everybody else was thinking. "I don't know about you, but I did like the place we've just seen. But unless we can build an extension to make downstairs accommodations for Steve and Laura, there's no point considering it. What do you think?"

"Yes, you're right," said Nobby. "In any case there are plenty more places to see and there's no need to reach a decision while we are on the island, is there?"

Rick shot a questioning look at Nobby, and later when they walked back to the car to drive to their next destination he pulled Isabelle by the sleeve to stay behind the little group and whispered, "Has Nobby changed his mind?"

"I was wondering the same myself," she replied.

The next property on their list was a true gem, they all acknowledged later. It was magnificent. Once more it was built using the local stone, and the original building dated as far back as 1870. Besides having an imposing entrance hall, drawing room and dining room, and a kitchen one could only dream of, there were three excellent accommodations on the ground floor. Each of them with French doors, and two rooms led directly onto the terrace and pool area. But the best downstairs accommodation was the one which had a private courtyard with seating, a sitting room, and doors to the pool area. It had two bedrooms instead of one, so it could easily be converted into a very large living area.

The lady owner was charming. Although the guests staying at the house seemed to be unaware of the possible impending sale, they were friendly and had no objection to their rooms being opened up and shown. As long as they did not have to tidy up beforehand, they joked.

All bedrooms on the first and second floor had en suite facilities; either showers or bath. Plus, on the top floor there was a self-contained apartment, clearly used by the present owners. From most of the rooms you looked down onto the garden towards the sea. The view was to be relished. They thanked the owner for letting them see her property, and told Nicola there was a possibility they might want to see it again later in the week.

The day had taken its toll, and they were exhausted when they reached Yarmouth and the minibus came to a stop outside the cottage. It made a grinding sound just before Bill turned the engine off.

"Even this bus feels worn out. I don't think I can face going out tonight," Ben said trying to ease his weary body down onto the driveway. "And the dogs need walking."

"I'll come for a walk, I could really do with stretching my legs." Isabelle had already put one of the dogs on a leash. Together they walked down the small footpath towards the water's edge. When they heard the patio doors sliding open they both turned and waved to their friends.

"Honestly, Isabelle, I am completely shattered. I wonder whether there is anything in the boxes Christine organised from which we could make a meal?"

"I doubt it, but it's worth having a look. We should have bought some bread. I know we have eggs, and I bet there is a packet of bacon somewhere. And baked beans."

"Stop it, Isabelle, you make it sound like a feast." Both were laughing when they returned and joined the others on the patio where Rick was busy pouring drinks. Upon seeing them he grinned. "Guess what, Nobby and Bill are going to get fish and chips for everybody, from the same place we ate last night."

"I could kiss you for this news." Ben walked over to him, pouted his lips and made kissing sounds.

"Isabelle, help me!" Rick shouted.

"Where is Nobby, anyway?" Isabelle said instead, and looked over to Laura and Steve. Steve had put his glass on the little table next to him. The long day had been too much for him.

"There you are." Nobby came outside holding the telephone in his outstretched hand. "It's Christine, she would like to speak with either Laura or Isabelle." He looked from one to the other.

"You take it, Laura, give her my love. I'll help with settling the dogs, so Bill can drive down to get the food sooner rather than later. Cod and chips for me Rick, and peas. Take my money out of my handbag. I'm starving."

Chapter 44

"Please tell me I am not dreaming, and it really is grilled bacon I can smell." Ben had entered the cottage through the back door, closely followed by Bill.

The dining room table had been set with a spread of fresh croissants, butter, marmalade, a jug of orange juice and a basket of fruit. Isabelle was standing at the stove placing a tray of bacon and sausages next to a dish containing baked beans in the oven to keep everything warm. Now she was in the progress of opening the carton containing the eggs and turned her head. "Anybody for fried eggs?"

"Wow, when did you get all that?"

"Isabelle took the bicycle and went down to Yarmouth before any of us was up," replied Rick, who had been put in charge of brewing the coffee.

"Which bicycle?"

"The one out front."

"We've just walked the dogs. I didn't see a bicycle, did you, Bill?"

Bill would not reply with a mouth full; he was devouring a banana he had picked up.

"Don't be silly, the one with the large shopping basket attached to the front."

"It's not there now," insisted Bill after a quick swallow. "And thinking about it, there was no bike last night."

Isabelle needed to check for herself and left the stove unattended for a minute to go outside. "Weird."

Rick had taken over her self-imposed kitchen duty.

"Over easy or sunny side up?"

"Over easy for me, I'll get the dishes from the oven, shall I?" Ben was ready before Bill had a chance to remind him that he should be on a diet.

Steve and Laura joined their friends.

"You two sit down, it all seems to be under control." Bill moved to pull up a chair for Steve.

"I'm fine, stop worrying. But Laura and I, we wondered would you mind if we don't come with you today?" Steve reached for the toast Nobby had brought over.

"It will be a long day with another three houses to see and further to travel," added Laura.

"Certainly, it's all right with us. In any case if we find another property we really like, we can go back and view it again." Rick placed a large dish with fried eggs in the middle of the table. "There you are everybody, dig in."

"Why don't the dogs stay here with us?"

"Are you sure? That would be great."

"It won't be a problem. And leave everything, we'll clear up. Have to make ourselves useful while you lot check out our possible new home," Steve volunteered and nobody objected.

"We'll see you tonight and don't forget." Isabelle hugged Laura before she took the seat next to Nobby. Steve and Laura waved them off and when the bus was out of view, returned to the cottage, "Now let's do it." Laura smiled, looking at Steve.

The first property that day was just west of Shanklin. Again, a Victorian building with plenty of land and a wonderful garden. However, the house itself was far too large but strangely the whole layout seemed to give an impression of being too closed in. Plus, it only had a partial view towards the sea. They knew it would not be the right place for them almost straight away and explained to Nicola it was because of its size.

The next place at Wootton Bridge, now this was

something else altogether. A wooden gate led to a gravel drive. The setting was spectacular. The location was right on the waterfront of a little creek and came with its own pontoon mooring. The property was set in stunning surroundings, nestled beside a small woodland which was shared with just one neighbour, and their house was at least five hundred yards away. And the house itself was beautiful. It was immaculate inside and out. From the hall, you entered into a very large open-plan sitting-dining room, wooden flooring throughout with a wood burning stove placed right in the middle separating the living from the dining area. From there you reached a conservatory which ran along the entire south-facing side, with glass doors which opened and closed via a remote control. This place had the 'wow' factor. The state-of-the-art kitchen with granite worktops had enough space for the pine table which stood partly on one side and could seat at least ten people if not more. A laundry room was a little further along. The house was empty, and Rick took as many close-ups as he could, including the bedrooms which were on the first and second floor. Only two of the bedrooms had en suite bathrooms; it was unquestionably a private house and not used commercially. This was a possibility for a revisit, although it would require some alterations to make it work for them.

Bembridge was about forty-five minutes further east. With hindsight, they should have made this their first destination for the day, since the drive back to Yarmouth would be more or less past the properties already seen.

Nicola suggested they stop for lunch at the Crab and Lobster Inn just a few yards from the centre of Bembridge. It would be easy to find, and they should just follow her part of the way. On the drive from Sandown they could see the windmill to their left, long before they reached Bembridge itself. It was one of the highlights listed in the brochure back at the cottage.

"Look at that! I'd like to take a closer look. We should drive around the island this week to get a better feel of the place. Who is up for it?" Bill suggested.

"I think that's a brilliant idea. Now turn right, there's a sign to the pub Nicola suggested."

"This is getting better and better, we'll also have to spend more time here. Look at this place. It says there it has rooms to let." Isabelle linked arms with Rick.

Upon walking inside, a friendly barman greeted them and took the drink order. He also inquired whether the group would like to see the menu. Bill, already having a good look around, was nowhere to be seen; but Nobby and Ben, drinks in their hands, found him in the garden a few minutes later.

"Local brew any good?"

"More than. We've ordered crab sandwiches. Came highly recommended by the landlord himself."

"Where did Rick and Isabelle go?"

"Inspecting the rooms. I think something is…" but Bill didn't finish. Isabelle appeared, followed by Rick.

"This is a lovely place. When we do a tour of the island we'll stop here for a slap-up meal. How far is the last place on our list today?" Rick took the map Bill offered him.

"Looks like only a few minutes from here, and this map shows that it could be walking distance into town."

"Let's drive through Bembridge first. From what I gather so far, it is a charming place."

Nobby put his mobile down. "Christine is not answering again," he added.

Bembridge did not disappoint. Although a small town, it had a definite village feel. The drive took them first to the harbour and then past the beaches. At one of them, Lane End beach according to the sign, there was a pier with a lifeboat station at the end.

They took a right turn before a left. Up a hill and the

property was straight ahead with an extensive garden to both sides. From the house itself a magnificent sea view. Nicola was already waiting for them and the front door stood open welcoming them inside. From a small hall into an open high-ceilinged room with a staircase to their left, there was a sitting room at the far end and dining room and kitchen to the side. Wooden floors throughout downstairs and every room except the kitchen had windows on two sides. The house was light and airy. A veranda to the south with rolling lawns beyond. All bedrooms were located upstairs, with three of them having en suite bathrooms. There was unfortunately no way it could be extended to give Steve and Laura easy access.

Isabelle glanced backwards when they were ready to leave. "It is a lovely place. I'm sure somebody would be really happy here."

Ben detected a hint of regret in her voice.

Instead of taking the more direct roads back to Yarmouth they drove the route through Sandown, Shanklin and Ventnor, past Catherine's Point to Freshwater before reaching the cottage.

Bill had to drive all the way to the beach house to park. An open top Audi had taken his parking spot. "Whose car is that?"

"I detect cooking," was Ben's reply. He was greeted by two excited dogs. He gave them a quick pat on the head and kept on walking towards the back, following the sounds of laughter.

"Christine! Lizzie!" He rushed forward, hugged Christine and gave Lizzie a kiss on the cheek. Nobby almost knocked him over and did the same, only the other way round. And it was not Christine's cheek he kissed, Ben observed.

Chapter 45

To Nobby's disappointment Christine slept on the bottom bunk bed with Lizzie securely tucked in on the top, in the room right next to his. He heard them giggling like naughty schoolgirls most of the night before he eventually dropped off. He was the first one up, and Christine found him at the coffee maker around 6.30am.

"I see you still wear that old bathrobe."

Nobby hadn't heard her enter, and there she was right next to him. He almost spilled the coffee he was pouring. He reached for her and pulled her towards him, placing his hand gently on her back under her 'Hello Kitty' short-sleeved pyjama top. He tried to kiss her but she turned her head and his lips brushed her cheek. She freed herself from his hold and started opening kitchen cabinet doors.

"Here, take mine."

Christine did, but instead of joining him she went back into her bedroom.

Nobby decided to take his drink onto the veranda and enjoyed the view. He was surprised how many vessels of all shapes and sizes, some of them with brightly coloured sails, were already on the water, not that he knew much about boating anyway. He heard noises coming from the front of the cottage. But he had no intention to check what it could be until he heard a rattle at the door itself. Reluctantly he rose, taking the empty coffee mug with him. Before going to the door he poured himself another drink. There was a slight draught when he opened the door; a newspaper lay flapping its pages on the ground in front of him and a bicycle stood to the right. No sign of anybody besides Bill and Ben leaving the boathouse to walk their dogs. But they were walking in the opposite direction; no point asking them whose bike this was. He waved at them and walked back inside. Armed with the 'Island Echo' and his coffee he returned to his seat on the veranda.

One by one they appeared in the kitchen. First Isabelle, then Rick, Christine and Lizzie.

"Are we going out for breakfast?" Christine wanted to know.

"No need for that." Bill entered carrying two large paper bags and emptied their contents into a large wicker basket. "We bought fresh bread rolls." The aroma of fresh baking filled the room.

"How come we always manage to arrive just at the right time?" Steve went over to the large fridge to retrieve the orange juice. "Are we inside or outside?"

"Outside. Come on Lizzie, let's lay the table." Christine had found the plates and was looking for the cutlery, just as Rick placed marmalade, jam, butter and bananas onto a wooden tray. Laura followed with the paper napkins.

"What do you think of all the properties we talked about yesterday, Christine?"

"I totally agree with your choices that we should see again; the third one you viewed in Ventnor and the one in Wootton Bridge. But, Isabelle, you were quite taken by the one in Bembridge, you said last night."

"It was really nice, and it had this feel about it; you know when a house says 'hello'? Yes, that's what it felt like."

"It's too small for all of us, Isabelle." Rick was sitting opposite her. "Though I must admit, I like Bembridge."

"Okay, I'll phone Nicola now and tell her to make the two appointments for today, and I'll ask her to check more listings in the Bembridge area if you like." To Isabelle's relief Christine was back in charge.

They heard Christine speaking to the estate agent from her mobile which she had left on the charger in her bedroom. After a few minutes she returned to the veranda. "She will be phoning us back soon, meanwhile Shane Ryan – or was it Ryan Shane? I couldn't quite make it out – anyway he will be checking for anything new to view."

"Oh, no," groaned Ben.

"Is this the weird guy you mentioned?" Christine remembered.

"The same, with the fake Rolex," Ben added.

"Never mind. Let's see whether he comes up with something. If he does we'll tell Nicola to show us the properties herself," Rick suggested.

"Besides Christine and Lizzie who will be going today?"

"Sorry, but I am not going. I am back on the Isle of Wight and I'm glad Christine persuaded me to come along. But looking for a property to live, no. I am sorry, I don't think I'm ready for that." Lizzie looked awkward as she told them how she felt.

Laura intervened. "Everybody totally understands, we're just glad you're here."

"I just want to totally relax today," said Rick. "I saw an advert in the local paper Nobby put on the table earlier. There's a country club not far from here. I'm going to check it out."

"I'll join you," added Isabelle.

"We'll walk the dogs on the beach."

"Laura, Steve, what about you?"

"The deckchairs on the veranda are beckoning."

"May I make a suggestion?" Lizzie had everybody's attention. "Nobby, why don't you take my car and you and Christine go alone?"

"That's the best idea I've heard so far. I'll help clearing up and go out with the dogs, why don't you come along, Lizzie?" Ben was up already. He gathered the plates together and left.

"Are you sure you don't mind me driving your car?"

"Why would I? I'll get the key." Lizzie pushed her chair back, rose and went back inside the cottage. Christine immediately got up and followed. She caught up with Lizzie when she went into the bedroom for her handbag.

"What are you doing? Sending me off with Nobby?"

Lizzie turned round smiling and dangled the car key in front of Christine's eyes. "I have only been watching the two of you for a few hours, but it is blatantly clear to me that it's about time you and Nobby spent some time alone together." She laughed and threw the key towards Christine, who caught it with ease.

Chapter 46

Nicola phoned back within ten minutes to confirm the times the properties could be revisited. There was a three-hour gap between the first viewing at Ventnor and the one in Wootton. Nobby said that would give Christine and himself enough time to explore the island. Possibly it had changed a lot since Christine had been here all those years ago.

Christine knew exactly what she wanted to do in the extra time. Wootton, there was that ping again, every time she either thought the word or spoke it out loud. She hoped nobody saw the heat rising in her face and noticed her heartbeat increasing. Wootton! What was she thinking of when she persuaded Lizzie to come with her to the Isle of Wight yesterday? But Lizzie hadn't even blinked when everybody spoke very enthusiastically about the two places they really believed did have possibilities. Either Lizzie had not clicked where one of them was, or it was really as she said; time has passed and it no longer haunts her. Christine was not entirely convinced about the latter.

The only destination they entered in the GPS was the place in Ventnor. For the island itself Christine insisted she would follow the map Bill had given her. Nobby slid his bulky frame into the driver's seat. He hadn't driven a car with a manual gear box for a while and crunched the gears at the first try. Christine shot a nervous look in the direction of the cottage, but nobody had come outside to watch them leave.

"This must be the country club Rick was talking about

earlier." The West Bay Country Club sign was on the right-hand side on the road to Freshwater. "He's right, you know, we should check it out ourselves."

She glanced back at the entrance. It indeed looked very well maintained. She smiled to herself remembering her theory about gates; something which had served her well ever since that nudist camp in France. They had taken an old VW camper van; Henry, Christine and a couple they had met and become friends with when Henry went through his 'I need to feel free and don't like wearing restrictive clothes' phase. His liberal upbringing with artist parents the sure instigator. Christine even agreed to join the official Nudist Camp Association, or whatever it had been called. There was a site they used to visit in the summer in Hertfordshire, not very far from Watford. Also, the local branch of the club had an active programme throughout the year and weekly nude swimming sessions at the local indoor pool on a Wednesday night. They became friends with the couple on one of the autumn fancy dress evenings. Yes, on several occasions even nudists met fully clothed. The four of them decided to book a place in France, near Dijon, if she remembered right. The camper van belonged to the parents of their new-found friends and would sleep all four of them at a push. Something Christine wanted to avoid at any cost, so a tent was bought but not too large; only enough sleeping space for Christine and Henry. A two-man tent would be easy to set up.

The ferry crossing was about five to six hours from Portsmouth to Calais and they reached their destination about lunchtime. The weather had turned from a bright sunny morning to a cloudy, cool afternoon. The camping ground was down a little country lane set inside woodland at a lake. It had looked idyllic in the brochure. The reality was something else altogether. They found it by chance. Nobody had taken care of the place, or so it seemed. The entrance was dilapidated with the sign only visible if you searched really hard. What had made her put a stop to this venture was the gate. It was hanging at an angle on one hinge. The slight breeze which had started made it move back and forth and with each movement the gate creaked. No way, Christine had insisted, are we going to stay here. If the gate is not in order, what will the rest of the place be like? To her surprise nobody objected. They had to drive in, since there was no way they could back the camper van down the road they had just travelled on. They sped inside, did a U-turn by the lake and drove out again. This must have taken them less than two minutes. Christine could still recall the faces of the campers as they'd sped past. They travelled further south. The weather became warmer, and they reached a site at Sérignan the next day. They had stopped at a bed and breakfast for the night. The new campsite Henry had found in the Nudist Association booklet was perfect. In fact, they returned there several times after the first visit. No, the theory about creaking gates had not failed her and it was something she implemented throughout her travels.

"Is there still an active nudist following in England?"

Nobby hit the brakes hard and Christine jerked forward. "What? Nudists? Where?"

"I must have been thinking out loud."

They followed the instruction given by Joanna Lumley's voice over the GPS as best as they could. On one occasion they went the wrong way anyway just to hear her voice, "No, darling, you took a wrong turn. Now don't do anything silly, turn back." But Nobby had no choice other than to carry on. There was traffic behind him. "Recalculating!" Joanna agreed to take them on a different route. "You've arrived at your destination, darling."

As promised Nicola was waiting for them outside and after the viewing, Christine agreed the property was indeed lovely and had real potential. The estate agent suggested a few places they should see in Ventnor and rushed off.

"Shall we have a look around here or carry on?"

"Nobby, what I really want is to go to Wootton Bridge."

"But the appointment is not for another three hours."

"There's a spa nearby at the beach, we almost booked to stay there. But when I rang to confirm the reservation, the accommodation was no longer available. It might be nice to have lunch there."

"Sounds good, let's enter the details so Joanna can guide us."

"I want to find it on the map." Christine studied the map intensely, forgetting Nobby for a minute, just staring at it, retracing her journey with Lizzie.

"Which way?"

Christine was brought back from her thoughts. "Take a right at the end of the road. That will take us via Godshill. It's a little bit further but I believe it is really pretty there." She had just remembered the name of the place where the guy who creased her new baby doll nightie that weekend said he came from. The drive took them less than twenty minutes. The spire of the medieval church was visible behind a row of thatched cottages. A sign which read 'Godshill Model Village' pointed to the left.

"He was right, this is really quaint."

"Who was right?"

Christine thought it best just to ignore that question. "Follow this road and next take a right and a left. That will take us down a country lane. After that we are on the road to Wootton Bridge."

"Do you want to stop there or go straight on to this place of yours?"

"Which place of mine?"

"Christine, what is the matter with you? Lunch at a spa you suggested."

They continued through Wootton Bridge until they reached a crossroads. Woodside Road to the right and Upper Woodside Road to the left.

Nobby stopped the car. "And now, which way now?"

Christine sat in silence staring ahead. Suddenly, she raised her hands towards her face, covering her mouth. "Oh, my God." Her voice was shaky and Nobby detected a tear rolling down her cheek. She unclipped her seatbelt, opened the passenger door and got out, walking towards a dirt road straight ahead. Nobby was at a loss as to what he should do, he couldn't just stop here; the car was in the middle of the road. He spotted a little layby and rolled the car forward, stopped and got out. Christine was kneeling on the ground, brushing away some brambles with her hands. The sharp thorns must have cut her hands. Nobby saw blood dropping on the ground.

"Christine?" He spoke very softly. "What is it Christine?"

"It is here, don't you see, it's still here. I thought where the new spa is, that's where it was. But it isn't, it's here." She got up and first walked, and soon ran ahead. Nobby had difficulty keeping up. The path led to a clearing. It was apparent that buildings must have stood there once, although they had been demolished and the rubble cleared away some time ago. There was no denying from the layout on the ground that this had been a major site.

"Here, this is where the outside pool was. And over there the reception and clubhouse. You know there was a bar, a café and shops, even a ballroom and a discotheque. Yes, here. And a games room, with large pool tables. Drinks got smuggled in no end. And the smell of pot almost made you walk backwards. The indoor pool was across there. Let's explore, come on, Nobby."

To his relief she now reverted to walking briskly rather than a jog, over the uneven ground until they could go no further. Up and down she walked, back to the end, counting out loud like she was measuring the distance. "Here. It was here."

Nobby stood back and observed her from a few feet away.

Christine had calmed herself and turned towards him. "Let's check out the beach." She brushed her hands on her jeans, leaving red smudges. To his surprise she put her hand in his and together they returned to the centre of the site. Before they took the footpath down to the beach Christine pointed to her right. "There was a footbridge leading to the other campsite."

They sat on the sand looking across the water to Portsmouth, still holding hands.

"I have often wondered about this thing of yours."

"Which thing?"

"You know, you and this thing; The Isle of Wight Thing."

Chapter 47

Dinner that night, they had decided, would be at Salty's on Quay Street, not far from the ferry terminal and next to the George Hotel. Rick had heard about it, but couldn't remember who had told him that he should go there if he visited Yarmouth. He had also been told it would be advisable to book a table, as the place is very lively and can get busy. He took this advice and phoned to make the reservation.

Bill and Ben planned to spend the day at Osborne House in East Cowes. Queen Victoria had lived and also died there. She had been a virtual recluse, only leaving her hideaway when absolutely necessary after Prince Albert's death in 1861. Bill was keen to walk through the actual house and the extensive grounds. He also wanted to have another look around Yarmouth. He had spotted this great bakery and was going to surprise Laura and Steve by bringing back some locally baked apple cake, he confided to Ben.

Isabelle really wanted to see the Needles, the famous landmark on the south-west point of the island; something Lizzie said she'd like to do too. But Rick could not be persuaded. He wanted, as he'd said the day before, to look at the facilities at the West Bay Club and really hoped Isabelle and Lizzie would come along. In the end, both women walked with him to the club but insisted on only having a quick look, before catching a bus which would take them where they wanted to go. Rick would have to make his own way back. Their plan almost changed when they arrived at the club. As soon as they walked in they knew this would be an excellent place to spend some time. The houses to the left and the smaller bungalows facing them looked immaculate. The whole site was spotless and well kept. They wanted to find out more about it and went to the spacious office. Sunlight shining through the windows lit the whole room. Behind a reception desk two young women in health club uniforms smiled and greeted them.

If Rick was disappointed that they were too young to recognise him, he did not show it. With his best smile he asked them about the club. Was there a membership? Were any of the properties for sale? Could you live in them all year? Isabelle seemed taken aback by all the questions and indicated to Lizzie it was time for them to go, just before the manager arrived, greeting them with enthusiasm and after a few words with his staff offered to show Rick, Isabelle and Lizzie around. He took a couple of keys from a board on the wall.

"These properties are for sale right now, one with two bedrooms and a one-bedroom bungalow. Both are located a few steps from the clubhouse."

Rick made further enquiries. Are these freehold or leasehold? Could you bring pets? Who would arrange for letting if that was what you decided to do? How much is the ground rent, service charges, insurance? His list went on. Lizzie shot a questioning look at Isabelle who shook her head in return. But both had to agree, the properties were indeed lovely. More friendly staff greeted them in the clubhouse. Even before entering the spa, they spotted a good size indoor swimming pool to the right.

"Heated, as you would expect," confirmed the manager.

In the modern building was a brasserie and a bar, and a receptionist available to book various treatments. From there they were shown the gym, sauna, steam room, treatment rooms, and the badminton courts. Isabelle suggested it would be great if they could indulge themselves there tomorrow. Lizzie agreed immediately. They booked massages, facials and manicures for the four of them but with the proviso if either Christine or Laura didn't want to come along, they could cancel the next morning. When they noticed an excited female pointing to her friend, saying, "Is that who I think it is?" Isabelle took that as a sign to disappear. She pulled Lizzie by her arm, nodding towards the exit. Both hurried away, leaving Rick to his adoring fans.

A bus was just pulling up to the stop diagonally opposite the West Bay Club entrance road. The bus driver noticed them running across and opened the door which he had just closed a few seconds ago. Isabelle was still rummaging in her shoulder bag for the fare as he pulled away.

"Pay me at the next stop."

When the bus pulled in again Isabelle asked for two tickets to the Needles.

"Sorry, love, you're on the wrong bus. Don't worry, I can drop you off at Freshwater Bay, from there you take the Needles Breezer. It will take you straight there." Relieved, Isabelle sat down once more. At Freshwater Bay a group of hikers got out before them.

"I overheard you speaking with the driver," said one of the ladies. "We're walking to the Needles."

Isabelle looked surprised. The lady in front of her must be at least the same age. Her elderly companion helped her with the weighty backpack before he put his own back on.

"Yes," he confirmed. "We do this route quite often, and we'll walk all the way back to Yarmouth to catch the ferry."

"All the way back to Yarmouth?"

"It's not too difficult, not on a lovely day like today. Why don't you join us?"

"How long do you think it will take?"

"To the Needles or all the way to Yarmouth?"

"Both."

"To the Needles? Bertha, what do you think? About two hours?"

"A lot is uphill, don't forget."

Bertha pointed to her right. Isabelle had not noticed the steady stream of walkers climbing the hill to what looked from this distance like a tall structure.

"What is that building up there?"

"It is a memorial, the Tennyson Monument."

"The poet lived around here?" Lizzie was curious; poetry was one of her passions. She wrote some herself. Something she hoped one day would be good enough for publication.

"Yes, he lived not far from here at Farrington House, but it is still undergoing extensive restorations."

"I'd love to visit there one day," Lizzie said. "Isabelle, can we walk to the memorial?"

"When you have mastered the hill you'll enjoy the walk all the way back down the other side. You will be amazed at the views from there. You'll be able to see right over this part of the island towards the sea and the Solent. A sight we never get tired of, do we Bertha? No, we don't. Now we'll have to leave you. Otherwise we'll never catch our ferry back this evening." The couple set off. As an afterthought the man turned around one more time, "Before your walk, you'd better buy some water in the shop over there." He pointed behind them.

In the shop they also purchased a nylon bag which could be used as a small rucksack, big enough for two bottles of water, a couple of energy bars and two bananas.

"Just in case," Isabelle said.

Lizzie volunteered to carry it on her back, although Isabelle did her best to protest. The first half mile was a steep incline and Isabelle fell behind. Lizzie had not noticed at first but then heard her shouting her name. She stopped, turned and realised she had walked too fast. Panting, Isabelle caught up. After a brief pause to catch her breath she said, "You are very keen to see this monument?"

"Sorry, I was deep in thought, trying to recall some of the poems he wrote. But as it is, only the first couple of lines spring into my mind." Lizzie didn't wait to be prompted and started reciting:

Once in a golden hour,
I cast to earth a seed.
Up there came a flower,
The people said a weed.

Isabelle continued.

To and fro they went,
To my garden-bower.

Lizzie smiled. "Now what?"

And muttering discontent,
Cursed me and my flower.

Both stood there laughing. "I didn't know you like poetry, Isabelle?"

"And I think you're quite a dark horse, Lizzie."

"He was right, the rambler, just look at this view."

Both stood there for a while taking it all in. Open sea to the left and the Solent to their right. From where they stood they could see from Southampton over to Milford on Sea.

"Over there, surely that is Hurst Castle. So that must be Keyhaven and Milford on Sea," Isabelle pointed out to Lizzie.

"Can you spot where you stayed?"

"Yes, with binoculars but not like this. We'd better get going, we can't even see the Needles yet."

At the Tennyson Monument they sat on a bench and

opened the backpack. They shared a muesli bar and each had some of their water. Lizzie had taken the label off one of them so they could identify which one was whose.

"In Memory of Alfred Lord Tennyson, this cross is raised as a beacon to sailors by the people of Freshwater and other friends in England and America," read Lizzie out loud.

"Look at the white chalk cliffs. Back there and over here. It is truly stunning. I am really glad we're doing this Isabelle." She picked the bag up and slung it back over her shoulders. Isabelle rewarded her with a grateful smile.

It took them almost two hours from there to reach the Old Battery. This had been a Victorian coastal defence. And from the top you had the best view of the Needles itself.

"Look, there's a board showing the opening times and entry prices. It says Old and New Battery. And there's a café." Isabelle was surprised but pleased how relaxed Lizzie was today, and agreed they should definitely go and have a look. Plus, having a coffee and something to eat was just what they needed. They bought the tickets and Lizzie studied the folded brochure they were handed.

"Those underground tunnels look intriguing. And it says here from there you have a bird's eye view of the Needles."

"More important still is the café in the old lookout tower," joked Isabelle. "But seriously, I think Bill and Ben will kick themselves for not coming with us today."

"But we wouldn't have done the walk, would we."

"No, you're right. Come on, let's explore the Old and New Battery."

Chapter 48

Isabelle and Lizzie were the last to arrive back at their accommodation.

"I was about to arrange for a search party," said Rick.

Isabelle laughed it off. "You should relax, we're quite capable of looking after ourselves. And we've still got at least an hour before going out together."

Lizzie apologised, she felt guilty that she had used up so much time at the Battery and also had stopped to take a look at Alum Bay before returning. They'd done the tourist thing and carefully selected some small glass ornaments at the Alum Bay Sand Shop, and painstakingly filled them at the Needles Park store with layers of coloured sand. A gift for each of them. That had taken quite some time, although Isabelle had helped. Alum Bay was famous for its multi-coloured sand cliff. Twenty-one different shades could be found there. This had been an attraction dating back to Victorian times. Nobody was allowed now to take any of the sands from the cliffs themselves. This was far too damaging. The Sand Shop however had most of the colours of the fine sand, in large trays placed throughout the store where you could recreate the coloured layers in the order of your liking. You had to hand the filled glass ornament back to the cashier, who added some more sand if yours was not full enough and put a stopper onto it. This way the layers would stay intact. A very popular activity for children and adults alike.

Lizzie and Isabelle wanted to see the cliffs for themselves and walked down the steps. How many had that been? As it was, it took over half a mile walk to the top of Alum Bay after they left the Battery. They had giggled like little girls when they took the chair lift back up. It was sheer luck that the big carousel Lizzie wanted to go on was just closing for the day. So was the glassblowing demonstration, otherwise they would have been even later.

Isabelle was furious. They'd both had such a lovely time and Lizzie for once didn't seem to have a care in the world. And now this. "See what you've done, you've made Lizzie feel uncomfortable. Thank you very much, Rick, and actually we had a great day, thanks for asking. Plus…"

"Whoa, whoa, whoa. Let's calm down, everybody is here, right? After all it is our last night together." Christine thought it was best to stop any argument which seemed to be brewing.

Nobby panicked. "What do you mean our last night together? We don't leave until Saturday."

"Lizzie has an appointment."

Isabelle couldn't believe what she was hearing. "You didn't mention that, Lizzie, when we booked the treatments."

"Christine and Nobby had already left. I cancelled my appointment, I'm staying."

"Really? That's wonderful. So, let's stop this bickering." Christine, they knew, was their peacemaker.

Rick walked over to Lizzie and hugged her, his way of saying sorry. "What's in that backpack, did you bring us anything back?"

Lizzie retrieved her treasures and could do nothing other than laugh. "I can see when you all move in together there will never be a dull moment."

Curiously enough nobody said anything, apart from Isabelle suggesting the two of them had better freshen up, ready to go out again.

At Salty's, the owner had greeted Rick by name. He must have realised who he was, when he checked the reservations for the evening. The best table, upstairs, had been set aside for them. Complimentary glasses of bubbly appeared out of nowhere as soon as the friends had sat down. Rick happily obliged having his photo taken with all the staff. One of them volunteered to run home and print it out, so that Rick could sign it for them. The end result would be displayed on the wall downstairs. The waitresses also posed for a second one with Bill and Ben, but later on wondered, who the two of them were. The meal was exquisite. Oysters for starters, followed by local lobster for Rick and Nobby, surf and turf for Ben, grilled sardines for Bill, and the rest tried the traditional beer battered cod and chips. All helped down by generous glasses of wine.

Christine agreed the two properties she'd seen were ideal and it would be quite difficult to choose between them since both were totally different but equally appealing. Nobby suggested they shouldn't rush into anything right now, but reflect on their time here after they all returned to their daily grind. Rick thought for once he made sense. One could easily get carried away on the spur of the moment. Laura commented that, if they were really serious, they should discuss a time frame, to which Steve nodded in agreement.

It was Christine who again came up with a plan they all agreed upon. They should meet in two weeks' time. By then they would have had the chance to take a step back, and everybody should air their feelings at that stage.

Nobby suggested they should come to his place in Hemel again and make a weekend of it; there was plenty of room for them to stay. He asked Lizzie whether she wanted to come as well. And to Christine's delight, she said she would love to.

No objections were raised when Christine wanted an early night, the emotional strain had caught up with her. Lizzie and Isabelle were also exhausted from their day of walking and called it a day.

When Lizzie had climbed up to the top bunk Christine

said, "I went to the old holiday camp today."

"No, you didn't? Really, it's still there?" Lizzie almost toppled over, she was hanging her head down from above trying to look at Christine. Christine swung her legs back out and sat on the floor. Lizzie climbed down the ladder attached to the upper bed and joined her. "Tell me all about it," she said. And Christine did.

Their last day was spent relaxing. The bookings for the treatments were kept and Nobby and Rick came along and had a good look at the complex, as well as relaxing outside until they all walked back together. They only wanted a small lunch and the back garden of the George Hotel had looked ideal when they'd looked into it from the Castle in Yarmouth on their first day there.

One thing they did all agree on was that the Isle of Wight was a great place to be. The bakery and deli were still open when they left the George; and French bread, more pâté, salami and cheeses were bought, together with cherry tomatoes and a cucumber. Whatever else they wanted for their dinner was still in the fridge in the cottage. The last evening was spent on the veranda watching the sun setting and reflecting on their time together on the island. They went over all the properties again, including the ones Christine had not seen. They showed Lizzie everything they had taken with Bill's camera, and she appeared to be genuinely interested and took an active part in all the discussions which followed. Clearly, she wanted to convince Christine that she was really ready to move on after all, although a move to the Isle of Wight was not something she had considered.

To Nobby's dismay, Christine travelled back the next morning in Lizzie's car. He knew it made sense, but he wanted her to sit next to him, all the way. He held her tight, a bit too tight and too long, but he just did not want to let go. He consoled himself that he would see her again soon.

Chapter 49

Events took over after they left the Isle of Wight, and the friends did not meet again for over a month. When Rick and Isabelle returned to Rick's and Isabelle put her mobile back on charge she heard an urgent message from Carmella. All she managed to understand was 'Come home and quick.' Rick wanted to accompany her but Isabelle told him not to worry, she would sort out whatever Carmella was so excited about. Carmella must have spent most of the days in the sitting room behind the curtain in her own house opposite Isabelle's, for she came rushing over as soon as Isabelle appeared, still in her onesie. Her words somersaulting from her mouth as she wobbled across, not even realising she was speaking her native Sicilian dialect. But Isabelle could make out "Polizia, Polizia," and came to a sudden stop, which made Carmella bump into her with the full force of her weight. Both women almost tumbled against the front door.

"Police? What do you mean?"

Carmella now realised that nothing she had said had been understood. "Sorry, Miss Isabelle. The police came two days ago, I telephoned you."

"What did they want?"

"We must go inside, Miss Isabelle." Carmella looked nervously around. The neighbours who had moved in two doors down last year were a right nosy lot. And look at the state of their front lawn. That old settee must have been there for almost one week now, having joined the rusty fridge and two deckchairs. But they were a crafty lot, having worked out that this neighbourhood did not tolerate such filth and would complain and contact the council immediately. Nobody wanted their houses to be devalued by people bringing down the area, which could easily happen. The council arranged for a van to come along taking it all away. At no cost to them, no doubt. How they could have afforded to buy the place with those four rowdy children was beyond her. Their fierce looking Alsatian dog seemed to be tied up most of the day. If you dared to walk on that side of the street it would pull on its chain and growl at you. Maybe they had been evicted somewhere else and were just put here to make everyone's lives a misery.

A committee had been formed which met in secret in the house right at the end. They had made it their mission to find out who these people were and if necessary get rid of them. A neighbourhood watch had already been put in place. Signs had been placed strategically throughout, stating this was a 'Neighbourhood Watch Area' and the men were taking it in turn to occasionally walk through the streets at night. Carmella was of the opinion this was taking it a bit too far, but decided it was wise to shut up and wait and see. No, best those neighbours didn't find out about the police knocking at Isabelle's door.

Isabelle fumbled for her keys and dropped them on the floor. Carmella despite her shape was quicker, retrieved them, stepped in front of Isabelle and unlocked the door.

"The policeman and woman were kind enough. There is a letter on the table in the hall. I did tell them you would be back this weekend, I did not want to have an arrest warrant out for you. You know they do that if you don't respond to their requests?"

"An arrest warrant, what for?" Isabelle was beginning to panic.

"I hope you don't mind, but you did not say your children

would be coming to the house while you were away. So, I had the feeling they are up to something when they came along with that big car, it had 'Rent a Van' written on it. I wrote down the telephone number which was printed on its side."

"They arrived with a pick-up?"

"Yes, but they could not get in. They sped over to me, but I did not open, just hid behind the door. They gave up eventually, having walked around your back garden and rattled on the door and window. The alarm went off, that must have spooked them. Shortly after that the police arrived. I did go over to your house, but I did not let them enter. You know they did not have a search warrant."

"Why on earth would they want to search my house?"

Carmella was beside herself. "I don't know, all they said was that this was a private matter, and you should contact them on your return. They handed me the letter which I had to promise them to give to you. I'll put the kettle on." She had already gone ahead into the kitchen.

Isabelle dropped her case in the hall, sighed and picked up the official looking envelope. She ripped it open, pulled up a barstool and sat at the breakfast bar.

Carmella for once kept silent and busied herself by getting the tea mugs, opened the fridge door and taking out the plastic container of milk. She undid the screw top and pulled a face. "Phew, that's off."

"I prefer peppermint tea anyway, it's up there on the top shelf. There's a whole selection of different flavours."

Carmella inspected several labels, chose two different teabags, placed them into the mugs and added the boiling water. She then pulled up a barstool opposite Isabelle, sat down and waited. Isabelle was still silently reading the contents of the letter. Carmella could stand it no longer. "Miss Isabelle, what does it say?"

"A complaint has been lodged, that I did not comply

with an arrangement which had been made for my children to collect their belongings. And that upon their arrival they were unable to enter their home, due to the fact that all the locks had been changed without their knowledge."

"Miss Isabelle, you did not tell me that I should let them in?"

"Carmella, they are lying. I will never let them in here now. Anyway, none of their things are here anymore. They took everything years ago."

"Oh, why are they doing this?"

"Carmella, I have absolutely no idea. You are truly a friend, and I must thank you for the care you take of me."

Carmella blushed. "Oh, Miss Isabelle, I don't want to cause you any upset. I best be going. You tell me if there is anything you like me to do, won't you?" She surprised herself when she stood up and gave Isabelle a quick hug. Embarrassed by her outburst, she quickly departed.

Isabelle sat there for a little while longer, but had to get up to reach her landline and entered the quick dial for her solicitor.

Chapter 50

Laura planned to drive home from Nobby's via Rickmansworth. From there she would head towards Slough, Windsor, Egham, Virginia Water and Sunningdale, down the A30 to Bagshot. It was a route they both preferred and far less busy than using the M3 motorway. Laura and Steve had stayed overnight at Nobby's. The journey on a Saturday from the Isle of Wight back to Hemel Hampstead had taken its toll on Steve. As soon as they arrived at Nobby's house at Piccotts End he'd gone upstairs for a rest in the bedroom they always used when they were there. Isabelle and Rick transferred their own luggage to Rick's car before they helped unloading all the boxes from the bus which were to stay with Nobby. Bill and Ben set off almost straight away after that, they wanted to return the bus that evening if at all possible. Ben was not clear about what the arrangement had been. Isabelle and Rick decided to stay until early evening. Nobby went down the road to pick up some Chinese take away.

The trip they had just undertaken was on everybody's mind. They talked about each property in detail again, and yes, those two they had selected were real contenders. Although Isabelle admitted she was quite taken by the last property in Bembridge, it was unfortunate that this one was too small for all of them. Christine had said on the phone that she was going to speak with Nicola again on Monday to stress the point should there be an offer made on either of those two before they could reach a decision to contact her immediately.

Nobby was relieved when Christine rang from her house in Hanwell to let them know Lizzie had dropped her off there over an hour ago and Lizzie was also home. Lizzie wanted to thank everybody again for the great time she'd had and was looking forward to seeing them again in a couple of weeks.

On Sunday morning Nobby managed to rustle up some fried eggs and bacon, accompanied by baked beans. He had taken a loaf of white bread out of the freezer the night before. The toaster had just sprung into action when Laura arrived in the kitchen.

"Good morning, you didn't need to go to all this trouble."

"No trouble at all, how did Steve sleep?"

"Really good, from what I can make out. But you know him, he seems to worry a lot these days."

"Who is worrying a lot?" Queried Steve, walking over to Laura and giving her a peck on the cheek.

"You, my dear. Coffee?" Laura didn't wait for a reply and had taken the jug already, pouring the steaming brew into the mugs and adding milk to hers and Steve's. Nobby liked his black with sugar, or sweetener which he had changed to lately. Nobby had these fantastic roast beans which he ground fresh each morning. The aroma filled the house. His coffee was too good to miss.

"We'll be setting off soon," Steve said after breakfast, having helped clearing the table as Laura went back to the room and packed the overnight items back into the small canvas case, which had been a gift from Berliot. The only item she'd ever received from her daughter which was actually of any use.

"See you in a couple of weeks." Laura kissed Nobby on the cheek and climbed into the driver's seat of their Peugeot. After Nobby waved and watched them turn into the road, he went back into the house and walked over to the telephone in the hallway. He had seen the red light of the answering machine blinking when they'd returned yesterday afternoon. Several messages from the same caller. He had recognised the number instantly: Australia. But had switched it off and ignored it until now.

Shortly after Hemel, Steve asked, "What do you think? Do you really believe this will happen, all of us moving in together?"

"I hope it does. I know it is an enormous decision not to be taken lightly. If you think about it, in reality it would mean all of us leaving our old lives behind. I know we talked about it during the week. Now, taking a step back, what is your opinion?"

"It concerns me that they are getting carried along because of my condition, and later on might regret it."

"Do you really think so?"

"It has crossed my mind."

"Look, we know our friends well enough to tell them how we feel. After all, the next two weeks are supposed to be a cooling off period. After that we can voice our concern."

"I want to go to Norway."

"What!" Laura almost hit a bicycle and only averted a serious collision by turning the steering wheel hard to the right at the last second. Shaken, she stopped the car a few yards further on and waited for the cyclist to come along beside her. She wound down her window. "I am so sorry, are you alright?"

"You gave me quite a scare, but you didn't hit me."

"Thank God for that. Is there any way I can help you?"

"You can take more care when driving in future," he replied, mounted his bike and drove off.

Steve was looking at Laura with concern. "Sorry, I should have waited until we were back home."

"Or, you should have told me much earlier. What exactly

do you mean, you want to go to Norway? You? After all this? What, you want to live there?"

"I don't know, let's not discuss it right now. Maybe I feel a bit homesick."

"Homesick? I think you are hallucinating. How many tablets did you take today?"

"Laura, please let us not argue. Please, just drive home."

She restarted the car, put it into first gear, checked the rear-view and side mirrors, indicated and looked out of the still open window, and slowly joined the rest of the traffic.

"Home, you said. I assume you want me to drive to Bagshot. That is still your home, right?" Laura could not let it rest now.

Chapter 51

Isabelle replaced the receiver. Rick wanted to come over straight away, but she'd reassured him she was fine. Although it was Sunday, she had reached her solicitor at home. He was going to contact the police station in Wimbledon where the complaint had been lodged. Was there any significance that it was Wimbledon and not a police station nearer to Wandsworth? He wanted to know. She had no answer for that.

Isabelle went back into her kitchen and looked into her empty fridge. She would have to go to the supermarket today but was at a loss what to get. How many days would she stay? She resolutely walked over to the utility room and unlocked the chest freezer. Still a lot of frozen food in there. She removed a chicken, tore several sheets of kitchen roll from its holder and placed the chicken on it on the drainer of the sink unit. That accomplished, she walked over to the oven and removed a large baking tray from the shelf beneath. Back to the chicken, she placed the paper and chicken in the baking tray leaving it on the sink unit for defrosting.

On the side cabinet she found the pen attached to a writing pad and started her shopping list. It was time she took charge of her own life again. Shopping list done she stepped down from the barstool and looked around her. Searching for a sign. But nothing, he was no longer here. He had moved on and so must she.

She walked back into the hall and retrieved her case

which she had dropped there earlier. Hers were the only footsteps to be heard on the wooden floor. It felt eerie. An emptiness overcame her, she felt dizzy and weak for a moment. But it passed. She steadied herself as she carried her case upstairs to unpack.

She passed her bedroom door which was slightly ajar, and continued into the guest room. It had been Janette's before she moved out, shortly after Edward. The twins had stripped their rooms of everything, as though they knew even then there was no coming back. Isabelle had hoped there would be a reconciliation, and she had tried in vain to heal the rift. It had been Isabelle and Patrick's fault, not the children's. They should have told them the truth earlier. But Isabelle had begged Patrick again and again there was no need to unsettle two small children, and the opportunity passed. What had they been thinking of? That the children would never find out? They'd never seen their birth certificates as teenagers when they were needed for passport renewal. In any case, Patrick and Isabelle were listed as parents. One sunny day in Italy, Edward had been involved in a motorbike accident and needed urgent blood transfusions. His blood group was rare; AB Negative. The hospital wanted to transfuse directly from Patrick or Isabelle, since their stock was low. That was when it all blew up. She was surprised and somehow pleased that both had come to Patrick's funeral. But Edward could not be persuaded to say a few words.

She thought she heard a noise and stood still. Nothing, she must have imagined it. There it was again. At the back of the house. She tentatively moved towards the window. A movement at the back next to the wooden shed, which Patrick had made into his den when the kids were small. As foreseen, this did not last long. The children were drawn to it like magnets, especially when it was explained their daddy was in there to create models of a layout for a very important auction which the company had been commissioned to hold. Curious at what their father was doing, they stood on tip toes looking in through the window. Patrick had laughed and scooped them both up and brought them back to the kitchen. He gave up on his den after that, and it was converted into a play area. All three of them had built the model railway which was set up on a specially erected wooden platform, and enjoyed it for many years.

There was that movement in the bushes again. She could make out some shadows moving from the shed towards the back of the house, but lost them from sight. Unless she opened the window and leaned out she was unable to see straight down onto the patio. She knew she should; whoever was there would hear and hopefully disappear. But she was frozen with fear. She thought she heard whispering coming from below, but she must have been mistaken. There was no way she would be able to hear anything from the garden below where she stood. Her eyes travelled towards the top of the window frame. The latch was open. She had been right, there was somebody there. She wished she had not declined Rick's offer to come over. Another sound, yes, somebody was trying to get in.

She would have to go down and confront the possible intruder, although she'd rather hide under the bed. She willed her body to move, cursing herself for being so far away from Edward's old room. His cricket bat was at the back of the built-in wardrobe; the one the English cricket team had signed when Patrick took him to Lords Cricket ground to watch England winning the Ashes back from Australia in the series of test matches. Edward had left his bat behind, accidentally or on purpose it did not matter now. They had kept it, and she wished she had her hands around it now. Maybe it would not help her with any outcome of what might happen when she confronted the burglars, but it would make her feel stronger. As quietly as she could she moved slowly forward. But running down the stairs and leaving through the front door seemed a better option.

Breaking glass. The back door. Now run! She didn't know where she got that speed from but two steps at a time she was downstairs. A backwards glance into the kitchen and beyond. Two men, then a flash across her sight. A dog seemed to appear out of nowhere, landing on one of them. Isabelle jerked the front door open, to be faced by her new neighbour with one of his sons. Isabelle screamed.

Rick was sitting on the sofa next to Isabelle holding onto her hand. Carmella was busying herself in the kitchen. "What you need is a strong cup of tea," she had suggested. Rick asked for his to be without milk but with sugar and a shot of rum. She knew where the drinks were kept. Earlier on Carmella went upstairs and fetched a sweatshirt for Isabelle, who'd said she was cold. Rick had felt her shivering when he held her close. She was undeniably in shock. Isabelle freed herself from Rick's hold, pulled up the hood and placed her hands inside the pocket of her top. The lime green colour suited her. 'Hoonah, Icy Strait Point' read the writing. She'd bought it when the family went on the Alaska cruise.

Rick left his seat and walked over to the patio door. A couple of police officers were inspecting the garden. He stepped outside and watched another one dusting for fingerprints on the kitchen door. There was a bright red stain which Rick could see from where he stood. One of the burglars, the one who broke the glass, must have put his hand out to steady himself before running off, leaving his companion, pinned down by the Alsatian on the floor, to his fate. As soon as the neighbour had given the command to the dog to release, the man had legged it. Despite some injury he was quick and made off towards the shed and the undergrowth before the neighbour's son could reach him.

All he could do was run after him; but he was too late to stop the blue transit van that had been parked there, revving its engine, speed off into the distance, tyres squealing. He'd hurried back to the house to write down the partial number plate he'd managed to see.

Carmella came with the tea and biscuits which she placed on the little coffee table in front of Isabelle, who had pulled her feet up and covered them with a blanket.

The police were still in the dining room taking statements from the neighbour and his son. What was taking them so long?

Isabelle had said very little after her initial hysterical outburst.

"I have to put a stop to it, Rick," she'd said after the first sip of the hot drink. "I will put the house on the market and sell my shares in the business. I will pay them out."

"But…"

"Rick, I have made up my mind."

"But you don't know that this is connected. This could have nothing to do with Janette and Edward."

"You know what the neighbour told us. These people were clearly not from here but originated from the Eastern Block. He understood what they said. It would be a strange coincidence don't you think, with the twins digging up their past and now all this."

Carmella was listening but did not say a word.

"What will you do?" Rick wanted to know.

"I will ask my solicitor to set up a meeting with them. Will you come with me?"

"You know I will, as long as you're sure that is the right thing to do."

"Yes, they are still my children, who have been hurt and feel confused and angry."

The police investigators entered, followed by the neighbour, his son no longer with them.

"Mrs Flitcroft, there is nothing more we can do here today. We will be in touch with you. If there is anything else you can remember please give me a call." He handed Isabelle his card. "Somebody should stay here with you tonight. Thanks to your watch scheme and a very vigilant Mr Lubrinski, who apparently had noticed these people loitering here before, he was able take swift action and avoid a more serious incident. I'll see myself out. Good day."

"I think we need a drink," Rick said to the neighbour. "Please sit down. How about you, Isabelle?" She nodded yes. "Carmella?"

"Yes, thank you. I'll get the glasses."

Rick retrieved the decanter containing the whisky from the sideboard and poured four generous measures.

All four sat with their glasses in their hands, Carmella and the neighbour in the comfortable armchairs. He raised his and looked at Carmella. "Yes, lucky we are now a neighbourhood watch area."

Carmella cleared her throat. "I am sorry Mr Lubrinski."

"Please call me Oleg." He noticed the questioning look between Rick and Isabelle. There must be something there they both did not understand.

"Yes, please," the neighbour repeated, now looking and smiling at Rick and Isabelle. "Call me Oleg."

Chapter 52

Bill and Ben wanted to get home that Saturday and said their goodbyes as soon as the bus was unloaded. The shortest route back to their house was via the M1 motorway, which Bill joined at junction 8 which was the nearest to Nobby's place. They had only driven about thirty minutes when a red warning signal lit up.

"What the hell is that?" Bill shot a worried look at Ben who was fiddling with the knobs of the radio to select a local station.

"I think it's the oil warning light. There is a Welcome Break service station in two miles, we just passed the sign. Let's hope we can make it that far."

As soon as there was space to move into the slow lane Bill did so. The speed of the bus was reducing although he did his best to keep it up. But the vehicle only responded by sputtering and jerking.

"Only three hundred yards, don't give up now." Ben fixated on the angry red flashing light. They limped the vehicle towards the parking lot, and almost made it but not quite. It stopped short just before the entrance. With a last effort Bill managed to get it as far over to the left as he could. At least that way it wasn't blocking cars trying to enter. As a precaution Bill had, as soon as the red warning light came on, activated the blinkers to let others know there was a problem. This avoided angry responses from fellow drivers behind them. When their transport had come to a complete stop, Ben climbed out clutching his mobile phone but left the dogs inside for the moment.

"Do you have a signal?"

"My battery is flat."

"We'll take the dogs and secure the bus but leave the blinkers on. We'll have to go to the complex over there." Bill pointed ahead. "Let's also take the chargers with us."

Carefully avoiding the traffic, they walked as close as they could to the kerb. A steep slope at their side made walking difficult. Bill wished that Ben had chosen a more subdued outfit, but there was no point commenting on it now. Ben seemed oblivious to the stares some of the drivers shot in their direction. One car full of young men wound the windows down and whistled. Bill hoped they wouldn't wait at the entrance and cause them any problems. It was distressing how often this still happened, even nowadays. He was relieved when they weren't at the entrance, but he spotted their car at the petrol station which was a bit further on to the right. One of them must have just gone in to pay for their petrol since he walked out of the door towards the car and opened the driver's door. He must have felt that Bill was studying him from the distance. The youth looked round and waved. Ben smiled and waved back. He watched the rainbow sticker on the rear bumper getting smaller and smaller as the car gathered speed. They found a place in the corner which had some electrical sockets and the dogs could lie under the table. Bill went to get some coffee from the Starbucks counter, while Ben connected the charger to the electricity. He came back with two large caramel macchiatos.

"What did you get?"

"Your favourite. Let me ring the RAC." Bill removed his phone from his trouser pocket, and went down his contact list. He found RAC and pressed the contact button.

"If you are ringing to renew your contract, press one, for new membership press two, for…" the female voice said. He dropped the phone. Damn! He hadn't selected the option for recovery. Now he had to go through the whole process again before he could actually speak to a real person. And he had nothing to write with. Phone back in his hand he ended the call. "I might need a pen and paper, I'll be right back."

"Your coffee will get cold."

"Ben, we have greater problems than cold coffee. Plug my phone in, I don't want to be cut off halfway through." A few moments later he was back.

Phone still on charge he started again. After several instructions to 'press this, press that', he was put on hold. An agonising wait, eventually a voice. A real person at last. He quickly responded. "Please don't hang up, I know I've reached the wrong number but our car broke down…No, it's not my car…No, not a friend's; a hire car…Which hire company? I don't know. Ben?"

Ben looked blank. "We borrowed it from a friend." he mouthed.

"Eh? Yes. Sorry, we borrowed it from a friend."

"The registration?"

"Ben, do you know the registration number?" he whispered.

Ben left his seat, took the pen and paper and went outside, close enough to the parked vehicle so that he could make out the number. The dogs took that as the sign it was time to go. As a safeguard, Ben had tied their leashes to the table which moved forward, spilling the drinks. Bill managed to hold on to the paper cups and stopped them tipping over. His phone call ended when the phone landed on his lap. "Blast."

He held the dogs by their collars, unable to leave the table to grab some napkins and clean the mess until Ben returned. Bill was relieved to see Ben coming back, but was surprised to see a uniformed man accompanying him.

"Now this is what I call a stroke of good luck. This is Mr Jackson from the RAC."

Bill stood up to shake his hand. "Oh, that's great. How did you get here so quickly?"

"No, I have a stall outside, trying to sell RAC memberships. I saw you coming in, but I don't think you noticed I was there. You were looking at the petrol station. I remember because I admired your dogs."

"Timmy, Tommy, say hello to the nice gentleman." Ben encouraged his pooches, who dutifully left their places with tails wagging and licked the hand of the stranger, who bent down scratching them behind the ears.

Mr Jackson stood up and addressed Bill. "I believe you have a problem with a van you are using. Do you have a membership card?"

"Yes I do, why did I not think of that before?" Bill retrieved his wallet, pulled out the card and handed it to the RAC representative.

"That's good, you have a personal based membership that means any vehicle you travel in is eligible for recovery." He used his mobile phone and pressed one button. "It's Jackson here, from station Zero X at the Welcome Break. I have a member here whose family transit has broken down. Yes, hold on, I'll hand you over." He gave his phone to Bill, who was now calm and explained the problem, giving all the required details including his membership number.

"They said they would be here in an hour."

"There you are, sir, I will be able to see them from my stand. Why don't you make yourself comfortable? I'll let you know when they arrive."

"Thank goodness. Thank you so much."

Ben gave a sigh of relief. "Shall I see what there is to eat?"

"Let's just take the dogs for a walk first and get them some water."

"You stay here, Bill. This is a good little corner to sit, besides Timmy and Tommy will be out of the way of other customers. I'll be back in a few minutes."

They had not been waiting long and hadn't decided what they should have, which by now would be dinner, when Mr Jackson reappeared. "The pick-up truck is here."

They hurried the dogs and went as fast as they could back to their transport. A large vehicle was positioned in front of it.

"Ben, take the dogs over there to the bench." Bill went over to speak with the mechanic, who was already on his knees checking the underneath of the minibus.

"Good evening, do you think you can fix it?"

"No, sorry, mate. No chance. From the description of the problem when they booked us to come, we knew it wouldn't be repairable on site. That's why they radioed me. You're fortunate that I wasn't far from here. Can you loosen the handbrake so I can winch it up onto the trailer?"

"Yes, yes, hold on." Bill did as he was asked. "What happens next?"

"We take it to your address or somewhere else, it's your choice. Do you have somewhere it can be parked?"

"I'll just check whether it should go straight to the place where we got it from."

Bill walked over to Ben. "Do you know whether we can drop it off outside at their office?"

"No chance. They don't even know we've got it."

"What?"

"Ahem, my friend sort of just gave it to us. He told me nobody would miss it."

"This is getting better by the minute."

Chapter 53

The estate agent from the Isle of Wight had phoned. Nicola was excited about a new listing. A manor house had come on the market. It might just be what they were looking for. Should she send the details by post?

Christine agreed it would be a good idea, but they would only consider viewing should their two chosen properties no longer be available when they were ready to take it further. She reminded Nicola that, as discussed, she was to let her know if either of them had been sold, or had a serious offer.

Christine was in a hurry. Sunshine Living, the home for retired artists where Henry's mother lived, had tried to contact her urgently. But Christine as usual had switched off her answer machine at home. She did not like coming back after a few days away to find several messages were waiting for her. It had happened before, during her divorce. She had not picked up a message left by her solicitor for several days. And when she did, she'd missed the deadline for lodging the demand for part of Henry's pension. The solicitor had assumed because Christine had made no contact to the contrary, that she had sent the notarised paperwork directly to the private pension company. Christine was livid with her solicitor. It was sorted out eventually but ever since that incident Christine would not leave the answering machine on if she was away for more than two days. Her friends suggested she invest in a system whereby you could phone your own landline, type in a code and retrieve any messages.

Why? Christine asked. If the person who is ringing me does not reach me, they will just have to try again. In any case, people who know me personally, would surely e-mail me or reach me via my mobile phone. Something she had argued with the solicitor at the time. Sometimes it had felt that the woman who should be representing her was actually favouring her opponent. Whose side are you on? she had asked her at one stage. Christine had calmed down after that outburst, but told her to her face when she paid her final bill she would never recommend any of her friends to make use of the services of that solicitor's office.

When the manager of Sunshine did reach her, it sounded really urgent, and could Christine get there if at all possible. Pippa, Henry's mother, had fallen last week. They had called an ambulance which took her to the hospital. The X-ray showed there were no broken bones, which was good. However, Pippa had remained in the hospital for two days for observation. She was back now, but did not want to come downstairs nor would she eat any of the food delivered to her room. She kept asking for her 'daughter Christine' every waking minute. Christine told the manager she would leave right away. She sent a quick WhatsApp message giving Lizzie a brief version of what she had been told and apologised for not coming over for the second estate agent visit to view the house which was going to be put up for sale. Lizzie replied immediately, saying not to be so silly and to give her love to her mother-in-law.

Just after the roundabout going to Greenford, Christine noted a quick, bright flash in her rear-view mirror. Oh no, not again. She kept forgetting that the speed limit had changed here. And she had been caught by the same camera before. Too bad that this time they would not offer her a driving awareness course, but instead it would be a fixed penalty payment plus three points on her licence without a doubt. Her car insurance would punish her for that slip up when it was up for renewal, she was sure about that. No point worrying about it now. The traffic seemed especially heavy, and there was a hold-up further down the road. All cars had come to a complete stop. Roadworks again. The triangle shape with the red border and a workman inside using what must be a shovel appeared on her side of the road. She was mystified why there were hardly ever any workmen to be seen. Plenty of signs, always followed by cones but no workmen? It was one of those mysteries in life, similar to the crop circles. Somebody or something must have put them there overnight without explanation.

It was one and a half hours later when she parked her car in the last available parking space, furthest away from the entrance and next to a puddle. But she had no time to contemplate why she had not changed out of her black strappy Jimmy Choo high heels. Maybe because they'd fitted like gloves, when she tried them on, after spotting them on the shelf of the Red Cross charity shop. She had dropped off a box she'd had ready under her bed for ages. It was in the way when she'd wanted to put her empty suitcase in that exact spot.

But Jimmy Choo? Come on, she just had to have them. Who would give a pair like that to a charity shop, for goodness' sake? She happily paid over the odds but now she had to tiptoe in order to avoid scratching them. Thankfully she could see the paved area was only about fifty yards ahead. She loved the sound her heels made on the flat stones once she reached them. Click, click, click, up the stairs, into the wide reception area. Karla raised her head and looked at her over her glasses. She had been busying herself with some paperwork at the reception desk. Her face lit up when she spotted Christine but she nodded to her left indicating for Christine to have a look. At a small table holding a bone china, flower pattered teacup, her little finger elegantly pointing up, sat Fiffi l'Amour, Henry's long-standing fiancée. Time had not been kind to her, Christine noted with some satisfaction. Christine tried to reach the reception desk without being noticed, but the click, click, click of her Jimmy Choos on the wooden floor gave her arrival away.

"Christeeeene!!"

Oh no, not that phony French accent. Christine tried to back away, but was out of luck. Fiffi had the audacity to hold her by the shoulders and plant a kiss on each cheek. "Are you here to see Pippa? 'Enri is up there now."

To the delight of Karla, who was following the encounter with great interest, Christine played dumb.

"Who?"

"'Enri, my 'Enri. You know, your ex."

"Oh, sorry. Didn't get that. You mean Henry is up there?"

"Yes, yes."

Christine had no intention of remaining in the presence of Fiffi, but before walking away she casually remarked, "Has he made an honest woman of you yet?"

From the expression on Karla's face, Christine was sure Fiffi's mouth had just dropped. Christine walked up the elegant staircase and took a left turn at the top. Pippa's room was the third on the right, with a Juliet balcony overlooking the back garden. She heard Henry's voice through the slightly open door and was in two minds to leave and come back later. But Pippa had spotted her. "Christine, there you are, come and sit with me." Henry's mother raised herself on her bed and stretched her arm out towards Christine, welcoming her with a warm embrace.

"Here, Henry. Take the paperwork back, I am not signing anything right now."

"You want your mother to sign something? What is it?"

"Nothing, it's nothing. It can wait." He hastily put a folder back into a brown briefcase. The same one Christine had given him as his fortieth birthday present. He turned to face her again, and looked her up and down. "You look different." Christine was glad she'd worn her tight cropped trousers and even tighter lacy top. These and her heels certainly had the right effect.

"You look…" She tried to find a suitable reply but could only come up with "You look…you." Followed by, "Lovely Fiffi asked me to tell you she is done with waiting."

"She's not here, is she? I told you I don't want her here." Pippa's voice had a panicky ring to it.

"Mother, calm down. I am done here anyway, I'll ring you later. Bye Christine, nice to have seen you."

"Hold on, I want a word." She went after Henry and closed the door so that his mother couldn't hear what she had to say.

"Henry, I don't know what you are up to, but from the speed you hid that document, I take it that it's not good. If you dare to cheat your mother the same way you tried to cheat me, you have another thing coming." She didn't wait for a reply, but returned to Pippa's room and shut the door.

Chapter 54

The meeting for the two parties to come together had been arranged. After consultation with the twins' solicitor it was confirmed that the venue would be the conference room at Patrick's old office. It was not exactly neutral ground but better than meeting at one or the other's solicitors. Apparently, Janette and Edward felt comfortable at their late father's place of work. They had spent so many hours there, and those memories were happy ones. During the years they had also formed a friendly relationship with the people there.

Rick was not so sure about any of it. He did not like this sudden change of attitude the twins were demonstrating. The ridiculous claim of kidnapping no longer existed. In fact, it had never been lodged. It had been nothing but an idle threat. He did not even believe a DNA test had ever been done. Or, they were foolish enough to have arranged for one and the result was not what they had been expecting. He would love to know. But he didn't want to discuss this with Isabelle. One of his former security guys was now a private detective. Rick decided to make contact with him, depending on the outcome of the meeting. He did not have a good feeling about the situation but thought he should wait and see. At this stage everything sounded too good to be true. But Isabelle did not want to hear any more and wanted it settled.

Her house was now on the market, and not surprisingly she'd had several viewings already. Wandsworth was an ideal location for professionals working in the City of London. Her estate agent, who was in Clapham, told her he was expecting an offer for the house any day now. Isabelle had told Christine over the phone that she was in two minds about selling so quickly, when the friends had not yet reached a decision. It had been the family home for many years. But with everything that had happened lately, for her, the time had come to move on.

Christine contacted Laura, and they decided to go to Patrick's office on the day of the meeting and leave a message at reception that they would be waiting in the café a couple of doors down. Laura declined Christine's invitation to stay overnight. She didn't want to leave Steve for too long, she reasoned.

It was a sunny day, unlike the last few which had been as gloomy as Isabelle's mood. Not sure what was required of her today, she gathered the leaflet about the house, but decided to leave last year's accounts from the auction house, where she was still the majority shareholder. The company had shown a much-improved profit and had paid a good-sized dividend to its shareholders. The changing of their shared bank accounts into solely her name had already taken place. There was only one private account of Patrick's to consider, but closing it would take some time because it could only be done when the probate was ready for submission. Since she was the sole beneficiary mentioned in Patrick's will, no problems were foreseen. Documents for both the apartments, Janette's and Edward's, Isabelle's solicitor would bring along. Isabelle had already started the process of handing them over to her children as gifts. She had been warned that this meeting could be one of many. Isabelle felt foolish not knowing exactly how selling her shares would work and how much the actual business was worth. One thing she knew, this was something which could not happen overnight. She hoped the twins did not envisage taking a large cheque back with them today.

Isabelle was going to take the number 49 bus to Clapham Common and from there travel by Tube, the Northern Line to Waterloo Station. Having to change there to the Bakerloo Line. At Waterloo she changed her mind. She realised she would be far too early and it was a lovely walk from there, over the Golden Jubilee Bridge to the other side of the river. She would even have enough time to make a little detour and visit Covent Garden. That always gave her a buzz.

She entered the office block just as Christine and Laura were leaving. Before Isabelle had a chance to ask what the two of them were doing there, Christine volunteered, "We are here for moral support. We hope you don't mind. We'll be in the café waiting. Rick is already upstairs."

The friends hugged. "I am glad you came, see you soon." Isabelle had to go.

Rick was sitting in an armchair close to the reception desk. After greeting him, Isabelle said hello to the receptionist and asked about her baby, dutifully looked at the latest portraits of the little boy which the young mother had taken on her mobile phone, before entering the offices and speaking with Patrick's colleagues and staff. Rick followed her into one of the side rooms where her solicitor and his legal team were waiting and going through some paperwork. There was enough time for them to brief Isabelle on anything that had happened since they last spoke.

Janette, Edward, and their solicitor with his assistant were waiting when the group entered the conference room. Isabelle seated herself opposite her daughter. Cordial greetings were exchanged and Isabelle's solicitor spoke first.

"We appreciate you coming here. We hope this gives us the opportunity to settle as much as possible today."

"There is nothing to settle," replied his opponent and handed him a folder.

"I see this is a copy of Patrick's Last Will and Testament. You are aware that Isabelle is the sole beneficiary?" He directed this statement to the twins, who until now had not spoken.

"What my clients want is a share in the business."

"What?" Rick could not contain himself.

"But I am selling the shares." Isabelle was confused.

"Mum," started Janette.

"Let me handle it," intervened the twins' solicitor.

"No. Actually, I'd like to speak with my children alone. Is that all right?" She first looked at Edward and then at Janette. Both nodded in agreement.

"Hold on a minute." Rick tried to stop this from happening. Who knew what Isabelle would agree to?

"What has this got to do with you? You are not my father." Edward shot him an angry look.

"And nor was Patrick, according to you."

"Enough, all of you, out." Isabelle stood up and ushered them through the door.

Defiantly, Rick remained in the corridor which enabled him to watch them through the glass panels. He observed them sitting closely together now, each taking it in turn to speak. At one stage Isabelle reached over to Janette. He almost re-entered the room when after about twenty minutes Edward's gestures became animated and he stood and walked towards his mother. Rick already had his hand on the door handle, ready to go in and stop Edward's possible aggression. Rick watched in amazement at what Edward did next. He put both arms around Isabelle's shoulders. Janette joined them, and there the three stood in a group hug, tears running down Isabelle's face.

Chapter 55

"There is an e-mail from Isabelle, come and have a look."
"What does it say?" asked Bill.
"I'll read it to you."

Dear All, guess what, I have sold the house.

"Isabelle has sold the house?"
"Apparently so." Bill walked over to join Ben in their small office and stood behind him, looking over his shoulder and bending down so he could read it at the same time.

The new owners are cash buyers with no house to sell. Right now they live and work in Singapore, but are relocating back to England. Still, I think the whole process until the sale is completed will take the usual two months minimum. I will be homeless after that. Maybe by then we will have given the Isle of Wight more thought and will be ready to make a move? But meanwhile most of my furniture will be auctioned off since I don't intend to take any of the dark coloured wood with me, wherever I will end up. The items I keep will go into storage. I, most likely, will be living out of a suitcase somewhere, hint, hint. (No, Rick, not your couch.) I so look forward to when we are all together again. Oh, by the way, I met up with Janette and Edward with

solicitors in tow. Thank you, Rick, for being there, and thank, you Laura and Christine, for surprising me by turning up and our chat afterwards. Things on the home front look much better now, but I'll bore you with all the details when I see you.
Love from Isabelle xxx

"I wonder what she has worked out with the twins. The e-mail sounds quite optimistic, don't you think?"

"It definitely does. I'll reply that she can come and stay with us if she likes."

"Yes, why don't you, Ben, and we could fill her in about our plans at the same time? Brilliant idea."

"But it's not concrete yet. Nothing might come of it. We have not even been approached about it officially, have we?"

"Sorry. Yes, you are right. Tell Isabelle she can come and live with us, and give her my love."

Bill knew their agent well, and when receiving such great news knew she would not give up that easily. Let's face it, it was far too good an opportunity to miss. An offer for Ben to direct a new musical and Bill to be the costume designer. The world premiere was planned to be right here, in the West End of London with Broadway next. The possibilities were endless. On the other hand, hadn't they retired from the world of show business altogether? Bill knew he and Ben working together would be a challenge for most of the team. Arguments and tears, mainly Ben's, as everybody would expect; especially when he didn't get his own way. Both of them quarrelling at the rehearsals and this being carried on at home. It always started about something ridiculous. Once, when Ben wanted a dancer to change a position, which had looked completely awkward, the dancer had insisted the costume design was to blame, and Bill was summoned. By the time he arrived a full-blown argument had developed, and the choreographer was ready to throw in the towel. Ben was the director, and known to be the best in the business. Therefore, more often than not, things got smoothed over quickly.

Bill felt confident that this new show would go ahead and had secretly started the first drawings. It was after all his favourite era; late 19th/early 20th century. And all circus related. A dream come true. Bill would definitely not let this one pass. He would have to discuss it with Ben soon in more detail. But both were, like the rest of the performing arts world, superstitious, and until a contract was signed anything could happen. It was one of those things which went with the art of entertainment. Where else would you wish someone to 'break a leg', instead of good luck? Never, ever, ever whistle on the stage, unless it is part of the show. One of the singers found this out to his cost. He had whistled on stage, and that, at the dress rehearsal. Ben had gone ballistic. Whistling on stage means nothing less than the audience will do just that at opening night and the show will be a flop. Ben insisted the singer was replaced. Even Equity, the union, was at a loss at first but a solution was found. A hastily arranged audition for a different production came up. Luckily, the whistling singer was chosen, and as the one of the principal parts no less.

If all went to plan the writers, a brother and sister from Adelaide, Australia, would arrive together in London with their musical director within the next few days. Bill and Ben's agent had told them she believed there was a connection of some sort between the writers and a British circus. It occurred to them that was why the siblings were so keen to produce it over here. Although she was not supposed to say it, they already had a producer who was willing to come up with the money.

Living on the Isle of Wight and working on a West End production might prove to be impossible if this move went ahead soon. It might be an idea to join the group over there at a later stage. But there would be a problem with the finances. They would have to re-mortgage their house to get the funds needed to pay for their share. Another question had come up during the days they'd spent in Yarmouth. How would the shares be allocated? Each person having one share? Or one share per household? Something which needed to be addressed before anybody got too excited. Ben had suggested that the two of them start to prepare a list of all the items they wanted to talk about when they met at Nobby's.

Chapter 56

"I spoke with Berliot. She said she would be in all day, would you mind ringing her?" Steve told Laura after she unloaded the shopping and carried several bags into the kitchen, placing them on the table. It had been raining all morning, but they had run out of essential supplies and the new Waitrose which had recently opened on the A30 was only a five-minute drive, if that. In good weather she could walk there, but never did. For items which could be carried home she would always do her shopping in the village itself. Waitrose had built their supermarket on the site of the former Notcutts Garden Centre. It had taken about two years to complete and was excellent. The company must have also given considerable thought to customer parking because provision was ample. Mind you, Laura had loved the old place. All their Christmas trees used to come from there. Well, almost. Not the one year when Steve, together with a neighbour and Steve and Laura's friend, Cliff, decided it would be a good idea to cut their own in the nearby woodland. Their neighbour, an artist, insisted that there was an old English law allowing people in this section of Surrey to cut their own trees. Laura had doubted it very much but there was not a lot she could do about it. Armed with axes and saws off they went. After about an hour they returned and when Laura opened the front door the first thing she noticed was their friend standing there with a smile so intense that she immediately realised something was up.

"Where is Steve with our tree?"

Cliff pointed to his left. There was her husband holding up what could only be described as a dilapidated imitation of…? She could not come up with the right description. It was not a tree as such, but a large stick from which two needleless branches swung.

"I am sorry. I found this lying on the ground covered by some bushes. I just could not bring myself to cut one down." He was Norwegian, for goodness' sake. A country where even the tree in Trafalgar Square came from.

Laura shrieked. Her parents in law were arriving the next day. She almost forgot about Cliff, who was happily picking up his treasure, a beautiful small firm little pine, grinning and waving before shouting, "Have fun, see you in a couple of days."

"Tell Joan I'll phone her later," Laura managed to reply.

They'd raced to Notcutts before they closed for the holidays. There was just one tree left for sale that Christmas Eve. It was not much better than the one Steve had brought home. But when they cut the top branches off and nailed them firmly to the tree trunk at the bottom, and hid everything with silver lametta, red baubles and real white candles, it didn't look too bad.

"What did Berliot say?" Laura shouted from the kitchen and hoped Steve would be able to hear over the sound of the television in the living room. From the roar and applause of the crowd Laura guessed it was cricket he was watching.

"Just ring her back."

Berliot usually called on a Sunday over WhatsApp or Skype, because it was free and they could see each other. Phoning during the week on the landline sounded alarming. Laura wanted to know more before she picked up the receiver. She put the kettle on. Both of them liked a cuppa in the afternoon and Laura had purchased some fresh apple cake from the bakery counter.

"Tea is on the table." She was convinced Steve would

hear that one. And sure enough he appeared in the kitchen, pulled up the nearest chair and sat down.

"That smells good."

"So, Berliot rang out of the blue without needing anything?"

"Not exactly."

"So, what seems to be her problem?"

"I rang her."

"That's good. But why do I need to ring her back?"

"I don't know."

Laura sighed, cut two large portions of the cake and placed them on plates, walked over to the dresser to remove the small forks and teaspoons. She then got the milk and sugar before placing the teapot strainer on the patterned plastic tablecloth.

"Pour the tea, my dear, I'll get the phone."

She glanced around the kitchen before entering the hallway. This house is in desperate need of updating; something she had said many times before. But Steve loved it the way it was, he would argue. Being a little ramshackle was the attraction of it. Who still had an original Victorian bathroom upstairs? A large free-standing bath in the middle of the room, the toilet and sink unit white with a painted blue flower design. The toilet cistern was high up with an arm you had to pull down with a chain which had at the end a white and blue original porcelain pull matching the rest. It was great when they were young, but no longer practical for Steve. They'd had a quick job done converting the junk room, which was reached through the kitchen and the small conservatory, into a shower room. This was anything but ideal. Isabelle had taken the first step, and they should consider the same. One way or another it would have to be done eventually.

Laura took the phone and went back into the kitchen, sat herself opposite Steve and pressed the redial button.

Berliot answered after the second ring.

"Oh, Mum, I am so excited. The kids will love it. We are so glad you have reached this decision."

"What decision?"

"Mum, what are you talking about? Dad phoned, he told me you are coming over soon to stay here with us. And we have just the right cabin for you. Don't worry, there's a wood burner inside, it will be nice and cosy in the winter. Will Dad be up to the long journey? You would need to come by car bringing all the little items you want to keep. You know, all those trinkets you've collected over the years. Oh, Mum. We are so happy, all of us together here."

"Berliot, sweetheart, there's somebody at the door," she lied. "I will have to call you back later. Sorry about that, bye." She hung up before her daughter had time to say anything else.

"Do you really want to live in Lillehammer?"

"I'm scared, Laura."

"I know you are scared, my love, but I am here, right with you, and so are our friends. You are not alone, Steve." She took his hands in hers, feeling the slight tremor. "Isabelle has already sold her house, and we should do the same. You are right about one thing. We cannot stay here much longer."

Chapter 57

Christine was looking forward to a visit from her brother Matthew. They hadn't seen each other for quite a while. Christine had only visited him once since he'd been posted up to Newcastle. That was supposed to be only for a few months to set up a new office for the software company he worked for. At that stage neither his wife nor children had come to live with him. The temporary posting lasted nearly two years. After that, he was asked to make it more permanent, whatever that was supposed to mean. To Christine's surprise he agreed. She also liked Newcastle as much as he did. It had become a vibrant city not only famous for its grand Georgian architecture and an exceptional university, but also as a business metropolis and for its arts and science. It was a young city. Students flocked to it and the nightlife was very active. Yes, it was a great place to live. But Christine doubted this was her brother's real reason. Somehow, she felt there was another woman involved. If that was true, no wonder he hadn't put up a fight when his wife decided to stay in Brighton. She insisted she had made a life there without him. Besides, their teenage children had no desire to uproot from their friends. Despite those two living so far apart, they'd never divorced and visited each other frequently. An arrangement which evidently suited them. At least in Christine's mother's eyes, only one of her children had failed in their marriage.

Christine liked his wife and occasionally they met in London for a girls' day out. They also sometimes saw each other at family do's at her mother's in Exeter. And Christine made a point of seeing them over Christmas. This gave her the ideal excuse for not going to Exeter and spending time with her mother and stepfather. It was a place best avoided. Christine still missed her dad terribly. He had died of pneumonia not long after arriving in Hong Kong. He'd been a Lieutenant Colonel in the British army. He had not been healthy when Christine saw him the very last time. It had been dismissed as a cold, which unfortunately left his illness undetected. Christine's mother, immediately after his death, suffered a nervous breakdown and was hospitalised over there. She did not even accompany her husband's coffin back to England where he was buried. Nor did she make any contact for several months after that. She reappeared years later, remarried. Something she had forgotten to tell her children in her letters. Whether Matthew spent more time in Devon, she never inquired. His own children had long flown the nest, and he and his wife were proud grandparents. Her brother on reaching retirement age was ready for his return down south, as he called it. Could Christine put up with him for a while, until he found the right place for himself?

She was intrigued about his future plans, she knew her brother would be up to something. There was always some sort of surprise lurking round the corner. It would be really good to spend some time together, and she would use the opportunity to tell him about the plans she and her friends had made. She had left a message on Lizzie's phone to tell her about Matthew's visit and would she like to come over and stay a few days. The three of them had always been very close. Her brother would arrive tomorrow, and she planned to surprise him with his favourite cuisine; Spanish food. She would make several tapas: Albondigas, the meatballs in a tomato sauce, Gambas al Ajillo, prawns in garlic sauce, plus little spicy sausages, and a paella. Accompanied by white bread sticks, to scoop up the tasty sauces. There would be plenty even if Lizzie did decide to come over.

Christine's next-door neighbour, Olivia, had a rented garage nearby but had no vehicle at present. She'd offered that either her brother's car or Christine's could be put in there. Parking in the street outside the houses was getting more difficult every day. Commuters were catching on that the road they lived on was more or less between Hanwell and West Drayton railway stations. The journey from there into London Paddington would take as little as fifteen or twenty minutes, depending on which station was opted for.

Normally, if at all possible, Christine would not move her car from outside her gate before 9am. When she had to, she could be sure somebody would take the spot, and it would be up to her to drive around until she found another one. Several people in the street had placed traffic cones there. This did not fool everybody, but some took notice since it was so close to the school. A couple of houses further down had contacted the council and for a fee they'd adjusted the kerb to create a driveway; just as they had done at Bill and Ben's. The garden had been paved over, forming a parking area outside the dining room window. There was a drive between her house and Olivia's but Christine had been blocked in there before and could not take the risk unless she knew that she wouldn't need her Mini all day.

Her brother could be quite unreliable with his travelling plans, which was one habit of his she could not get used to. He could arrive tomorrow as he said, or otherwise not. It had been known for Christine to sit in for three days in a row waiting, dinner in the oven ready to be heated up. She'd had to destroy the food and her brother was at the receiving end of her fury when he eventually waltzed in. This was part of the reason she decided to use her Spanish cooking skills. She could freeze the meatballs, the prawns would be frozen anyway, and the paella would only be prepared once he had actually arrived. If Lizzie turned up before him, they would go to the pub or have a takeaway. Olivia had a house key and unless she was at one of her 'New Age' group meetings she'd be at home meditating. Her beau would be there in any case.

Christine checked her shopping list first and her drinks fridge. The light had gone out again in there so she added bulbs to her list. She would not have bothered replacing it right away if Matthew hadn't been coming. This job was a real pain because she had to unplug the fridge, for which she needed to pull it forward. Take out all the drinks, remove the shelf and she had to lie on her back and wiggle her body inside the cold fridge. With a screwdriver ready to remove the light fitting at the top, she had to then replace the bulb and repeat the procedure in reverse. Christine was always glad when the job was done. The fridge with the glass door was the focal point of her kitchen. Nobby had one, but his was massive, around six feet tall she thought, filled from top to bottom with the finest champagne. Not to be outdone, hers contained white and rosé wines and several bottles of Cava.

Christine went to the storage cupboard in her hall to retrieve the bags she used to carry her shopping. She picked up the car key from the unit under the mirror and unlatched her front door. That was when the phone call came.

Chapter 58

Lizzie felt a shiver run through her body. The same feeling you might get if you believed you were being followed by someone. She turned round again, but apart from the normal foot traffic of the folks living in this part of London, nothing unusual. It was early afternoon and Lizzie had gone to the small shop on the other side of the park. She didn't really need anything but she'd been stuck indoors all morning on a lovely day. She loved the walk through the park and used getting the local paper as an excuse. Not that she needed one. Nobody was waiting for her at the house. Somehow, she had stopped calling it 'her home'.

She felt a little dizzy. It must be the after effects of all the bubbly she drank last night at a champagne reception, held at the intimate gallery in Mayfair she frequented. She had purchased one or two items there over the years. Now she was invited every time they had a new exhibition in their one room. She had to admit that the guy who'd chatted her up was rather dishy. But she declined his invitation to continue their evening at a bar he knew. Lizzie would not trust a man again for a long time. Especially since her fateful encounter with Emilio had occurred on such a night. And look how that turned out. Now she'd been told if his latest assault went to trial, she would have to give evidence in open court. It had been suggested Lizzie should be questioned in a separate room via a camera without having to face the accused. But that had been dismissed. In any case what was the point? He would know it was her. She feared that prospect. Emilio had powerful friends. What had possessed her to get involved with him? The attention she got? His charm? Yes, he had been charming, at least in the beginning. The flattery that at her age she had a boyfriend much younger? Or the lifestyle she had craved?

They had met at a fundraising event at the golf club. It was held to raise money for a football training centre which would be built at the local secondary school. It was a much-needed facility in the area, and Lizzie was happy to help. The guest of honour had been kept a secret to avoid onlookers turning up, blocking the street. When Emilio was announced and entered the stage, he was accompanied by a group of children wearing football gear, the shirts bearing his name, each of them clutching a football. Each wore sparkling gold coloured football boots. These alone must have cost more than a parent could earn in a week. Lizzie had been shocked at first. What a show-off. Not the type of person she would associate with. But then, after the speeches, the meal and the lottery, where a staggering £150,000 had been raised with a promise of more to come, he had made a beeline for her when she went to get her coat.

"Let me get that," he whispered, took his own and said to the organiser, "The lady and I are just leaving. Thank you for a pleasant evening." He put her coat around her shoulders and guided her outside, where his car arrived instantly. He ushered her to the back seat and slid in after her.

"Now what is a lady like yourself doing at a function like this?" was his opening line. They both laughed. After that, Lizzie started to move in circles she would have not imagined in her wildest dreams. She was accepted by the rich and famous, went on holidays to private islands, on private yachts the size of houses. Lizzie loved her new life and believed it would last forever. She was never in any doubt that this was the life she was supposed to live. She was overwhelmed when Emilio suggested they should make it more permanent. She had this massive house after all, why not live there together? Lizzie eagerly agreed. This was really happening, he was making a go of it. In any case he was right, staying overnight in his rented apartment was no longer an option. It was spectacular, true enough, but the walls were so thin you could hear the neighbours coughing. That did not suit their lovemaking, which was extremely noisy and a bit adventurous to say the least. Emilio was a very clever man, she realised too late.

At first, she'd thought nothing of it when he'd said, "Let's experiment." At her age? She showed no inhibitions and followed his guidance. In turns they tied their wrists to the bedposts. But there came a time when he changed. He turned violent for the first time. Slapped her in the face while she lay there defenceless. She asked him to stop, but he was working himself into a frenzy. He put his hands over her mouth, and she struggled. She tried desperately to free her hands. But the ropes only became tighter. She lay quietly letting fate take over. He forced himself upon her and after satisfying himself, simply got up, leaving her where she was. It must have been thirty minutes before he returned, still naked. He dabbed her face with a cold wet flannel, kissing her all over, freeing her from the restraint, apologised and carried her into the shower. There he made love to her gently, whispering and drying her tears. "You must not do that again," he told her. Over and over again. She was confused, it must have been her fault for sparking it off. She was to blame. So, she bought him the car to make up for what she did.

Lizzie checked her watch, it was getting late. The photographer taking pictures for the impending sale had taken far longer than he had told her beforehand. He'd also said if necessary he'd be back tomorrow to take some more. The light had not been favourable. Favourable? What was that was supposed to mean? It had been bright and sunny most of the day. She hoped that at least the bloke who was due late afternoon to assess the energy rating would be on time. Apparently, estate agents were now required to issue an energy performance certificate. Whatever next?

The uneasiness returned and Lizzie started to hurry. The park was emptying. Mothers with children had hurried home. She reached the gate and paused on the pavement. A bicycle went past, one of those racing ones, ridden by a man in Lycra. He carried on, carefully avoiding Mrs Kaschinski with her pushchair. Her family ran the shop Lizzie had just been to. The mother and child had arrived from Krakow to join her husband less than two months ago. As far as Lizzie could work out she spoke very little English. She relied on waving and smiling as a greeting. But Lizzie wished she wouldn't use her mobile, speaking or listening to somebody the same time as crossing the road. Lizzie looked to her left and saw that about twenty yards away, the same car was still parked. She had noticed it earlier since it had been left blatantly on the double yellow lines. Obviously, when the school children were on holiday no traffic wardens were to be seen. She did not notice the person inside. He was hidden from her view but now slid up on his seat, starting the engine. An engine which could not be heard. The car was a soundless hybrid. The road was clear, she stepped forward to cross it. Too late she felt the rush of air. She turned to face the driver and then the car hit her. The force was such that it threw Lizzie upwards, and she landed on the other side of the road. A scream rang out before the car sped away.

Chapter 59

Mrs Kaschinski remained frozen on the pavement, her body twisted towards the scene. She was still clutching her phone. Several people came running out of their houses and from down the street. Lizzie's next-door neighbour was the first to call for help. Two others stopped the traffic and persuaded the drivers to turn around. A teenager was sent to the bottom of the road to make sure no more traffic would come that way.

Lizzie lay perfectly still. A blanket had appeared to cover part of her body to avoid losing too much body heat. Sirens blaring, first the police arrived followed by the paramedics and the ambulance. It took the ambulance less than eight minutes to reach the scene.

Bystanders were told to make space. One of the policemen began asking questions, looking for witnesses. There was only one person who had seen it all. Nadia Kaschinski. She was in shock and in no fit state to even tell them her name. The baby started to cry. Lizzie's next-door neighbour, having left his position at the top end of the street, walked towards the police.

"Sorry, you cannot come here. Please stand back."

He pointed to Lizzie. "Officer, this is my neighbour. I live right there."

"You know this woman?"

"Yes, she lives next door."

"Can I have your name please?"

"Paul Smith."

"Please give all your details to my colleague over there." His outstretched arm indicated a female officer who was speaking to a group of youngsters and writing something down.

The officer changed his mind. "Wait. You wouldn't by any chance know her? She seems to be our only witness."

Instead of replying to the policeman he faced the young woman. "Nadia, are you all right?" She looked at him, and he saw the tears running down her face.

"No, not all right." She handed him her mobile.

"What's that?" The policeman took it instead and scrutinised it. There it was, a partial photo of the fleeing car. "We need to hold on to that."

"Wait a minute officer, you cannot just take her phone. This woman is clearly in shock as it is. Nadia, come to my house, my wife will make you a cup of tea." Willingly she let him lead her away. The officer went with them and spoke to his female colleague, then turned back to Paul. "My colleague here will go with you and take the statement. I will follow as soon as backup has arrived. They will be here shortly. Please, Mrs…?"

"Kaschinski," said Paul.

"Mrs Kaschinski, can I hold on to your phone?"

Paul looked at him with suspicion. "Nadia's English is not very good and you're frightening her."

"I am trying to avoid the picture being wiped off accidentally. We have a team of experts who will need to go through everything."

The phone started ringing as Nadia watched Lizzie being carefully placed on a stretcher. Her head in a brace and her body strapped onto a firm, secure board.

Paul laid his hand on Nadia's shoulder. "Nadia, come on. Let's go, we can ring your husband from our landline." The officer followed them to the house. Nadia picked up the crying infant and left the pram beside the stairs.

The policewoman knew straight away how traumatised Nadia was, and that coaxing any valuable information from her might take time and patience. Some trauma victims blocked out whatever they might have seen or been part of. She spoke to her supervisor, and he agreed to let her handle the situation, but would send in a fellow female officer to assist. She let Paul's wife settle Nadia on the settee and bring her hot tea and biscuits.

Meanwhile her colleague phoned for Nadia's husband to come over, assuring him nothing had happened to her. They took as much information as Paul could give them about their neighbour.

Paul replied to the routine questions as best as he could. Does Lizzie have family? Friends? A place of work? How long had she lived next door? He was glad for the interruption of the arrival of Nadia's family. Her mother- and father-in-law stood outside next to her husband. A roaring noise came from above. A helicopter arrived and skilfully touched down on the green in the park. The extra police who had come on the scene had cordoned off the whole area. Paul watched as the first of the television vans arrived. The London News team set up their position as close as they were allowed. Bright lights came on and the makeup crew touched up the female reporter's face. The cameras turned towards the park where Lizzie was being transferred to leave by air. Paul watched until the helicopter departed. He re-entered the house and joined his wife in the kitchen. In the sitting room Nadia was slowly putting the pieces together for the police.

"I was listening to what Nadia had witnessed," his wife greeted him with when he sat down, totally drained.

"She said it was not an accident."

"What?"

"Yes. Lizzie was crossing the road, there was no car apart from the one parked at the kerb. She waved at Lizzie and the next thing she knew the car drove into her. The police were asking whether Lizzie has any enemies."

"What did you say?"

"Nothing yet."

As if on cue the officer who had talked to Paul earlier entered the room. Did they know of anybody who could be contacted?

"Lizzie has a good friend," said Paul. "Her name is Christine but we have no phone number for her. Maybe it's in the telephone book in her hall. We could go and get it."

"You have a key? Why did you not say that earlier?"

"Officer, as far as I am concerned I cannot just give it to you. I'll go in and get the book." It was apparent that Paul was not a great friend of the police force.

"I'll accompany you," the policewoman said.

"Sorry, I can't let you enter the house. You have no right to do that."

"I just want to make sure that nothing is moved. From what Mrs Kaschinski has told us, this might become part of a crime scene."

Ten minutes later Christine received the phone call.

Chapter 60

As though possessed Christine stormed next door, banging with both fists so hard that Olivia checked for damage when she opened the door.

"It's Lizzie," Christine gasped while trying to catch her breath. "She had an accident and has been taken by helicopter to King's College Hospital."

"Oh my God, what happened? Come in."

"I can't, I have to get there. I don't know when I will be back. I'll try to text my brother."

"You're in no fit state to drive, I can drive your car."

"I'm taking a taxi. I'll phone you when I know more."

And she was gone. Back inside her house Christine frantically searched for the number of the nearest taxi company. Something she hardly ever used but promised herself in future to leave in a prominent position on the mirror above the telephone table. She had a quick check there just in case, since everything else was attached to it. No, nothing there. Where were the Yellow Pages? After a fruitless search in the obvious places she found it on the shelf in the kitchen next to her recipe books, of which she had plenty, but never looked at any of them. With shaking hands, she pressed the buttons on her house phone. They would be there in a few minutes they said. She grabbed her bag, keys and phone and as an afterthought went to get her jacket.

She went outside to wait. Olivia joined her. Wordlessly they stood together. The car arrived promptly. The two women hugged and Olivia went back inside once the car was out of sight. Christine texted her brother. She was in no mood to speak with him in person. She might break down and cry. She just needed to sit for a while and go over the conversation with the police.

The accident made no sense. Why was Lizzie knocked down by a car virtually outside her front door? She understood the bit that the neighbour had a key and knew her name. But the police hadn't wanted to tell her any more. They'd said if possible could she come to the hospital straight away and go to the Accident and Emergency entrance. There somebody would notify them when she arrived. The traffic was bad, it was nearing the peak of the commuter time. The driver did his best and took the fastest route possible, via the M4 motorway, through Hammersmith into town and crossing to the south side of the River Thames at Vauxhall. Even so, the fifteen miles took nearly one and a half hours. She texted Isabelle, Laura, Bill and Nobby, just telling them Lizzie had been in a car accident and that she was on her way in a taxi to the hospital. She would let them know more when she found out how Lizzie was and what happened. Isabelle immediately phoned. Christine was relieved to have somebody to talk to and cried as she relayed what the police had told her.

"I am so worried, Isabelle. Being taken by helicopter, and the police having sent an officer to the hospital, sounds really bad. Oh, my God, I hope she is all right."

"The police told you the driver sped away. Surely, they want to ask Lizzie some questions, that's why they are there."

"I hope you're right, but why King's College Hospital, is there none nearer?"

"It could be they wanted a helicopter because of rush-hour traffic, and I think King's College is one of the few with a helipad."

"Yes, that could be it. I'll let you know as soon as I know some more. Can you tell the others we spoke? That way I won't need to ring around. Isabelle, I am here now, I have to go. Bye."

Christine paid the driver and rushed through the door. She went straight to the counter and ignored that the nurse behind the desk was attending to a couple. "My friend has been brought in by helicopter. The police said I should come straight away."

The two people in front of her gave her a dirty look, but before they could complain the nurse asked, "Are you Christine Henderson?"

Christine nodded.

"I am sorry," the nurse said to the couple. "I just need to get a colleague." She returned straight away and nodded towards Christine. "Anna, please take Mrs Henderson into waiting room three, and tell the constable that she has arrived." She then returned to her task of taking the details of the other couple who had been waiting in line. Christine received a sympathetic look from the woman who had been waiting.

"Would you like some tea or coffee?" asked the pleasant young nurse.

"A cup of tea would be wonderful, thank you."

"No problem, I'll let them know you're here."

A man and a woman arrived before the tea, the woman was in uniform. "Thank you for coming, I am DC Platt and this is PC Whetherford. Do you mind if we ask you a few questions?"

"I am sorry, detective, I need to see my friend."

"I totally understand but your friend is in surgery right now, and it could be a while, that's why we would like to speak with you now."

The door opened and Christine's much-needed mug of tea arrived. The nurse had put it on a small plate with biscuits, which she placed on the little coffee table next to the armchair. "I'll be waiting outside if you need me," she said to Christine.

"Please," said the detective. "Sit down and drink your tea, I realise how anxious you must be."

Christine took the offered chair. Her hands were shaking and the mug rattled on the plate when she picked them up.

"Can you tell me what happened?"

"Mrs Henderson…"

"Please call me Christine."

"Christine, you must appreciate that any details we can divulge are for family members only."

"Besides an elderly aunt and some cousins, Lizzie has no family. I have no idea where they live. I am her best friend."

"I see. Now that is established, I can tell you your friend was involved in a serious incident, and from what an eyewitness described we believe it was an attack carried out on purpose."

"Attacked? What do you mean by that? How is she?" Christine's hand flew to her mouth.

"I am sorry, but from the first information the doctors gave she suffered multiple injuries. We really do not know any more at this stage, only that she is in the best hands with the team here and right now they are doing everything possible."

Christine staring crying. PC Whetherford took a couple of tissues out of the box which stood on a shelf on the wall. She took the chair next to Christine and glanced at her boss, who nodded. "Christine, the doctor will come directly to this room as soon as your friend is stabilised. I know you want to help her, is there any person you can think of who would want to harm her?"

"Emilio Gassiamos," replied Christine without hesitation.

"The football coach?"

"Lizzie is supposed to give evidence in court against him."

DC Platt pulled a chair over and sat down facing her. Now all three sat in a semicircle.

"Could you give us the whole story? PC Whetherford will take the notes."

Christine began to speak, and after every few sentences he interrupted with a question. When Christine could not think of anything more he asked her to slowly read through everything which had been written down. And if something was not as she remembered to let them know. Then he gave her his card. "If you think of anything to add, please call me."

He rose. "If you'll excuse me now, it is important that we act on this information immediately. My colleague here will stay with you. Thank you for your help." They shook hands and he left.

Christine sat back in her armchair and closed her eyes. She must have dropped off because when she opened them next a team of doctors had entered. One was speaking with the police constable. Christine shot out of her seat. "How is my friend?"

"I am Mr Bridges, the chief surgeon." Christine took his outstretched hand. "Your friend sustained multiple internal injuries. Please don't be alarmed. We successfully repaired the damage and stopped the bleeding. Now she is in ICU where she will be monitored overnight." Christine breathed a sigh of relief. "However, I am sorry to tell you, either the impact of the car or when she was thrown on the road broke her back in several places."

"Oh no!" Christine screamed.

"I know how distressing this news must be. If your friend remains stable during the night we will arrange for a transfer by helicopter to Stoke Mandeville Hospital tomorrow, where the National Spinal Injury Centre is located. You may be aware this is the best and largest specialist spinal unit in the world, and we believe that transferring her there would give her the best chance for recovery."

"Can I see her?"

The doctors looked at each other. "Normally we don't let anybody into ICU, but we'll arrange for you to have a gown and mask. You'll only be able to stay for a few minutes, and you must be aware that she might not realise you are there."

Chapter 61

Stoke Mandeville Hospital was not far from where Nobby lived, only twenty miles or so. It made sense, he suggested, for Christine to come and stay with him. The next date for all of them to meet was approaching. He further suggested she should come to him first and he would take her to the hospital. He knew exactly where it was, it was easy to find. But he didn't want her to go by herself. Armed with a bunch of newspapers he patiently waited in the hospital restaurant situated in the main lobby. Christine had not checked whether the hospital had regulated visiting times, but that would have not deterred her from seeing Lizzie immediately.

As it was, Lizzie was being kept in the intensive care unit where visiting was restricted in any case. However, the professor in charge was very aware of Lizzie's situation and allowed Christine to see her friend every day for a short time, and made sure she received regular updates on her condition. Her friend was being kept in an induced coma which would continue for at least a couple of weeks. This would help Lizzie's body to heal without her becoming stressed or uncomfortable. Slowly they would start to reduce the medication until she was fully awake. That process could last several days. The X-rays taken at the spinal unit had confirmed that indeed her back had been broken. But the extent of those injuries could only be assessed after the initial swelling had gone down. Only after that could further investigation be carried out.

❀

A sombre group met on the weekend. It had been ten days since Lizzie was hospitalised and her situation had not changed. Christine visited her daily. She sat there holding her hand and talking to her, not knowing whether Lizzie could hear her or knew that she was by her side. Everybody embraced Christine in turn and tears were shed. Christine filled them in on what the doctors had said. Also, the detective had been in touch. Thanks to Mrs Kaschinski's instinctive action, the team were able to identify the registration number. It was a rental car, picked up at Heathrow airport three days prior to the attack. They found it abandoned in a residential street in Hounslow. That was after a resident had phoned in that there was a vehicle left with a dented bonnet and blood spatters. That car was now with their investigating team. The police also said that chances of finding the actual perpetrator were slim, since he would have long fled the country. However, they retrieved the security footage from the rental company for the day the car was collected. If Christine wouldn't mind coming over to go through it, there might just be a chance that she would recognise somebody. Nadia had agreed to do the same, although she was still very traumatised and was receiving counselling.

Christine and Nobby had cooked for everybody and they served the meal at a long mahogany table in the dining room next to the kitchen. The estate agents' leaflets from the Isle of Wight remained untouched in a plastic folder on the floor. Nobody seemed interested in looking at them at this stage.

It was Christine who felt she had to address the moving situation after the dishes had been cleared away. Everybody remained at the table with their glasses of wine.

"With the situation Lizzie is in now, and her recovery possibly taking a very long time, right now I cannot make any decision about living on the Isle of Wight."

"Don't worry, we can put it on hold. There's no urgency to move, is there, Bill?" asked Ben, looking directly into his partner's eyes.

Bill put his hand to his mouth to avoid a coughing fit. Isabelle noticed his hesitation in replying and shot him a questioning look.

Bill took a large sip of wine. "I'll say it straight out. Ben and I have been asked to work on a new West End project. And we have signed the contract."

"But that is marvellous." Rick was getting excited. "Is it a new musical?"

Bill filled them in about the new venture, a world premiere which Ben would direct and he would be the costume designer, with opportunities that were beyond anything they had ever worked on together. They had met with the writers and musical director. At this stage, he stressed, everything was hush, hush.

Everybody talked at the same time and wanted to hear all the ins and outs. Bill finished his story by saying, "Sorry folks, but that means we cannot join you on the Isle of Wight for at least a year, maybe even longer. We could still put some money into it," he added quickly when he saw Isabelle's disappointed face.

"Tell us what's happened about the situation with you and the twins." It was time to divert the subject away from them, Ben decided.

"Things are much better now. Edward's still having a difficult time and is exploring his family history. But we speak. Janette has come round totally. We are now working on a stronger relationship. The house as you know has sold, and I will be moving out soon."

"Will you pay them out?"

"Not directly. I have given each their apartments plus they will both have a ten percent share in the business."

"I understood you would be selling your shares?" Steve queried.

"I am. Thirty-one percent of my shares will be sold to the existing shareholders. That will give them the majority they want. Everybody seems to be happy with the solution. To my surprise the twins want to work actively at the auction house. With Janette having a Master's Degree in Fine Art and Edward already running a small but international transport company they will be a welcome addition, I have been told."

"That sounds really good, I am so happy for you, Isabelle," Laura joined in. "Steve wants to move to Lillehammer."

For a moment there was stunned silence, they all looked first at Laura and back to Steve.

"What brought that on?" Christine thought she had to get Laura out of what could develop into an awkward situation.

Steve's hands, which had been resting on the table, started to shake, a movement they all felt. Christine to one side of him laid her hands over his.

"I sort of feel homesick. I can't explain it."

"We thought we'll try it for a few months. See how it goes in the winter before we reach a decision. We can't stay where we are, you all know that."

Surprisingly the mood became lighter after that and several more drinks were poured. That was until Nobby said, "I am moving to Australia."

Chapter 62

The leaves on the trees had all but gone. The park was a little gloomy this time of the year. Christmas was only a couple of weeks away. Christine pulled the blanket around Lizzie's shoulders. It was fresh at this time of the day. Even so, the sun was high up in the sky and there was not a cloud in sight.

A nurse came onto the patio carrying their lunch. Christine had ordered and paid for hers on arrival, although she had been told there was no need. Before the nurse went back inside she moved behind the wheelchair ready to position it close to the table.

"Sue, you know I can do this myself." Lizzie looked up at her and started to move the wheelchair using her gloved hand.

"Yes, you're making fantastic progress. Soon you will leave us, I am sure of it." The nurse walked back inside through the open door.

"I stood up today," Lizzie proudly announced. "All by myself, but only for a brief moment. My legs ache like crazy now from that effort and the exercises after. But I'm not complaining. To be honest I enjoy feeling them again, and I don't want the doctors to dull the pain."

Christine bent over and kissed her friend on the cheek. "You have no idea how happy that makes me, I can tell you. Matthew is converting my front room into a bedroom for you, so you don't have to negotiate the staircase when you come and stay with me."

"You do know it won't be for several weeks, right?" Lizzie reminded her. "And it will be temporary."

"By all means, but we have to start planning."

"How is that brother of yours enjoying my house?"

"He loves staying there, but only until the sale goes through, he is aware of that. Do you still want Isabelle's old company to auction the furniture?"

"Yes, everything except the items on the list I gave you. You have given it to Matthew so he can pack them up?"

"Yes, and I will do your clothes. You are sure about that? There will be hardly any left since most of them, on your instructions, will be going to charity."

"I want a completely new start, and I have given a great deal of thought to where I should live. I've decided what I want is a penthouse flat in the London Docklands area. I've already put my feelers out with Rick's agent. Now tell me the latest of what has been going on."

"Isabelle, believe it or not, is moving to the Isle of Wight by herself. Rick will spend most of his time there with her, I'm quite sure about that."

"Where will she live there?"

"Remember she fell in love with the house they saw in Bembridge? I didn't go there at the time, but I saw it last week. The house is wonderful. It will really suit her. She was right when she said she felt it say 'hello' to her when she first set eyes on it."

"Hello?"

"Apparently so. As you know, Laura and Steve have been in Lillehammer for nearly a month now and we believe things are looking good. There is an excellent medical centre. He seems to be settled, said Laura, although she desperately wants them to come back."

"And their house?"

"That is on the market." Christine tasted a bit of her smoked salmon pasta dish. "This is delicious."

"True, the food is great and the treatment fantastic but I cannot wait to get out of here."

"Any news about your case?"

"Yes, Emilio goes to court in three weeks' time. I will give evidence via a video link from here. They have found his involvement with the guy who tried to kill me. He was a notorious hit man. They can't locate him, but there is an international arrest warrant out. Emilio was stupid enough to leave a paper trail and bank statements. All the payments could be traced. Apparently, there is other overwhelming evidence. He will remain in custody until the trial for attempted murder. It's an open and shut case. That is what the detective said."

Then Lizzie wanted to know, "What's going on with Bill and Ben?"

"Would you believe it! They are the proud owners of a cabin. Guess where? Yes, none other than Shorefield Country Park, in Milford on Sea. One came up for sale recently. It was too good to miss, especially since it's one of those with an outside hot tub. We are all invited, they wouldn't dare not to. Besides that, they send the odd e-mail. Busy with the new show. But we'll forgive them when we receive our tickets for the opening night. Laura said, come what may, she will be there for that." Christine took another bite. "By the way, Nobby is leaving for Australia today."

"Today? He's going to Noosa today?"

"Not directly there, he will be flying to Sydney and staying a few days. He knows a fellow retired surgeon over there and intends to spend some time with him. I'm not sure when he will travel on."

"But Christine, you should go to the airport and see him off."

"No, I cannot bring myself to do that." The sound of the 'pink panther' theme rang from her handbag. She bent down to retrieve the phone and looked at the caller. "It's Nobby."

"Answer it for goodness' sake."

The ringing stopped, she'd left it too late. She placed the phone face down on the table.

Lizzie sat there open mouthed. "Ring him back."

Christine did not move.

"If you won't, I will." Lizzie grabbed the phone and before Christine had a chance to protest, pressed redial and handed it over.

"Christine, Christine, is that you?" They heard Nobby's anxious voice.

"Say something," Lizzie insisted.

"Yes, Nobby, where are you?"

"I am at the airport, I will be checking in in a minute. Christine?" Suddenly there was an issue with the connection. The signal was in danger of being lost. "Christine?"

"Yes, I can hear you, Nobby."

"Christine, I need to ask you something?"

"It's a very bad line, what did you say?"

"Christine, will you marry me?"

"What?"

"Will you marry me, Christine? Are you there?"

"I am here and I heard you."

"What do you say?"

"Nobby, why did you wait nearly forty years to ask this question?"

"Christine, I honestly never believed I would be good enough for you."

"Nobby, are you crazy? You are the best thing that ever happened to me. Come home, Nobby."

Printed in Great Britain
by Amazon